CW00956449

THE FIFTH GIRL

PAUL J. TEAGUE

Storm
PUBLISHING

To request permissions, contact the publisher at rights@stormpublishing.co

Ebook ISBN: 978-1-80508-493-8
Paperback ISBN: 978-1-80508-501-0

Cover design: Lisa Horton
Cover images: Trevillion, Shutterstock

Published by Storm Publishing.
For further information, visit:
www.stormpublishing.co

ALSO BY PAUL J. TEAGUE

The Fallen Girls

Her Last Cry

The Fifth Girl

ONE

'Jenni! Jenni!'

Her colleague lay lifeless on the pavement. Hollie checked for a pulse. Her hands were shaking too much to be able to tell if there was anything there. She hadn't even thought about the motorcycle rider. Was he gone? She thought so.

To her side, the man with the birthmark stirred. 'Is she alive?' he croaked.

'I can't tell. I'm shaking too much. Are you all right? Your head is bleeding. I-I just don't know what to do.'

He moved over to her and placed his hand on her shoulder. For a moment, it was reassuring, but then the horror of everything came roaring back.

'You have to think clearly. We don't have long.'

'We need to get an ambulance for Jenni—'

'Yes, do that right now. But you have to decide what's happening to me.'

Hollie's phone was in her hand. She shook so much she could barely re-activate the screen.

'Let me hold it. You place your finger on here.'

She did as she was told, and he dialled the number for her.

'Emergency. Which service?'

'Ambulance. And the police.'

'You must decide, DI Turner. Are you going to give me up right now? Or can we carry on working together?'

The call handler ran through the checks.

'Is the patient breathing?'

Was she? Hollie had only checked for a pulse.

'I can't tell. I don't know. She's sustained a severe head injury. She might also have broken bones, perhaps a fractured skull. She was struck by a motorcycle and thrown into the air—'

More questions came, but Hollie was overwhelmed by the speed of them.

'Try to stay calm, please. Where are you calling from?'

Hollie had attended so many emergency scenes in her professional life, and it was usually her who calmed down members of the public. Now, she felt herself falling to pieces. Her world was caving in on her. Jenni might be dead; she'd certainly sustained a terrible injury. And all because she'd allowed herself to be led a merry dance by this man. A man who might be, for all she knew, up to his ears in all this. Yet, the person on the motorcycle seemed to be the main source of threat.

'Where are we?'

'Is somebody else there with you?' the call handler asked. 'Are they calm enough to talk to me?'

Hollie's entire body was shaking now. She knew that might be a sign of shock. She had to wrestle her mind to the ground; that was the only way through this. If she couldn't get a grip, that bastard would not only get away with murder, but he'd also walk away from injuring her colleague, too.

She made the split-second decision, knowing at that moment it might change the course of her life. Her job was on the line, but she was in too deep now.

'No, I'm alone. I was just talking to myself,' she picked up. 'I'm in The Pathway. The ambulance should park at the Bowlalley Lane end to gain the fastest access—'

As she spoke, knowing the die was cast, her hand stopped shaking, and shortly after, the strength returned to her body. She felt surer and steadier now. She'd set her course, and this would have to play out, come what may. She had to trust this man. And she was going to risk everything to protect him.

'Can you give me a Three Words location?'

'Yes, I have that app on my phone. One moment.'

Hollie found the information and passed it on to the call handler.

'An ambulance is on its way. What number are you calling from, please?'

Hollie finished off the call after the operator gave her some basic suggestions for how she could be ready when they arrived. She held Jenni's hand, which was cold and limp now.

'You must go to my car. This place will be crawling with cops soon—'

'You're not giving me up?'

'I ought to... I'm going out on a limb with this. But you'd better tell me everything you know. If you don't, I'll march you directly over to HQ and we'll arrest you on the spot. If you don't have some watertight information for me, that's it. Your time's up.'

'Okay, I promise. I'm feeling pretty faint. And sick—'

'You look terrible.'

His face was white, blood dripping down his cheeks. He looked in shock, too, even though he was managing to speak coherently. Hollie found her car keys and handed them over to him.

'Were you watching for CCTV?' she asked.

'Of course,' he replied.

'Don't let your guard down now. I'm going to instruct my

3

colleagues to get their hands on every bit of CCTV in the area which might give us an ID on that prick on the motorcycle. If you get identified during those checks, your time is up, and I will lead them directly to you. I won't protect you from the natural course of the investigation. Do you understand that?'

He nodded, looking like he was about to vomit.

'Your blood is likely in this alleyway, too. Are you on any police databases?'

'No, why would I be?'

'It'll take a little time to get the results back anyway, so you're on the clock now. You come up with something useful or we make this official—'

Hollie heard the sirens heading their way. She told him where her car was parked.

'Sit tight until I'm back. Keep your head down. And watch out for CCTV.'

The man stood up from his crouching position, unsteady on his feet at first.

'Careful how you go.'

It was still early morning. Hollie spotted something resting under Jenni's leg. She slipped her hand underneath and pulled out the key she'd loaned her colleague after their night on the town.

'Oh, Jenni, what the hell were you doing? Why didn't you call it in if you thought someone was watching the flat? Why did you have to follow me here and get yourself in a fix like this?'

The first paramedic had to prise Jenni's hand out of Hollie's when they arrived minutes later.

'We've got this now. Have you got any injuries, my darling?' the paramedic asked.

Hollie shook her head. This was the second time in twenty-four hours she'd been next to someone close to her who'd needed help like this. She felt cursed, like everybody she cared for was thrust into a nightmare, which clung to her like the ancient mariner's albatross.

'Just move to the side, if you would, and we'll get your friend sorted out.'

Hollie stood out of the way and let them get on with their work. Uniformed police officers arrived shortly afterwards, and she followed their lead, taking a back seat. She was guided through the information-gathering process in a trance.

Name, contact details, what happened, timings, description of the assailant, did she get a number plate for the motorcycle?

The number of times she'd cursed witnesses for not even noticing a part of a number plate, yet here she was, without a clue. It had happened so fast; she'd been more concerned about Jenni. She couldn't even be entirely certain how the motorcyclist was dressed.

Hollie felt rage creeping over her body. She'd been in touching distance of the man who'd snatched and drugged her son and the psycho who'd killed Sister Brennan. He was there, right in front of her, and he'd slipped through her fingers. Not for the first time in her policing career, she could have kicked herself. She knew it was completely irrational but she scolded herself anyway.

The uniformed officers' tone changed the moment they realised her job and rank, but she urged them to carry on and forget her presence. She needed them to treat it like any other crime scene.

The medics were about to take Jenni away. She'd been transferred to a special stretcher, one which Hollie knew was used for serious head, neck, and spinal injuries.

'May I?' she asked as the medics braced to lift Jenni from the ground.

One of the medics nodded.

Hollie took Jenni's hand once again and she knelt, placing her mouth close to her friend's ear.

'I'm so sorry, Jenni,' she whispered. 'I wish this had happened to me, instead of you. But I promise you, I'll get this bastard. It's not just the nun now. This has become personal. I'm going to get this prick for you and for Noah.'

TWO

'Do you need to come in for a check over?'

'What?'

The medic's voice drew Hollie from her distraction.

'Are you all right? You've had quite a shock.'

Her head was pounding, her legs felt like jelly, her heart was beating so fast it was in danger of exploding out of her chest, and she'd just experienced a sudden rush of over-whelming anxiety.

'I'll be fine, thank you,' Hollie replied curtly.

'You don't look too good.'

'Honestly, get the ambulance doors closed up and be on your way. Jenni is the priority here.'

The medic nodded and headed out of the alleyway to the road beyond, where the vehicle was waiting. A constable was still hovering nearby, the place crawling with officers now. It was not yet opening time for the shops. They'd have to wait an hour or so before they could start moving door to door, searching for CCTV footage.

'What will you do now, ma'am?'

It was a good question. She'd seen colleagues injured in the line of duty before, but the suddenness and violence of what happened to Jenni had shocked her. Hollie could still hear the crunch of her head striking the ground. The body could be patched up and fixed, but the head could not. She had to come up with a story about the man with the birthmark. Why was she there at that hour in the morning? Why was their murderer there? So far, she'd given details that indicated the man she'd been meeting had gone by the time Jenni and the motorcycle arrived. If the timeline on CCTV footage questioned her version of events, she'd find herself in deep shit in no time at all. She'd stall for now and blame the shock of recent events if CCTV showed anything that contradicted her. One thing was for sure: if her informant didn't come up with something useful by the end of the day, she was giving him up to the investigation without hesitation.

'I need to get some breakfast and clean myself up,' she replied to the constable at last. 'My team will want to know what's going on, too.'

Hollie cursed that she was so new to Humberside Police that she didn't know the scene of crimes officers who were present at the scene, taking photographs, checking for evidence, and scoping the area for witnesses and cameras. She checked in with as many of them as possible, introducing herself and thanking them for their work. They had the advantage of knowing who she was already. She wondered what they were thinking.

At just past seven o'clock, Hollie excused herself from the scene and headed back to her car. She checked around her before getting in. There might have been plain clothes officers in the area. It was quiet in the Old Town, with a steady trickle of office arrivals beginning to make their way through the streets in the early morning light. Hollie checked one more time, making a secondary scan for CCTV, and then climbed into the driver's seat.

'Is it safe to sit up?' came a voice from the back.

'Yes, it's clear. Have you been crouched down there this entire time?'

'Yes, and I'm cramped now, too.'

Hollie exhaled slowly, relieved to be sitting down at last.

'I'm so sorry about your colleague,' the man said. 'She can only have been in her mid-twenties. What did the ambulance crew say?'

'It's not looking good—'

Hollie began to cry. She'd never have done so in the office; her team had to know she was reliable under stress. But now, away from their gazes, she had to get this out of her system if she wasn't going to crumble.

The man in the back let her get on with it.

'You're married, aren't you?' she said at last, after composing herself. She checked her eyes in the wing mirror; they were red and tired.

'Yes, I have a family, too.'

'I thought so. It shows a sure hand, letting me get it out of my system, without offering empty platitudes. You're an expert at this sort of thing.'

'I wouldn't say an expert. I'm not sure you ever get used to the shit life throws at you. But if you need to have a good cry, please don't stand on ceremony. I've been shaking with fear in the back here for the past hour.'

Hollie sat in silence for a couple of minutes, and he let her.

'I'm taking a huge risk now in not handing you over. You're an intelligent guy. You get that, don't you?'

'I do, and that's why I'm going to tell you something that will help you understand why I'm being so secretive.'

'You need to, because my career is resting on this.'

For a moment, Hollie considered that it might not be so bad if they threw her out of the force. They could probably survive on Léon's money, and she'd have all the time in the world to be with the kids. Perhaps she could work at a supermarket checkout while they were in school. It would be a hell of a lot safer, that was for sure.

'If you can trust me – and I know you have no reason to – but if you can find the courage to follow your gut, I believe this will work out fine for you. I can't promise, but you'll have to take that chance.'

'I'm listening. You need to give me something compelling enough not to hand you over to those police officers along the street. Something that's going to mean I can get the bastard who nearly killed my colleague.'

'I've met him—' he began.

'Okay, you've got my attention now.'

'He came to see me at my home in Chester—'

'You live in Chester?'

'Yes. It's where I work, too. I'm taking a leap of faith even being in this city. I reckon my wife's beginning to think I'm having an affair.'

'Okay, you have skin in the game. But not as much as Jenni.'

'I have more than skin in the game. I was one of the children who was born in the mother and baby unit. I was adopted and never knew my birth mother, not for years.'

'Whose child are you?'

'That's what I can't disclose – not yet. You found the photograph when I dropped it during our first encounter near the river. You're talking to the right group of people, and it'll lead you there, eventually.'

'Who is this man?'

'That's what I don't know yet. I thought he was one of the girls' sons, but as you've worked out already, he's not. Besides, I've followed them and watched them. None of those men came to visit me in Chester.'

'So, who did? What happened?'

'I've been in touch with my birth mother for some years

now. Our reunion was... difficult. Two months ago, an aggressive and angry man turned up on my doorstep. He said his name was Doug. Somehow, he'd managed to figure out my connection with the mother and baby home. He was hell-bent on finding his birth mother. His adoptive parents had died, and he'd found all the adoption paperwork when he was sorting out their house. The only lead he'd got was a link to the girls' home and a couple of names. He might have been researching his family tree, for all I knew. It was just his manner – it unsettled me – that's why I was so reticent with him.'

'Were you able to help him?'

'No, not really. And I certainly wasn't going to give him any details about my connection with the place. It's not like I know first-hand. I just know what my birth mother told me.'

'Do you have paperwork from your adoptive parents?'

'I do. My mother is dead now, but I have power of attorney over my father's affairs.'

'Have you looked at it?'

'I have, but in no detail. Why?'

'Could you get me a copy?'

'Yes, in theory, but I'd have to conceal the names—'

'Is it really that important?' Hollie was growing impatient with this secrecy now.

'Yes, DI Turner, it really is. Please respect that part of it. I will give you any help I can, but I can't reveal that final piece of information yet. It won't help you find your killer. I promise. Once we figure out who his mother is, that may assist us.'

'Is there any chance you could meet with this man again? Do you have his contact details?'

'No, but he has mine. He managed to find me on Facebook. He has a fake profile, so I don't think that'll get you anywhere either. I blocked him because I didn't have a good feeling about the guy.'

'Can you unblock him? Maybe ask him for a meeting and draw him into the open?'

'Yes, I can try. That's a good idea.'

'We'll have your back on this. I know he's dangerous; we won't leave you on your own. And you're certain when my colleagues scout the CCTV footage, they're not going to get a beautiful, full-frontal picture of your face?'

'I wear this all the time.'

Hollie looked in the rear-view mirror and saw him pulling up his snood. She let out a long, deep sigh.

'Okay.'

'What?'

'I'm going to find a place where you can get patched up and recover. But if you draw a blank in the next twenty-four hours – or if my colleagues get a clear picture of your face on CCTV – I'm handing you over. Understood?'

The man nodded. Hollie started up the car. There was only one safe place she could take him.

THREE

1968: SOPHIA BRENNAN'S STORY

Sophia skipped school to watch it. The line of formidable women making their way to the dockside was a sight nothing short of inspirational. She'd seen Lillian Bilocca as she'd been going about her business along Hessle Road, but never imagined the deaths on the trawlers would make such a celebrity of her. Sophia felt proud to live in the fishing community.

She knew many of the women there, too, each with their headscarf, some carrying handbags, others pushing prams, their dignity and anger all directed at the port bosses. The fifty-eight deaths hit the community hard. Her own father had lost his life at sea two years previously, so she understood their grief extremely well. It was too late for her, but she hoped some other families would be protected from being torn apart like hers had been. She hated the sea and blamed its cruelty for the life she now led. But what choice had her father had but to make a living on the trawlers?

She followed the march as long as she dared, steering clear of the police officers who'd been assigned to accompany the women. She admired them all but didn't yet feel old enough to be one of them. Three trawlers down in a matter of weeks.

They'd never known anything like it. And so many lives were lost in such a short period. The entire community was reeling from it. And it had made life at home worse than she could bear.

Sophia observed the line of women make its way off into the distance, and she found a wall to sit on while she watched them disappear. She hoped that one day, she, too, might find the spirit to fight like that. And in her darkest and most hateful moments, she wished her stepfather Martin could have replaced one of those good men who'd died at sea, so an innocent man could have gone home to a loving family.

It was cold and Sophia wished she'd stayed at school. If she had thought things through better, she might have dressed a little warmer. Eventually, she gave up and went home. If Martin had gone to the pub, at least her mum would give her some peace.

They lived above a shop on Hessle Road, and she hated it. Before her father's death, they'd been in a small terrace. The remains of the old outside toilets were still out the back, but they'd been happy enough there and they could just afford the rent. When her dad died, they'd been thrown out on the street, kept alive by the charity of strangers. And then her mother had done a thing she would never forgive her for. She'd met Martin in the pub, taken up with him, and got pregnant with his baby soon after. She knew why her mum had done it, but she still couldn't forgive her. And now they were all stuck in his one-bedroom flat above the shop: a screaming baby, a teenage girl, a miserable mother and a hateful man. Sophia despised her life, and she resented her mum. She wanted to kill Martin. If she only had some of the courage that those women had, she would do it.

She spent a few moments looking in the window of the shop immediately below the flat, then rubbed her hands and opened the building's side door. The hallway was narrow and dark, the wallpaper damp, with the edges beginning to come away from the walls.

She could hear two babies crying. Four families were in those flats, with only one bathroom between them. Two of the women had babies; there were several toddlers in there and a couple of teenagers like herself. She waited outside the door for a moment before opening it. She couldn't hear Martin. Thank God for that.

'You're home early,' her mother said as she stepped inside.

'The boiler's broken at school.'

Her mother didn't very much care. Three terry nappies were hanging off a chair in front of the small fire on the far side of the room. The air was moist, and the windows dripped with condensation. The baby was teething, her cheeks red and raw and her complaining continuous. Sophia noted how tired her mum looked. She hadn't seen her smile in months, not even when she and Martin got married. It was the cheapest wedding ever; they could barely afford the licence. The moment her mother knew she was pregnant, she'd cornered Martin and tied him down. She'd even apologised to Sophia.

'We don't have a choice, girl. With your father gone, we'll be on the streets if I don't do this.'

'Do you even love him?' Sophia had asked.

'It's not about love. It's about survival. We have a man in the house. We'll be taken care of. That's all there is to it.'

'But you loved Dad, didn't you?'

'Of course I loved your father, but he's been taken by the sea. You and me, we have nothing now. And so that's that. Love is for the lucky. It's not for people like you and me.'

And so, she'd got herself a stepfather: a violent, drunken, waster of a man whose sole saving grace was that he could stay sober long enough to earn a paltry wage down at the docks. And that, at least, kept him out of the house for much of the time. That and the pub.

'Now you're home, fold that washing, please. And you can peel the vegetables for tea, too. I've not had a break from this baby all day. You were never like this when you were teething. She just makes Martin angry. I wish to God she'd stop.'

While her mum soothed the baby on her chair, Sophia walked over to the unfolded washing that had been abandoned on the table.

'Mrs Edwards let me use her twin tub again. Those things were sent by angels. They're a blessing when you have a baby in the house.'

Sophia folded the items, noting they weren't yet fully dry. They'd take their place in front of the fire later. Most of the time, she wore her clothes very slightly damp. In the meantime, she stacked them on one side of the tatty sofa, which doubled as her bed. Once the clothing was sorted, she went into the small kitchen to the side of the living room to prepare the vegetables. At least she had her own space, if only for a moment; a place where she was warm enough and where she could be alone in her thoughts.

They heard him before they saw him. Martin was hurling abuse at somebody in the street down below. It was probably the shopkeeper chasing him for the rent again. Sophia flinched every time she heard his voice, retreating deeper into her mind to protect herself from him.

'Martin's home. Get busy with that dinner. He sounds like he's been to the pub again.'

She heard her mother scurrying around the living room, tidying up some of the baby's things. She wished she'd stayed outside in the cold now.

Sophia heard him stagger through the door. She flinched.

'Will ya shut that damn baby up! I can hear her bawling right down them stairs!'

Sophia pressed the peeling knife deep into the potato, imagining it was Martin's head.

'She's just a baby, Martin. It's what babies do—'

'Well, tell her not to do it. It's doing my fucking head in—'

'You've been at the pub—'

'I'm entitled to, after a day at work. Besides, if you hadn't had that bloody baby, it wouldn't matter!'

'It's your baby, too!'

'That's what you say, but no baby of mine would make a noise like that. Take her into the bedroom. I can't stand that racket.'

Sophia heard her mother moving.

'And who left this fucking shit on the settee?'

Sophia peered around the side of the door frame to see what was going on. Her mother was making herself scarce. Martin had thrown the newly folded washing pile onto the floor.

'Ah, you're home, are you?'

He'd spotted her. She froze. Her mum moved into the bedroom, saving herself and the baby.

Sophia darted back into the kitchen and set about the vegetables again. She knew what he was going to do. Her mother knew about it, too, she was certain. She tensed her body as the bedroom door closed and Martin fell silent in the living room.

She could sense him getting closer.

'How are you, Sophia?'

He was in the doorway now. She kept her head down and carried on peeling. She thought of the women in the scarves. She thought about the knife he used to gut the fish that he would sometimes steal from the docks. It was just within reach.

'You're growing up into a lovely looking girl,' he said, speaking quietly, directly into her ear. It was a threat more than a statement. 'Yes, a beautiful young girl.'

He placed his hand on her rear, then, never lifting it, ran it around to her tummy, then up to her right breast. He grasped it firmly and pressed himself into her from behind. She could feel his excitement, and she despised him for it.

'You're sixteen now, girl. It's about time you started making yourself useful around here. It costs me to keep you, you know. Nobody gets a free ride in life—'

His hand had now worked down to her skirt and he was ruffling up the material. Sophia was rigid with fear, one hand on the potato peeler, the other clutching the potato, and Martin pressing himself hard against her. His fingers found the elastic of her knickers and he began to tug them down.

'Martin?' came her mother's voice from the bedroom door.

'Get back inside the bedroom and look after the fucking baby!' he screamed at her.

Sophia heard her mother pause, and then the bedroom door clicked shut. She thought she heard her sobbing but couldn't be certain. Her pants were half down now, and his hand had moved up to the bare cheeks of her behind. Sophia gagged, but he carried on, touching her, panting with breath that reeked of beer, his drool covering her neck. She thought of the women at the march, and she snapped. Sophia plunged the peeling knife into his leg. He lunged away from her like she'd just given him an electric shock. His trousers were unfastened, but he seemed more surprised than hurt.

'You fucking bitch. You know you want it really.'

He pushed his trousers down to his knees and was beginning to do the same to his underwear when Sophia grasped at the fish knife and held it out in front of her. With her spare hand, she pulled up her pants as best she could, adjusting her skirt, desperate to put something between herself and this monster.

'Don't touch me!'

His fist crashed into her jaw before she even realised it was coming, and she slumped against the sink from the power of it. His hands smelt of fish; Martin always smelt of fish. His underwear was down now, and she was cornered. Blindly, she slashed the knife in front of her and he screamed out. She'd caught him across the abdomen. There was a clean cut there, nothing too deep, but it was bleeding and looked bad. Martin shouted at her.

'Get out of this fucking house, you bitch, and don't come back! Look what you've done. Fucking get out! Get out!'

Sophia dragged herself off the floor, holding out the knife in case he came at her again. She backed all the way up to the flat's door, never letting him out of her sight. Her mother was at the bedroom door now, pleading with Martin to leave her alone, but he pushed her back into the room with such force that he almost swept her off her feet.

'I hate you, I fucking hate you!' Sophia shouted at him. 'I wish you'd drowned at sea, and we never had to see you again.'

With the knife still in her hand, she turned and ran down the stairs and out into the street.

FOUR

'If I didn't think he was safe, I wouldn't be suggesting he stays with you.'

Gilly was taking some convincing, but Hollie thought she was finally coming around.

'I haven't even eaten my breakfast yet. It's not every day you have a surprise like this sprung on you.'

'I'm only asking because you're involved in the case. I'm hoping you can confirm to me that he's not Theresa's son.'

'I've only seen photographs of him,' Gilly reminded her.

'Yes, but I trust you and this is a lot quicker than getting Theresa to send me a photo. He needs some medical attention, too. I wouldn't ever dream of asking this, Gilly, but I think he gives us our best hope so far of closing this case.'

'Okay, okay, you've badgered me into it. But no more than one day and not overnight.'

'I promise. I'll drive him back to his hotel myself. I assume he's staying in a hotel. I suppose it might be an Airbnb or something like that.'

'And you swear he's not dangerous?'

'He's not dangerous, Gilly. I wouldn't put you at risk like

that. Besides, our killer has already been in your home. This man is not the killer. But I believe he can lead us to him.'

Hollie could see she'd won her over at last so went back outside to bring him in.

'Can you give me your name?' Hollie asked as she opened up the car door to let the man out.

'Tony. It's my real name, but I'm not giving you a surname yet because I know what you coppers are like. Call me Tony.'

Hollie accompanied him into Gilly's house, noticing that his clothes were bloody; it was high time he had somebody look at the wound. Gilly was apparently thinking the same thing.

'This needs to be looked at by a doctor, surely?'

'Clean it up and get a covering on it for now,' Hollie urged. 'If it looks like it might be more serious than we think, Tony can go to the infirmary at the end of the day, en route to the cop shop. You do understand that, Tony?'

'Yes, I get it. It's painful, but it won't kill me. I can hang on here.'

He winced in pain as he spoke, but it didn't appear life-threatening to Hollie.

He waited for Gilly to move through to the kitchen, and then lowered his voice.

'As soon as I'm patched up, I'll try to get through to this guy on Facebook.'

Hollie checked one more time that everything was okay with Gilly when she returned to the living room.

'You have my phone number. If you need me for anything, just call.'

'You owe me for this,' Gilly reminded her.

'I know, don't think I take it for granted.'

Hollie left Gilly's house and walked back to her car. She reckoned it would be fine to check on Noah by now.

. . .

As she drove over to Hull Royal Infirmary, Hollie felt a swell of anxiety as she pictured Jenni being treated in the hospital, and how close her own son had come to being harmed. She thumped her steering wheel as she waited at a red light.

She had to stop this monster before he harmed somebody else.

The infirmary was already becoming too familiar to her, but it was easier this time to find Noah's ward and report at the nurse's station.

'He's barely stirred since you left him,' the nurse updated her. 'Once we've done the morning rounds, and the consultant has given the all-clear, he'll be fine for picking up. I think he just needs rest now, but he's had a good night. He'll be ready for collecting after ten o'clock. You can wait for him, or come back later, it's entirely up to you.'

Hollie looked in on her son, who was still fast asleep. He was so boisterous and full of life when he was awake, but lying there, still and innocent, he seemed fragile and vulnerable. She stroked his hair and kissed him. Her three children were so precious to her, it was like torture even considering that any harm might ever come to them.

Hollie didn't feel quite so bad now about leaving earlier. She consoled herself that she was right to leave the professionals to do their job. Besides, she'd got to spend a quiet night with Lily and Phoebe while Noah was in good hands. She decided to keep out of the way while they did the morning rounds; she knew how annoying it could be when members of the public got in the way of her doing her job. Besides, there was a Costa at Hull Royal, and she was ready for a strong hit of caffeine.

As she sat with her drink, Hollie checked in on Phoebe.

'You got my note?' she asked, her phone in one hand, her coffee in the other. 'I'm afraid I just had something urgent to attend to at work.'

'No problem, you sneaked out quietly, I didn't hear a thing.

How's Noah doing? Are you still fine to take Lily while I'm in my interview?'

Hollie said nothing about what had happened since she'd left the flat. That was a copper's life; people at home were best knowing only part of the story.

'I'm just waiting at Hull Royal; I can pick up Noah in half an hour or so. I'll come home via McDonald's and get us all breakfast. How does that sound?'

It was greeted much more enthusiastically than it ought to have been. She heard Lily giving a cheer in the background when Phoebe told her what was happening. Her brother was in the hospital recovering from being drugged, but the prospect of a Maccy D's made everything else pale into insignificance. She pictured her children working through their sorrow at her future death by tucking into a Big Mac. She ended the call and checked the time on her phone once again.

As Hollie nursed her coffee, the hubbub of conversation, coffee orders, the frothing machine and chinking crockery allowed her mind to drift, and she thought back to the events of the early morning. Her hand began to tremble, and she placed her coffee back on the table. Jenni was somewhere in this hospital; she needed to check in on her.

Leaving her half-drunk coffee, Hollie leapt up from her seat and crossed over to the main entrance of the infirmary.

She showed her ID as the receptionist looked up to acknowledge her.

'I'm wanting to make a condition check on Jenni Langdon. She was admitted just over an hour ago.'

The receptionist took Hollie's ID and studied it carefully. She began to tap her computer keyboard.

'You can't see her, I'm afraid. She's being prepped for emergency surgery. It'll be some time before we can give you an update—'

'Can I go up there and check?'

'No, officer, that's not allowed. The best thing you can do is call in later. We'll let you know as soon as there's news.'

Hollie felt useless. She'd let Jenni down and it was gnawing at her from inside. She needed to know that she would be okay.

Her phone rang. It was DS Anderson.

'What the fuck happened to Jenni?' he barked.

'Whoa, that's enough!' Hollie snapped as she exited the foyer and ducked out of the way to take the call. 'Let's have a little respect here, please.'

Anderson was livid.

'You've been in post for less than one month and already we've got a colleague fighting for her life in hospital. How did it happen?'

He didn't need to scold her; she was angry enough with herself already.

'DS Anderson, you'll address me as ma'am or boss—'

'How the fuck did it happen, ma'am?'

Hollie waited a moment. He'd got her hackles up. Having already lost a DI – a colleague – in the last six months, her rational mind could understand his anger. But she couldn't let this slip any longer.

'I'm at Hull Royal right now. Jenni's just about to go into surgery. When I'm back in the office, I'd like to schedule a catch-up with you, DS Anderson—'

'Yes, bring it on. I'd say that's long overdue, wouldn't you?'

'In the meantime, let's remember that the man who injured Jenni is still out there. And he's already killed Sister Brennan and may well have killed Father Duffy, if he hadn't been disturbed. Let's focus on the case and save the personal stuff for later. For Jenni's sake, if no one else.'

She sensed Anderson calming at the end of the phone line. She felt like one of the cowboys she'd seen on TV, settling a kicking horse by whispering in its ear. When she was certain he'd cooled down, she talked him through everything, leaving out all the details about Tony, and only saying instead that he'd left a message asking for a meet-up in the alleyway. It was time to introduce Tony as a bit-part actor, just in case he was spotted on CCTV.

'And you didn't think you'd need backup?' Anderson pushed.

Before she could answer, he rattled off more questions.

'Why did Jenni follow you? Do you have an email address or sample of handwriting from where this man contacted you? Why didn't you inform your colleagues?'

She was on the ropes; she'd have to take a leap of faith with him.

'DS Anderson, what made you agree to hold back information about the girl known as Twiggy? Why did you go along with that?'

'Because my gut instinct tells me it's the right thing to do for now. I'll get it checked out, and the moment I'm confident enough to share it with the team, I'll let them know.'

'I know you don't know me very well yet, and you have no reason to place your faith in me. But I'm working on my cop's instinct now. I want to solve this case as soon as we can. But we have nothing except for a dead nun, a half-murdered priest, and now, a seriously injured colleague. Whatever you think of me personally, DS Anderson, and however much you think my job should have been yours, surely you know I'll do anything I can to bring this man to justice?'

Anderson was silent at the end of the line. It felt like a long time, but it couldn't have been more than a minute.

'All right, I'll give you twenty-four hours. If we don't make some significant progress by tomorrow's briefing, this new information comes into play. I'll try to catch DCC Warburton myself after the morning briefing and probe her a bit—'

'Tread gently with that, or I won't be the only one hauling you in for a meeting.'

Anderson laughed at that. They were through the hostility. For now.

'I'll leave today's briefing in your hands. I'll be out of the office on family matters, but I want to know of any updates as soon as they come in. Oh, and keep on top of the case log, too, please.'

Anderson's voice softened.

'I'm sorry, I didn't ask after your son. How is he?'

'He's fine, thank you. I'm picking him up after they've made the morning rounds.'

'Good, that's good. I'll let you know ASAP if there's anything new to report.'

They ended the call. It wasn't even half past nine and, already, Hollie felt exhausted and worn out. But after a start to the day like that, she was certain things couldn't get any worse.

FIVE

Picking up Noah from his hospital room distracted Hollie for a while, and for a short time, she was able to shut out thoughts of Jenni from her mind and focus on her own child. Noah was delighted to see her and didn't appear to be any the worse for wear. He rushed in for a hug as soon as he spotted her walking into the ward. She'd missed the little things so much. The feel of him burrowing in deep, his small hands holding on tight like she was the most important person in the world, melted her heart.

'How are you feeling now?' she asked, wiping away a tear that had formed in her eye.

'The nurse said I might feel a bit weird, but I just feel normal,' he replied, his boisterous smile back on duty after its temporary break.

'I love you, Noah—'

It was harder finding the right moments to say it since she'd left the family home, but she had to tell him. The thought of losing him was unbearable.

He made a mock vomiting face but kissed her on her cheek anyway.

'You're so soppy, Mum. But I love you anyway.'

PAUL J. TEAGUE

He was a typical kid of his age; it was water off a duck's back. Abducted from the park and drugged by a dangerous man? No problem when you're a pre-pubescent boy, powered by being alive and without a care in the world. It was probably a good thing Noah was completely oblivious to the peril he'd been in.

Hollie was handed a list of things to look out for by the nurses, but Noah seemed to have shaken off any concerns about the previous day. He was up for a day of activities, and Phoebe had already promised the two children a visit to a museum and a trip to The Deep aquarium. Much as she craved being back in the office, Hollie decided to give herself that day. The children would be leaving shortly; she had to set the case aside for now and leave it to her colleagues.

They called in for food on the drive back to the flat, and Hollie could barely believe the restorative powers of a McDonald's breakfast; it was exactly what she needed after the morning she'd just experienced. She ordered two breakfast muffins, figuring that if she couldn't justify double helpings that day, there would never be a good enough excuse.

Phoebe, Noah and Lily chatted happily while they all tucked in, and Hollie observed how fast her daughter was growing up. It was the small things that gave it away. She held a sustained conversation now, rather than flitting from topic to topic like Noah might. She'd grown taller, too, but she looked more like a young woman than an older girl. She was growing her hair longer and it aged her, lending her youthful face a greater maturity. Time was slipping through her fingers. Lily and Phoebe were perfectly at ease with each other despite a seven year age gap. Their bodies were in tune as they walked along together, their faces engaged in lively conversation, and Phoebe stopping to sort out Lily's hair when it came loose from her hair band. Hollie took a moment to appreciate how lucky she was to have such awesome kids. But her mind began to cloud over with thoughts of Jenni. She felt a pang of searing guilt over what had happened, even though she knew there was nothing more she could have done. But she was angry with herself for not being able to protect her friend.

After the stress of the past forty-eight hours, the sheer mundanity of running Phoebe up the road for her interview was bliss.

'Well, good luck, Phoebe, I really hope your interview goes well,' Hollie said, giving her a hug. 'They'll be lucky to have you at the university. In fact, I'll walk in there myself and give you a reference if you want.'

Phoebe laughed.

'It's probably best that you don't.' She smiled. 'Wish me luck, kids!'

Lily gave her new friend a hug, and Noah gave her a high five. They watched Phoebe as she walked across the campus to the building where her interview was taking place. She turned and gave them a wave before walking through the entrance.

'If we take a shortcut through this pathway, I can show you where I went to university.'

'I think I'd like to go to university, Mum,' Lily said. 'Phoebe has been telling me all about it. It sounds fun. Why did you leave uni, Mum?'

Hollie liked the children growing up. As they did so, they became more interested in the parts of her life that were filed away as memories, like an old photo album. Sometimes it felt good to take them out for an airing.

'I wanted to join the police. And I'd had Izzy by then. I wasn't as interested in studying,' she replied. Noah was walking ahead, already bored with the conversation and eager to burn off some energy.

'I miss Izzy,' Lily remarked. 'I wish she'd come back; she's been away for ages.'

Hollie couldn't have put it better herself. She changed the

subject; she was barely hanging on over Jenni. If Lily made her talk about her absent older daughter, she reckoned she might fold.

'This is where my university used to be. It was called the University of Humberside then. It's moved over to Lincoln now.'

She thought back to her time in the city. Whenever she reflected on that previous life, it was more about the people and relationships, rather than the studying. She'd had a couple of casual boyfriends, gone wild, drank too much, had some crazy nights out and had thrown herself headfirst into everything the city had to offer. It hadn't been without incident, of course. She seemed fated to pass through life without being able to avoid trouble. Sometimes it felt like a curse. At others, it seemed more like a calling. In the nineties, she'd never have imagined herself walking through the grounds of her old university with two children in tow – three with Izzy. Izzy knew this place, but she couldn't remember any of it. Hollie could still remember pushing her through the campus in her pram, her tiny face staring out from above her baby blanket, as they headed to the main building to hand in one of her essays. Now, looking back, she didn't know how she'd coped. Somehow, she'd managed, but the lure of the police had been too great in the end, and she'd headed back to Lancaster. She'd met Léon, they'd fallen in love, and everything else had just slotted into place.

Once upon a time, not so long ago, they'd have made this trip as a family, with Léon accompanying them, listening to her tales of university life. It was one of the things she'd been looking forward to. Hollie had always liked Hull and felt that she wasn't quite done with the city just yet. Besides, she still had unfinished business there. There were ghosts in that place which still had to be laid to rest.

'What would you like me and Dad to do?' she asked, not

entirely certain why she'd been so blunt with Lily. Her daughter seemed to have thought it through already.

'I don't want you and Dad to split up,' she began, stopping to talk out of Noah's earshot. 'But lots of my friends have divorced parents and it seems to work okay. I don't want to go to France, though, and Noah agrees. We want to stay in this country.'

When Hollie really pushed herself on the matter, this was the issue that concerned her most. She was still in shock that Léon was having an affair, but she couldn't stop him, however much she wanted the marriage to work. She still loved Léon, however angry she felt with him, and she could see how her work had taken its toll on their relationship. She just wished he'd spoken to her rather than shipping in a newer, younger, faster model.

'If I can convince your dad to stay in Lancaster, would that be better?' she asked.

'Would you be able to visit at weekends and holidays?'

'Yes, of course. I'd see you whenever I could.'

'I'd be happiest if we don't go to France. I like it in Hull, too. We can come and see you. And Phoebe will be here, if she does well in her interview.'

Hollie ran through this information in her mind, keeping her eye on Noah all the time so he stayed in sight. Léon was right. However much she wanted it, she couldn't care for the kids around meals and school times. She could see that. But if the children stayed in Lancaster, and if Phoebe was travelling backwards and forwards to university, they could make it work. Léon had talked about mediation, and she would agree to it. Lily had offered her the solution that it might have taken weeks of rowing to reach themselves.

'Does Noah agree?'

'He's the same as me. He doesn't want you to split up, but he has friends whose parents have separated, too. Most people make it work. I just don't want you and Dad hating each other. That would be horrible.'

Hollie wondered if they offered courses in mediation at the university. Her daughter was a natural. They walked on, changing the subject. How had she missed Lily growing up? She was conversing like an adult now. Perhaps she had been too absent from their lives of late.

They made their way back to Canham Turner House, which Phoebe had marked on a printed map for her. It didn't take long to find Wilde's Café, where Phoebe had said they should meet. She was waiting for them already and had a hot chocolate, which was still cooling. The children rushed up to greet her like Phoebe was a long-lost friend. Seeing how easy they all were together made Hollie feel more positive about the future. If Léon could be convinced to stay in the UK, they might be able to make it work between them.

'How did it go?' Hollie asked. Phoebe wasn't giving anything away by her face.

'I got an unconditional offer on the spot!' She smiled. 'They rarely ever do that. I'm so happy.'

'Congratulations!'

Hollie leant in and gave Phoebe a hug.

'Did you tell your mum and dad?'

'Yes, I texted them. Mum says I can pay for my nights out by babysitting for you and Léon. She doesn't know what's going on yet, does she?'

'No, not yet. I'll tell her, I promise. I've only just worked out what's going on myself.'

'I'll keep quiet, I promise,' Phoebe replied.

Hollie's phone sounded. She drew a ten-pound note out of her pocket and handed it to Phoebe.

'Can you sort the kids out with a drink and snack while I take this call? It's the office. It could be important.'

Phoebe took them over to place an order while Hollie sat on

one of the comfortable chairs. She steeled herself. The fleeting time she'd had with the children had provided a wonderful oasis of calm. She answered the call.

'DI Turner.'

'Hello, boss, it's DS Patel. I'm sorry to disturb you on your day off with your family, but DS Anderson asked me to let you know straight away—'

Hollie's stomach knotted. She prayed it wasn't Jenni.

'Go ahead, DS Patel.'

'It's DCC Warburton, boss. She's disappeared. She went to walk her dogs at North Ferriby this morning and didn't come back. The dogs were found roaming the village and there's no sign of the DCC.'

SIX

1968: SOPHIA BRENNAN'S STORY

It was getting dark. Sophia felt the bite of the chill night the moment she stepped out into the street. She looked up and down the road, not sure what to do next, and still trembling from Martin's attack. She'd always been wary of the man, but never thought him capable of that. Part of her thought it might blow over, but deep down, she knew she could never return to that house and be left alone with him again.

Where could she go? She hadn't got a clue. Most of the families she knew were already struggling to get by, with too many bodies packed into the sham-fours along Subway Street and Hessle Road; they would not want another mouth to feed. There was the model lodging house near the docks. If the worst came to the worst, she could try for a bed there. However, Sophia could not bear the shame of that prospect. She had to speak to her mother. She could hear her rowing with Martin from out on the street. They'd been warned by the shopkeeper that the shouting was not good for business, and either they kept things quiet, or they'd be looking for new lodgings.

Sophia walked across the road and perched on a low wall opposite the shop and flats. If she was lucky, she'd catch her mother at the window. She could perhaps make an excuse to leave the house or, more likely, Martin would return to the pub. As it turned out, Martin slammed the front door ten minutes later, storming off along the road, no doubt to consume more pints at the pub.

Sophia took her chance. She watched Martin walking with some difficulty along Hessle Road until he was out of sight, then she darted across to the flats. She still had her key – Martin hadn't thought about that – so she crept up the staircase to their front door. She heard voices as she made her way up towards the shared landing. Mrs Brady, one of the neighbours, was talking to her mother. As Sophia stepped onto the landing, she baulked as her eyes caught her mother's face. It was bloody and bruised, and she was crying; Mrs Brady was tending to her wounds.

'I hope the bastard drowns in his beer,' her mum cussed as Mrs Brady dabbed away the blood from her cheek with a wet rag.

'Sophia—'

She'd been spotted at the top of the stairs. Mrs Brady looked at her, too.

'He hit you as well? His own daughter? I've a good mind to send our John around to give him a beating. A man can't go round behaving like that—'

'No!'

'What do you mean, no, Margaret? He can't carry on hurting you both like this.'

'I can't risk losing the flat,' she replied. 'I have to stay, for now, for the baby's sake. I can't walk away.'

'What about me?' Sophia asked.

'Look what he's done to your family,' Mrs Brady said.

Sophia watched as Mrs Brady continued dabbing her mother's forehead with the rag.

'I did worse to him,' Sophia went on, her lip trembling at the memory of it. 'Is there any chance he might die?'

'He made me patch it up, but it was worse than it looked. I got this because the disinfectant stung when I put it on the wound.'

Her mother pointed to the cut on her face.

'What did he say about me?' Sophia asked.

'You can't come back,' she replied. 'He won't allow it.'

'Do you know what he tried to do to me?'

'I can't deal with this now, girl. It's too much. The baby needs taking care of. If we're out on the street, I don't know what we'll do.'

'But what about me? Where will I go?'

'You'll be able to get yourself a job. You're old enough now. But you can't stay here anymore, you know that?'

Footsteps were coming up the staircase.

'Go into our flat, my dear,' Mrs Brady whispered. 'Just in case it's him.'

Sophia ducked into her doorway and kept out of sight.

She didn't recognise the voice at first, but at least it wasn't Martin.

'Mrs Brennan? Is your husband around?'

'No, he's off at the pub.'

'Well, I'll tell you then as we're closing the shop shortly. You'll have to move out of the flat. We can't have all that noise when we're trying to trade downstairs. We'll give you your papers tomorrow, but I thought you should know—'

'But where will we go?'

'I've warned your husband several times now about the noise. It just won't do. You'll have until the end of next week to be on your way.'

Sophia heard her mother start to sob, and the baby let out a moan from inside the flat.

'What will we do? Please, sir, Mr Stephenson, we really need this flat, what with the baby and everything—'

'Did you know your husband is behind with the rent?'

Mr Stephenson's expression suggested he hadn't come round for a negotiation.

'No, I did not. He told me we were up to date.'

Sophia saw Mrs Brady squeeze her mother's hand.

'By the end of next week, Mrs Brennan. Make sure you tell your husband.'

Mr Stephenson headed off down the stairs.

Sophia's mother was panicking now, clearly frantic that they'd end up out on the streets.

'I'll check on the baby,' Mrs Brady offered, walking over to the flat.

'What will you do?' Sophia asked. 'What will we do?'

'I can't cope with you right now!' her mother snapped. 'You'll have to sort something out, find somewhere to stay. See if they have a bed at the Sally Army. They'll help you out. I have to focus on the baby, Sophia. You're old enough to take care of yourself now. And don't let Martin find you here. He'll go mental if he sees you.'

Sophia saw what was left of her life unravelling. She could forget school for starters. She'd have to see what work she might get in the icehouses or the smokehouses along Subway Street. She could always help with the net repairs; they were always on the lookout for women to do that work.

'Can I take some things before I go?' Sophia asked.

'Yes, take what you need.'

Sophia felt like she was a problem her mother simply couldn't cope with at that moment.

She still had the fish knife, and she intended on keeping it. She took the blanket she used at night and her bobble hat. She made sure she had her gloves with her, and she put on her warmest jumper.

Mrs Brady stood in the living room with the baby in her arms, who had been soothed and was now picking up on the restored calm. Sophia's mother sat on a dining chair, her face blanched, a woman worn out by what the day had thrown at her.

'Try the Sally Army, as your mother suggested.'

Mrs Brady did her best to reassure her.

'They'll give you a warm bed and a meal in your belly there until you get yourself sorted.'

Sophia walked up to her mother, the blanket thrown over her arm.

'What am I going to do?' her mother sobbed.

'I love you, Mum.' Sophia spoke quietly.

Her mother said nothing. Sophia waited a moment or two, then walked off, down the shared staircase. It was silent as she made her way down the steps, and she'd never felt more alone since she discovered her father had been lost at sea. She'd felt a desolation that night when some of his crew members had come around to the house to break the news. That emptiness stayed with her, and her mother had never been the same since. What joy there had been in their lives was gone. When Martin had arrived on the scene, it receded even further. And now, here she was, at rock bottom.

Sophia had no idea what she was going to do that night. Her only plan was to make directly for the model lodging and see if the Salvation Army had a place for the night. They did not; they were full already. If she wanted a bed, she'd have to make herself known to them early the next day.

She was worn out, exhausted by the shouting and violence of the day. Walking back from the Salvation Army, Sophia detected drops of rain as she neared the underpass at Subway Street. She could shelter there, and there would be a steady flow of good, working men walking to and from the docks if she needed to call out for help. She took shelter at the side of the subway, out of sight, and pulled her blanket up around her, the fish knife in her hand. It would do for now. She'd try for a bed the next day. But for one time only, she could make do with the cold of the winter night.

SEVEN

When she walked into the office, Hollie could almost reach out and touch DS Anderson's resentment at her being there. His face said it all: he'd hoped to take the lead on the DCC's disappearance, and no doubt any credit that would come from a swift resolution.

Phoebe and the children were happy enough for her to leave them, especially with a visit to The Deep aquarium in the offing.

DCI Osmond intercepted her before she could get to him.

'A word in private?' he asked, leading the way to an unoccupied office. Hollie followed him, wondering what this was about.

'I wasn't expecting you in so soon,' he began, the moment the door clicked shut.

'I can't not be here for the DCC—'

'I want you to check yourself in for some counselling,' he continued. 'What happened to DC Langdon this morning was terrible. You might not feel like it now, but these things take a toll. I'd like you to sort it out ASAP.'

'Yes, sir, but it's not necessary. I've been shaking slightly all day, but the best thing to resolve it is to catch our man. Talking about it will only go so far. Seeing our killer locked up in jail will make things much better.'

'You know that DC Langdon is critical?'

'I do, sir.'

'And you know what that means?'

'Yes, I do. I'm trying not to think about it. I've just been over to the hospital to pick up my son. I asked after DC Langdon while I was there, and she was just being taken into surgery. I'm better getting on with the case, sir. Besides, DS Anderson and I think we can pull some of the strands together now. You'll be joining us for the briefing?'

'Yes, of course. Get that counselling booked. I mean it, DI Turner.'

She nodded and thought back to what Anderson had told her about Osmond's breakdown. It made sense he was a fan of talking things out, if that's what had brought him back from the brink. Hollie preferred action, rather than words. Experience had taught her it was a fine antidote to emotional trauma.

They exited the room and walked over to the briefing area where Anderson was getting ready to address the team.

'We need to talk after this,' Hollie suggested.

'Sure. Did you know the photographer from Beverley is in the building?'

'No, I didn't. That's good timing.'

'He's waiting in Interview Room 3 right now. He found some more pictures. I've stalled him with coffee while we get this briefing out of the way. Do you want in?'

'You bet I do. How about we delay the briefing for fifteen minutes? It makes more sense to speak to the photographer first, doesn't it?'

DS Anderson considered that, then nodded.

'I'll put the word out and tell the photographer you're on your way.'

As Anderson updated the investigations team about the slight delay, Hollie walked over to DS Patel's desk.

'Could you do me a favour, please, but only if you get a moment. Book me in a session with the counsellor, would you? Check the roster for my availability.'

'Counselling, eh?'

'Less of the judgement, please, DS Patel.' Hollie smiled. 'There's nothing like a bit of counselling to help you understand that things could be much, much worse.'

DS Patel laughed.

'I'm with you on that.'

Hollie walked off to the interview room. She heard the low hum of male voices through the door. DS Anderson was in there already.

'Sorry to keep you, Mr Maddison,' she said as she entered the room.

He had five photographs spread out across the table, all of them black and white. There were three different images of the netball team, with an additional two solo shots. Each showed the girl they'd been calling Twiggy. There was also some paperwork, most of it completed using an ink pen. It had the logo for David Lister School by way of a heading.

'I can confirm this girl's full name is Rose Watson,' he explained. 'I still have the records from the parents' purchase. I was taking images for a school brochure, but they were made available for sale to the children's parents. Her father was Harold Watson. He was quite a bigwig back in the day. I'd forgotten all about him, to be honest with you. It's so many years ago.'

Hollie immediately made the connection to what DI Burns had told her in his email. He'd mentioned DCC Warburton's father. This was the confirmation they needed, from two different sources, too.

'Did you know him?' Hollie asked.

'Sort of,' Maddison replied. 'I was always being called in as a freelancer to take pictures for the local paper. It went with the territory, meeting all the movers and shakers.'

'What was he like?' Anderson asked.

'He was a pain in the arse, if I'm being completely honest about it,' Maddison answered. 'He always struck me as a pompous man. He was very dismissive and cold. I can't say I warmed to him.'

'Was he unpopular in the city?' Hollie encouraged.

'No more than any other wealthy businessperson. He once bought a bit of land by the old docks, which caused him to fall out with the locals. The redevelopment of anything to do with our declining fishing industry is always a bit sensitive. Besides, it wouldn't matter if he was unpopular, he took care of all that himself.'

Hollie and Anderson looked at each other, then at Maddison.

'Go on,' Anderson urged.

'Well, he killed himself shortly after this picture was taken. Shot himself through the head in his office. It was quite a sensation at the time. In fact, it can't have been long after these photographs were taken. That poor girl, if only she'd known what was heading her way.'

EIGHT

'You lead this session, please. You're more on top of things than I am.'

Anderson seemed surprised. He nodded and called the room to order. Throats were cleared, papers shuffled, and seats taken. The Murder Investigation Teams were always deadly serious about each and every case, but when it was one of their own, minds sharpened, and attention focused acutely.

'As you know, we believe DCC Warburton was snatched from the shoreline at North Ferriby between 07.30 and 08.30 this morning—'

He must have headed to North Ferriby shortly after he'd hurt Jenni. He'd done a lot of damage in the past twenty-four hours. Whatever he was up to, past experiences suggested to Hollie that this heightened activity would result in a crisis point of some sort. Either he'd grow so brazen that they'd catch him, or... She didn't want to think about it. They had to find the DCC.

'We've had officers in the village all morning. We believe our suspect is now driving a car or van rather than the motor-cycle used to injure DC Langdon—'

The room fell silent. She'd never heard a roomful of cops sit so still. They all knew it could have been any one of them.

'Have we found the motorcycle he used when he struck DC Langdon?' Osmond asked.

It was the first time Hollie had heard him contribute a bit of policing to a briefing.

'Nothing yet,' Anderson replied. 'We're monitoring reports of stolen vehicles to see if we can get plate details, but he may be using his own wheels. We need to stay open-minded. DS Patel, have we gleaned anything from eyewitness reports or CCTV in the area?'

'From what I've collated so far, we have an unidentified motorcycle roaring along New Walk in North Ferriby that was picked up near the station entrance. It's not necessarily our man. There were no sightings at the shoreline, even though it's a popular spot for dog walkers.'

'Have we spoken to her husband yet?' Hollie asked.

'Yes, uniform has, but all he can offer is that she walked the dogs there most mornings and that she's been very distracted recently,' Patel explained. 'To save me wasting your time, we have nothing to work on as yet. We're assuming she was snatched, because of the dogs being found loose—'

'Have we considered that she might have run away?' Osmond interjected.

The entire room turned to look at him. His face reddened and he gave more explanation.

'I'm simply suggesting that we can't assume the obvious. Keep your minds open. Potentially, we might have an at-risk person.'

'He ought to know,' Anderson muttered under his breath.

Hollie glared at him. That one-to-one they'd got pencilled in couldn't come soon enough.

'Okay, so there's something important we need to update you about,' Hollie started, her mouth feeling uncomfortably dry.

'This is extremely sensitive information, and it stays between these walls, please. If I hear any leaks to the press that haven't been run through official channels, I will haul you over the chopping block myself. Is that understood?'

There was a chorus of *Yes, ma'ams*, and she was pleased to see the look of surprise crossing several faces in the room. They had to understand she was deadly serious about this.

Hollie took a deep breath. She was about to tell the whole room that one of their most senior bosses had, most likely, been a rape victim as a teenager.

'DCC Rose Warburton is the fifth girl,' Hollie began. She thought carefully about the words she was using. Some of this information had come from her colleague at Lancaster Police and she didn't want to show her hand. She held up an enlarged copy of the picture of the school netball team and pointed to the young Rose.

'The girl in this picture is the same girl who took the photo of Gilly, Mandy, Violet and Theresa in the mother and baby home. We've referred to her by her nickname of Twiggy so far—'

There were looks of disbelief among the team as she spoke. That was something you didn't often see in a briefing room.

'But the Beverley photographer, Stanley Maddison, just confirmed it to us and has the paperwork to prove it. Violet Farrow also told us the girl who took this photograph had the surname of Watson, but she was unable to remember her first name. DS Anderson and I grew suspicious of this connection last night, but we wished to discuss it with DCC Warburton first, due to its sensitive nature. If the DCC has been abducted, as I believe, then this confirms her direct connection with the case.'

'Are you certain of this?' Osmond asked.

'Yes, sir,' Hollie confirmed. 'The girl known as Twiggy was, we understand, the victim of a rape at the age of fifteen years old, or thereabouts. I know coppers aren't known for their empathetic wiring, but I'd urge you to consider the DCC in all of this. There's a very good reason why she might not have shared her connection with this case, and I'm going to insist you respect the sensitivity of this situation. From our conversations with him so far, do we know if her husband knows anything about her past at the mother and baby home?' Hollie asked the question and looked around the room for a response. 'Who spoke to her husband this morning?'

A hand shot up, but she didn't know the name of the detective constable.

'I did, ma'am, though uniform visited his property first after he reported her missing.'

'DS Anderson, you and I will conduct a formal interview with him due to its sensitive nature. DS Patel, make that happen ASAP, please.'

DS Patel jotted it down in her notepad.

'So do we think it's her child who did it?' somebody asked.

Hollie wished she knew more of their names.

'They have to be a suspect,' Hollie answered. 'We can't rule it out.'

'Do we have a name?' DC Gordon asked.

'I know the DCC has children by her present marriage,' DS Patel said, 'but if she had a child as a result of a sexual assault—'

It seemed she almost choked on the words.

'It's all right, DS Patel. All of us here share your shock at this news. We'll gently ascertain what her husband knows when we interview him—'

Hollie stopped dead. The man with the birthmark – was he the DCC's son? But he was with her at the time the DCC disappeared. None of it made sense. Hollie made a mental note to phone Theresa directly. She'd ask her if her son had a birthmark on his neck. She'd seen both Clive and Duncan with her own eyes, so Mandy's and Gilly's sons could be discounted. She considered Gilly; did she have the DCC's son with her in her home? She'd send her a text message to check in on her after the meeting was over.

'We must consider all angles here,' she reminded DS Patel while tapping on her phone screen. 'Who would want to snatch the DCC, if, indeed, that's what has happened to her?'

DCI Osmond gave her a small nod of acknowledgement. If she'd learnt one thing about being in a senior position, it was that you never ignored an idea proffered by the brass.

'What about Clive Bartram now, ma'am?' DC Gordon asked. 'He was in custody awaiting interview at the time of these events. I assume that places him out of the picture now?'

Hollie considered that for a moment.

'He may have been an accomplice, so I'd like you to go over to Clough Road and make sure he's formally questioned – I take it he is out of the infirmary after his soaking in the Humber?'

DS Patel put her thumb up to confirm it.

'We need to know how and where DCC Warburton was taken,' Hollie resumed.

'And, perhaps, most importantly, why has he taken her?' Anderson added.

Hollie wished this man wasn't so abrasive. He was clearly a good cop and they worked well together.

'Does she know something?' he continued. 'How was she caught up in the events at the home? And is she in danger?'

'Needless to say, we must now assume we're dealing with a kidnapping situation,' Hollie cut in. 'You know how this plays out. Time is of the essence. Does anybody have anything to add?'

'Have we profiled the killer yet?' a young DC asked.

'It's certainly worth considering, DC—?'

'Forsyth, ma'am,' the young man added.

'It's great thinking, DC Forsyth. Can we set that in motion, DS Patel?'

Hollie wondered if it might arrive too late, bearing the time sensitivity of the case, but it was a sensible idea and might give some useful insight into their killer.

'I think the line we've taken – that this relates to a mother and baby in some way – is the correct course in the meantime. This is about anger, loss, and a sense of broken trust. We still can't rule out the possibility it's connected with another intake of girls, but it seems most likely that we're dealing with the right group of people here. Everything leads back to that time.'

Hollie waited and looked out across the room. She could sense the eagerness to get going. They were like a pack of hounds who'd got the scent of a fox.

'DS Anderson and I will catch up with you individually where possible, but in the meantime, continue to feed everything through DS Patel. Thank you, everybody. Let's find the DCC.'

The room cleared fast.

Hollie sent a text to Gilly before she became embroiled again.

> Everything okay with you? How is your house guest?

DCI Osmond made his way to the front of the room.

'DCC Warburton is a professional through and through. I think it unlikely that she didn't flag up this potential conflict of interest with the Chief Constable. I'll schedule a meeting with him and see if that's the case. If she kept quiet about her connection with the case—'

'We don't need to crucify her, do we, sir? It's understandable if she didn't want to share those details, if it didn't prejudice the case in any way.'

'It's a tricky one,' Osmond answered. 'I'll let you know how I get on.'

He walked off. Gilly's text reply arrived on her phone.

All fine here. He seems better now. He's dozing in the living room!

As Hollie read the message, she realised something she'd missed. DCC Warburton had been keen for her to avoid Gilly Hodges. Why was that? Was she hiding something? Or was it just that Gilly might have identified her? It was almost half a century after the event. There was no reason Gilly should recognise the DCC out of context, years afterwards, and with a married name. So why had she chosen to withhold the connection?

NINE

1968: SOPHIA BRENNAN'S STORY

Sophia was woken by the sound of clogs echoing in the underpass. It was still dark and bitterly cold. Bobbers were making their way down to the docks to land the catch at the quayside. Sophia was used to the constant to-ing and fro-ing, but it seemed louder in the cold, night air.

Her breath shot out in ice-cold wisps, and she rubbed her hands, wishing her gloves were thicker. How those men got by in the Antarctic waters, she didn't know. What she was certain of was that she couldn't spend another night on the streets. She had to get something sorted out.

Sophia spent what was left of the night alert, doing her best to stay warm, retreating into the shadows so she wasn't spotted. Some of the men were still drunk and, occasionally, one would split off from the line of workers to urinate or throw up away from the path. None of them saw her: she made sure of that. But she wasn't so stupid that she couldn't see the trouble she might get herself into by the underpass.

The night seemed long, and she had a lot of time to reflect on her situation. She loved her mum and her baby sister, but she couldn't contemplate being in the same house as Martin, not after what he'd tried to do. Her mother had no other choice, she knew. The baby was too young, and she'd struggle to work if Martin left her. She was stuck for the time being. Sophia saw she was on her own for now; she had to get herself sorted out. She urgently needed to find a place to stay. The Sally Army would help. Then she'd get work. With work, she'd be able to rent somewhere small, perhaps even get on the list for one of the new houses being built on the council estates. It seemed so simple in theory, but the path before her was strewn with problems, she knew that.

Sophia was up on her feet by six o'clock. She felt like she'd freeze to the ground if she stayed put any longer. She hid the knife in bushes close to the underpass, so it would be there if she was forced to sleep in that spot again. As she walked along Subway Street, she called out as she passed the various commercial establishments.

'Any work going?' she'd ask, only to be told it was men's work, not work for a schoolgirl, and that she should seek netting repairs. But with neither a place to do the work, nor the equipment to work with, that was not a possibility.

It was school time. It seemed so irrelevant at that moment; besides, it was over for her now. She'd been a good student, but an academic life was the preserve of the rich girls. People like her had to get to work and contribute to the household expenses. Martin had been on her back about it ever since she'd turned fifteen, but her mother had resisted, dangling the carrot of a better-paying office job if Sophia achieved her examination results. For a split second, she considered going to school, merely to stay warm. But catching a reflection of herself in a shop window, she thought better of it. She hadn't even considered how she'd wash and stay clean.

For one moment, Sophia felt a blind panic. Her anger rose at her mother, throwing her out like that, choosing to protect herself and the baby over her older daughter. With Martin in the picture, nothing was likely to improve. She changed course for the Salvation Army building and decided to see what they could do to help.

The centre, close to the docks, was packed with former fishermen. Some had lost fingers from gutting fish, others limped or had lost eyes due to accidents at sea, and each one had been cast aside by an industry that required them to be fit and capable. Many were drunk, drowning the misery of their lives in pints of beer, which only exacerbated their problems. There were almost no women there, but any women there were came with babies or young children. Sophia resolved to visit her mother again that night, to urge her to leave Martin and seek a bed at the Salvation Army. They could get away from him if they stayed together. She'd find work, and they could make sure the rent got paid.

It was warm in the centre and Sophia got herself a hot drink and some toast. She'd never really understood what went on there; her mother had managed to secure them a floor at a friend's house when her father died. Martin arrived on the scene not long after. They hadn't even recovered her father's body from the sea.

Sophia was advised to return to the shelter later in the day if she wanted to secure a bed for the night. A kind woman warned her against sleeping on the streets again, especially at her youthful age. She used the bathroom facilities, washed her face, tidied her hair, and then headed into the city. She was not allowed to stay at the centre all day, so she decided to use the city library. It would be warm, and she'd be safe there.

The day passed quickly, and the library staff left her alone long enough to catch up on the sleep she'd missed the night before. She made sure she was in the queue for a bed for the night in plenty of time. She couldn't stay on the streets again; the weather was much too harsh. She was relieved to find that she'd got a bed. It was in a dorm room with two other women and their children, and another girl, a little older than she was. She was grateful for the company, though the children were young and fretful. It wasn't anything she hadn't had to cope with already in the flat, what with the baby being there.

As Sophia lay in bed, the children now asleep and quiet, she saw the other young woman was still awake, trying to catch her attention, without waking the others. Constant noise came from the male occupants, who didn't have to keep to the same routines as the mothers. Sophia followed the girl's lead, quietly getting out of bed, and then creeping out of the room. They leant up against the radiator in the hallway and whispered.

'I know of a place that we can stay in the city. It's a squat in an empty house. It's lovely round there. The owner is abroad or something like that.'

'What's a squat?' Sophia asked.

'It's a better place to stay than this, and much safer. The men here are always trying it on, given half a chance. I met a group of people in town yesterday. They said I could join them.'

'What about food? Is it safe?'

'They've got a boiler and six bedrooms. It's a huge place in The Avenues. I've been here for three nights, and I don't want to stay any longer than I have to. They said to meet them at the Queen Victoria statue in the city centre tomorrow at four o'clock. I'm sure they'd let you come along, too. The house is huge, they said.'

Sophia wasn't so sure. A part of her still expected the situation at home to resolve itself, and the Salvation Army didn't seem so bad. She didn't know what she'd do if there were no beds available. The thought of a second night on the streets terrified her.

'I'll see,' she replied. 'I'll need to have a think about it.'

Sophia and the girl – Kerry – spent much of the night chatting and it felt good to have someone to share her experiences with. Kerry's family had lost their home, too, but there was no love lost between the family members and Kerry was now on her own.

The next day, grateful for a warm bed and food in her belly, Sophia decided to speak to her mother again. Perhaps Martin had calmed down. There was also the issue of the eviction notice that had to be dealt with.

As Sophia walked up Subway Street, she sensed a spark in the air, a buzz of chatter. The last time she'd got this feeling was when the *St Finbarr* trawler had caught fire and the entire fishing community was rocked by the tragic news. The closer she got to Hessle Road, the deeper her sense of foreboding. Something was up, and she had a bad feeling about it.

She started to run towards the shop where the flat was located and, as she neared it, she saw a crowd gathered and two fire engines outside the building. Breathless, she reached the shop and joined the crowd. The top of the building was burnt out, smoke still billowing from the windows, even though the fire had been damped down. Sophia was desperate now.

'What happened? Was anybody hurt? Did they get out?'

Her frantic questions brought no replies, only looks of shock and sadness. Her stomach knotted as her worst fears reared up like monsters come to consume her.

She spotted Mrs Brady sitting on a doorstep further up the street, still in her nightwear and slippers, her face blackened by soot and a blanket around her shoulders. She was sobbing.

The sight of her shocked Sophia. Mrs Brady was usually such a strong and vibrant woman, but now she looked exhausted and broken.

'Mrs Brady, what happened? Is my mum all right?'

Sophia could barely get the words out fast enough. She wanted to know, but she was terrified to hear the answer. Her mouth was dry, the tears already welling in her eyes.

Mrs Brady looked up at her and tapped the step with her hand.

'Come here, you poor girl.'

Sophia felt sick. Her stomach convulsed; she wanted to throw up, but nothing would come. The pain was lodged inside her, stuck, unable to find a way out. She sat at Mrs Brady's side, her legs incapable of carrying her any longer.

'I'm so sorry, Sophia—'

The tears began to flow now. A guttural sound came out of her mouth, and she struggled to breathe. Her hands were shaking, she was sweating, her entire body gripped by the horror of the scene behind her.

'Martin came back drunk last night and set fire to the shop when he heard he was being evicted. Only, he collapsed in the hallway before he had time to warn anybody. We got out the back—'

'What about my mother and the baby?'

She knew already, but she had to hear it to be true. As Mrs Brady said the words, she descended into a pit of darkness.

'I'm so sorry, Sophia. They didn't make it.'

TEN

'We seem to be sinking deeper and deeper and getting no further forward,' Hollie said as the briefing room emptied.

'I'm wondering if we should have pushed harder to talk to the DCC yesterday,' Anderson said quietly. 'Might it have spared her this morning's events?'

'Who knows? Every case is a labyrinth of what-ifs. It's such a sensitive matter. I think she might have brick-walled us. We need to talk to her hubby ASAP, that's for sure.'

Hollie called over to DS Patel who was already back at her desk.

'Any progress on contacting Rose Warburton's husband?'

'You can call over in half an hour, ma'am. He's just gone to pick the dogs up from the person who found them.'

'Shall I get a pool car sorted, or are we going to have this pep talk you wanted?' Anderson asked.

There it was again, the attitude.

'Come with me,' she said, leading the way towards one of the side rooms. She pulled the door closed behind him.

'Listen, DS Anderson, I'm not going to speak to you like I would a younger member of the team—'

'I'm pleased to hear it.'

'I won't belittle your intelligence. I've seen enough already to know you're a good cop and you believe in what we're doing here.'

Anderson seemed surprised at what she said.

'Here it comes, the shit sandwich,' he sneered.

'No, I told you I won't insult your intelligence. You've been to the same managing people training that I have. You know all that bollocks already. And this is off the record. It's between you and me, two senior team members. So, tell me, what's the problem?'

'Off the record?' Anderson checked. 'You want to know the truth?'

Hollie nodded. She'd tried conversations like this using management speak, and it didn't wash with cops. It provoked them more than anything. She found blunt honesty worked best.

'You don't belong here,' he began. 'You don't know the patch. You don't know the team. You're a country bumpkin from a rural patch.'

'Okay, that's good, for starters. And I take it the job should have been yours?'

'Of course it should. Surely even you can see that?'

'As it happens, I can. I got lost in Hessle on the night Sister Brennan died. I don't know any of the people and places we're investigating, and I sure as hell don't know any of the history. And when I'm in briefings, I look out across the sea of faces and can barely remember the names of my immediate team, let alone the other officers who are part of this investigation.'

Once again, Anderson studied her, weighing her up, seeming unsure what to make of her approach.

'So, what do you propose we do about it?'

Anderson said nothing.

'It's just that you seem to think you have all the answers. I'll make no secret of the fact I'm floundering here. I'm out of my depth. I've been thrust into a massive case before I even had a chance to get my feet wet, and, you won't know this yet, but my husband decided to implode our family just as we were all about to move to Hull. So, yes, I'm feeling pretty fucked over at the moment, and it doesn't help me having a petulant DI on the team.'

'I'd rather have had the shit sandwich.' Anderson grimaced.

'I like working with you, DS Anderson. We work well together with interviewees. I certainly value your local knowledge and expertise. I also appreciate the way I can hand over to you and know things are taken care of, like the logbook updates. You'll get to DI rank. There's no doubt in my mind that you have all the skills you need. But for Christ's sake, take it on the chin. You didn't get the job. They gave it to me, who knows why, but they did. And we're both stuck with it. So why don't you put it down to experience and bide your time? If we get this case solved between us, I'd say your star is about to rise.'

Anderson digested what she'd said. She expected a snarky remark, but it didn't come.

'You're right,' he said at last. 'I've been a prick.'

'I haven't finished yet—' Hollie started again.

'Jesus, there's more?' Anderson asked.

'Did you ever consider you might not have got the job because you sound like you've just stepped out of a seventies TV cop series? The language you use and the references you make, they're not appropriate for a modern police force. You don't even respect the choices of your own son—'

'Damn, that was close to the bone,' Anderson said. 'I didn't know this was family counselling, too.'

'You've got to stop this shit,' Hollie asserted. 'I have absolutely no doubt you have all the experience you need to make DI. But you're in charge of a team. They must look up to you and trust you, and you have to show them some respect. A lot of the kids who pass through these doors are going to see their lives differently from our generation, just like your son does. As leaders, we have to work with that and adapt. If we don't, we'll go the same way as the dinosaurs.'

Anderson was nodding.

'I can't say I'm looking forward to this year's performance review now.' He shrugged. 'But seriously, you're probably right. I'm an idiot sometimes, I know that. My former wife reminds me of it constantly. Between you and me, I'm still getting over the boss – the old boss – dying like that. I blame myself. I guess I've been lashing out at other people.'

'Did you go for counselling?'

Hollie knew she was being hypocritical, but sometimes she had to resort to the management handbook.

'A couple of sessions.' Anderson shrugged again. 'Sometimes I think you have to resolve this stuff up here.'

He pointed to his head. She agreed with him, but she wasn't going to say that right now.

'There's one more thing—'

'Bloody hell, another? Haven't you kicked me enough while I'm down?'

'I'm trying to do you a favour here, DS Anderson. We can play management bullshit if you want, but I'm not the only DI in Humberside Police, and I see no reason why you shouldn't get the next promotion.'

'Go on then, let me have it. What else is there? You might as well finish me off.'

'I had a complaint from a female member of staff who felt that she'd been sexually harassed at work—'

Anderson was agitated. He'd taken everything she'd said to him so far and it had gone much better than she might have expected. But this had rattled his cage.

'Okay, it's my time to lay down the law now. I will admit I've been a dick and I will hold my hands up to everything you've said so far. But I absolutely do not harass women. I want to be really clear about that. Was my name mentioned?'

'No, I just thought it might be you—'

'Absolutely not. But I will tell you, this goes back a bit, to DI MacKenzie's time. He mentioned once over a pint that he'd had a couple of complaints.'

'Did he do anything about it?'

'He didn't have a name. You're as long in the tooth as me, and you know you don't point the finger at your colleagues. But if I catch a whiff of it, you'll be the first to know. That's after I punch the idiot's lights out and scupper my chances of making DI forever.'

Hollie believed him. If he hadn't taken everything else so well, she might not have done. She could see it in his eyes, though. This was clearly something he felt strongly about.

'What happened to DI MacKenzie?' Hollie asked, changing the subject. 'I mean, what really happened? Not the sanitised version that the brass gave me.'

'It was fucking horrible. I hate to think what he was caught up in. They cut off his head, his hands, and his feet to make an example of him. It was bloody vicious. I saw the body. I've never seen anything like it.'

'You should consider that counselling, really. I mean it,' Hollie said. 'So, are we good here? I need you on this case, and I don't want to be fighting you all the time. Is there anything you want to get off your chest while we're having a group hug and singing "Kumbaya"?'

He laughed.

'Not that I can think of. I'm sorry, I got all stressed out about you joining the team. I worked myself up into such a state. I'd already convinced myself you were going to be useless—'

'By my own admission, I'm not playing my peak game at the moment—'

'Yeah, but the troops like you. That's a pretty good result

after such a short time. MacKenzie used to hide behind his desk. It's a popular move, mixing with the troops, doing some leg work. I can probably learn a thing or two from you, to be honest.'

'We're not competing here, Anderson. We're on the same team. I sure as hell need your help. I'll make no secret of that.'

Hollie's phone sounded. She checked the screen; it was Gilly.

'Excuse me, I need to take this.'

Hollie walked out of the interview room, not wanting Anderson to hear any of the conversation. Gilly could barely contain herself. She was lowering her voice, clearly not wanting to be heard.

'Is everything all right?' Hollie started.

'He's Twiggy's son!' Gilly exploded. 'I just saw his birthmark while he was getting changed. I know it. I saw him when he was a baby. This man you've left at my house is Twiggy's son.'

ELEVEN

'How do you know this, Gilly?'

She'd already considered this possibility, but here was Gilly Hodges swearing it was true.

'Twiggy had her baby at the same time as Theresa. I can remember it as clear as day. We were in the doghouse with the nuns because we'd sneaked out of the home one night. Mandy and I saw the baby sitting in the hallway while they were bringing all Twiggy's things from the taxi. This man is Twiggy's son, I'm telling you!'

Hollie's mind raced as she worked through what they knew. Stanley Maddison had confirmed the fifth girl was called Rose Watson. Violet had independently confirmed the same surname. Gilly only knew Rose Warburton as Twiggy; she wouldn't yet understand the relevance to the case of what she'd just said. And Acting DI Burns had also confirmed details about Rose Warburton's past. It was all slotting together, but she still couldn't see the big picture. And why was it that DCC Warburton was so keen for her to stay away from Gilly?

'Can I speak to him?' Hollie asked. 'It'll need to be in private, I'm afraid.'

'Of course,' Gilly replied. 'You already know this, don't you?'

'No, I didn't. This is brilliant information, Gilly. But I can't tell you how it relates to the case. And I'm going to ask Tony not to say anything as well. I'm as certain as I can be he's not our man.'

'Well, I hope he's not.'

Hollie paused. Tony was with her when the DCC was snatched; she was confident he was no threat to Gilly. Could she risk asking Gilly about Rose Warburton without giving the game away? She wanted to know why the DCC didn't seem to like Gilly.

'Just before I go, what do you know about DCC Warburton? Do you encounter her in your line of work?'

'That's a bit left of field, isn't it?' Gilly asked. 'I don't know her. She was once going to attend a council event I'd organised, and she pulled out. But I don't have anything to do with her. Why? Is there something I should know about her?'

'No reason,' Hollie deflected. Gilly would sniff this out if she wasn't careful.

'Can you get Tony for me?' she asked, anxious to move things on. Perhaps the distrust of Gilly had come from the DCC. Was Rose Warburton trying to keep her identity a secret from Gilly? That would make the most sense. She hoped the DCC would be able to clear that up herself, as soon as they were able to locate her.

DS Anderson moved towards the door. It looked like their one-to-one was over.

'I'll get that pool car sorted, shall I?'

'Yes, check with DS Patel on the address.'

Anderson nodded, and Hollie pulled the door shut once again for privacy.

'Hi, it's Tony.'

'Tony, is Gilly out of earshot?'

'Yes,' he confirmed. 'How out of earshot does she need to be?'

'Can you go out to the garden, maybe? This needs to be private.'

She heard movement, and Tony explaining what he was doing. She heard a door shut.

'I have something to tell you. I think now might be the time to come out of hiding—'

She could sense him tensing at the end of the line.

'We know you're DCC Warburton's son—'

He cleared his throat, about to protest, but he was intelligent enough to know when the game was up.

'Damn, you're good. Rose said you were.'

'She knows about you?'

'Yes. Of course she does. It was Rose who I've been protecting all this time.'

'It might have helped if you'd said—'

'I'm not sure that it would, detective. Besides, my mother is a private woman. I need to know I can trust you, DI Turner. Can I?'

'Yes, of course. But if it relates to the case, you know I'll have to use the information.'

'Do you know about the circumstances of my birth?'

'Sort of. Tell me in your own words.'

'My birth mother was raped, DI Turner. At the age of fifteen. I am the product of that rape...'

'We've worked that out. I'm so sorry.'

'Don't worry, I've got a psychologist. I'm still working through all that shit. It helped when I met my birth mother—'

'So you have a relationship with Rose?'

'Yes, for seven years now. But it's our secret. Her husband and family don't know, and my wife doesn't know. We meet once every three months. My wife once thought I was having an affair. That was a tricky one to handle. We've taken it slowly, bit by bit. She has a lot of mixed-up emotions about me, as you can guess.'

'Why the secret?' Hollie wondered aloud. She realised what a stupid question it was the moment Tony began his answer.

'She's deputy chief constable of a large police force. She has a husband and children from a loving marriage. She put the rape behind her years ago, even though it still haunts her every day. But she rebuilt her life, DI Turner. She was not expecting her child to walk back into it after so many years.'

'I'm sorry, that was an insensitive question. You were adopted, then? Like all the other children at the home? Did Rose find you or did you find Rose?'

'I found her, through the priest. I'd never met him before this. We corresponded via phone and letter. I think he felt guilty about the past.'

'Which priest was this?' she checked. She had a pretty good idea already.

'It was a Father Duffy – Francis was his first name, but he preferred Frank.'

'And Rose's reaction when you contacted her?'

'Hostile, to say the least. It took three years before she'd even meet with me. Can you blame her?'

Hollie considered how lonely it must have been for DCC Warburton, carrying that terrible baggage with her for all those years.

'How did you get involved in the case?' Hollie asked him. 'Did your birth mother know?'

Tony hesitated at the end of the line.

'No, she didn't. I told her about the man who'd been asking questions. She urged me to keep quiet about it and not speak to him again. But the moment the news broke about the nun, she called me. She was terrified. She thought the truth would come out about her past. I didn't tell her I was coming to Hull. I've been working of my own accord. She gave me those photos a couple of years ago, you know, to help me understand her past. I wanted to protect her. I was worried about her. I thought she might be in danger. So, I tried to find out what was going on. I wanted you to see those photos, so you'd speak to the other girls. I'm convinced it's connected with Rose's time at the home, but I don't know how.'

Hollie waited a moment, bracing herself to deliver unwelcome news.

'Tony, I'm afraid Rose was abducted this morning—'

She heard him gasp.

'She was walking her dogs at North Ferriby when she was taken. There's a small possibility she might have run away—'

'You don't believe that, do you?'

'No, not for one minute—'

'She hasn't been... hurt, has she?'

'There's no evidence of violence, and I can confirm that no body has been found. At this stage, we believe her to be alive. We're about to talk to her husband—'

'What a mess. What a complicated, screwed-up mess. Who on earth would want to take Rose?'

'Well, on Monday, she was on the TV press conference, like me. My family have also been targeted, but it was just a warning—'

'I'm so sorry to hear that.'

'It's fine. My son is okay. But we have some lunatic on the loose here and I haven't a clue what he wants. There's no doubt in my mind it's all connected with the mother and baby unit. But how? And why? What does this man want?'

'I'll send another Facebook message,' Tony said at last, after a long silence between them. 'I'll see if I can bring him out into the open. You can use me as bait if he gets in touch. I don't mind, if it will help Rose...'

There was another pause. It sounded to Hollie like he'd just realised something.

'Will you tell her husband about me?'

Hollie swallowed hard.

'Nobody knows about you yet, other than Gilly and me. I'm going to tell my colleague on the drive over to Swanland, to see what he thinks we should do next. But I won't tell her husband. I think that's up to Rose to do that, don't you?'

'What about the reporters? They'll sniff it out, won't they?'

'Yes, eventually. But we'll keep it out of the press updates for now. It's confidential information and not something the public needs to know. I suggest you don't say anything to Gilly yet. You know she was with your mother in the home?'

'Yes, it's why I dropped off that photo of the girls at her house. I don't know her, though, and she doesn't know me—'

'She does now. She knew your birth mother as Twiggy. She saw you as a baby in the mother and baby home. She recognised you from your birthmark.'

Tony laughed.

'Of course she did. That's how Rose knew it was really me and not some gold-digger coming out of the woodwork. I thought I'd done a good job of concealing it, but nothing gets past you coppers.'

Hollie was anxious to move things on, but with Tony in the city, they had a way of reaching out to the killer and making direct contact. That seemed to her like their best bet for now.

'Tony, I want you to lie low. Please don't let Gilly know Twiggy's identity, for now. Just go along with the nickname. But reach out to this man on Facebook again. How's that wound, by the way?'

'Better, thank you, but painful and sore. I'll survive. Is there any news of your colleague?'

'No news so far. We're all waiting for an update from the hospital. Look, Tony, sit tight and, if I hear anything, I'll get straight back to you. We're off to speak to Rose's husband now. I won't beat about the bush with you, though. We need to locate her. Fast.'

TWELVE

1968: SOPHIA BRENNAN'S STORY

Sophia scanned the room. It was like nothing she'd ever seen before. There was a chandelier, for starters. The shaped glass caught the light and made a snowflake-like pattern on the ceiling. The dining table was built of sturdy, polished oak and the chairs were beautifully upholstered in a rich, mauve velvet.

'What do you think?' Kerry asked, coming back in. 'It's a bit posher than the Sally Army, isn't it?'

'How can someone own a house like this and be able to afford not to live in it?' Sophia wondered aloud.

'Well, that's why we're borrowing it, isn't it? It can't hurt.'

There were beer cans and cigarette butts left around the place. Ash and food debris stained the once pure-white linen tablecloth. Sticky rings lined the sideboard where drinks had been left, and somebody had drawn black marker moustaches on a family portrait presiding over the room. They weren't borrowing this house; they were systematically wrecking it.

'I'm still not sure,' Sophia said. 'Look at the place. Won't we get in trouble with the police?'

'So long as we keep a low profile and the neighbours don't

realise what's going on, we'll be fine. Just do what the others showed us, and everything will be okay. As they said, always enter over the fence at the back and get into the house through the storeroom window. Nobody can see us from there. Besides, when Cillian comes back, it'll be much better. He's in charge, apparently. I've been told it all runs much smoother when he's around.'

Sophia moved over to the large iron radiator, which was belching out heat. It was glorious compared to the gnarling cold she'd endured next to the underpass.

'Come upstairs. I'll show you our bedroom.'

Sophia followed her, her clothes still hot from the radiator. There were signs of the squatters everywhere: torn pictures hanging lopsided on walls, cigarettes discarded carelessly on carpets and burn marks where they'd been stubbed out. There were discarded tins and food packets, as well as slogans and song lyrics written on the wallpaper. Sophia knew it was wrong, but she couldn't see what other option she had. It would suffice for now until she could get herself sorted out.

There were six bedrooms upstairs. She and Kerry were sharing a children's bedroom, which was equipped with a bunk bed. The room was Rupert the Bear themed, with annuals and posters all over.

'See,' Kerry began. 'I'll bet you never had a bedroom like this as a kid. These people are loaded. It won't hurt them to help us out while they're away doing whatever rich-person thing it is they're doing.'

'Top or bottom?' Sophia asked.

'So, you'll stay then?'

'For now, yes. It's hit or miss whether we'll get a bed at the Salvation Army tonight, and there's no way I'm sleeping outdoors again. I'll say yes for now. Thank you for asking me.'

Sophia spent the rest of the day catching up with her sleep.

The sheets and blankets were crisp and dry. She only ever experienced that in the summer when it was possible to get the washing properly aired. In winter, without radiators, everything had a cold, damp feel to it. The bunk bed felt luxurious to her.

As she dozed, she allowed herself to weep over her mother's death. It was the first time she'd been alone and felt safe enough to do so. She didn't even know what would happen to their bodies; it wasn't as if they could afford to pay for a funeral. She prayed her mother wouldn't be buried with Martin. She couldn't stand the thought of her never being able to get away from him, even in death. The poor baby, too; it must have been terrifying.

Sophia woke to the sound of a male voice downstairs in the hallway. It was immediately confident and commanding; it had to be Cillian.

Kerry burst into the room.

'Cillian's back. We'd better get down there and introduce ourselves. What he says goes in this place. We can't stay unless he says so.'

Sophia hadn't realised that; she'd thought her place there was assured. She threw back the sheets and tidied her clothes and hair. Her mouth felt dry and stale, and she knew she badly needed a wash.

'So, here they are, our two new additions to the household.'

Cillian scrutinised the two of them as they walked down the stairs. The atmosphere was different with him there; everybody seemed more guarded.

'You're both very young,' he said. 'And pretty, too. The question is, will you be prepared to contribute to the household?'

Cillian didn't seem to be down on his luck. He wore a tan leather jacket and a Wranglers shirt and jeans. His shoes were sturdy and looked like they'd seen polish in the last couple of weeks.

'Of course we will,' Kerry answered on their behalf. 'We'll do whatever you need us to do.'

'We'll see about that,' Cillian sneered. 'It means we're a bit crowded in here if you stay, though.'

He looked at the other squatters who'd gathered to greet him in the hallway. Sophia noticed a slight boy doing his best to blend into the background. He jumped as Cillian called his name.

'Clifford!'

'Yes, Cillian.'

He looked like he was about to wet himself.

'You'll need to fuck off.'

'But—'

'Fuck off!'

'I'll sleep on the floor—'

'Fuck off, Clifford.'

The boy began to cry. Sophia reckoned he must be a similar age to her. She started to panic. Suddenly the mood had changed, and she didn't like it. This is how things turned at home.

Clifford looked around the room. A woman a similar age to her mum started to walk over to the boy. Cillian raised his hand.

'No, leave him. He's a useless waster of a prick. Get out of the house, Clifford. And if you cause any trouble, I will personally find where you're sleeping rough and take a piss on you at night when you can't see me coming. Understood?'

Clifford nodded and walked towards the kitchen, behind which the storeroom was located.

Everybody was silent. Sophia wanted to reach out to Clifford but she daren't move or make a sound. Had she made a terrible mistake coming here?

'Can I collect my bag?' he asked, sniffing as he struggled to maintain a steady voice.

'Can I collect my bag?' Cillian repeated, using a baby voice to mock the boy. A couple of people fidgeted while others looked down at their shoes.

'Get your bloody bag and piss off!' Cillian shouted, his words dripping with contempt.

Sophia wanted to walk out of the front door, but she was rooted to the spot. Cillian had complete command of the room. He turned to face them.

'So, yes, you can stay, but as I said, you'll have to earn your keep. We're going out tonight and I want you two to come. All right, Billy?'

A man of a similar age to Cillian came out of the living room. His shirt was hanging loose around his trousers and Sophia could clearly see his chest, which was covered in thick, black hair.

'Sure,' he sneered. 'Might as well get them trained up quick.'

'Eleven o'clock,' he said to Kerry. 'Make sure you're both here. In the meantime, feel free to make the most of the facilities.'

As Cillian left the hallway, there was a collective release of breath and mumblings between friends.

'Poor Clifford,' the older woman whispered. 'I'll make sure I send him off with some food.'

'He's a nutter. I wish he'd just get lost and leave us to it,' said another.

'There's a rumour this place belongs to his parents,' one of the men mumbled. 'They threw him out, apparently, and this is how he's getting payback.'

Sophia looked at Kerry. She didn't know what to say. She wanted to run, but she knew how it would play out if she tried to leave.

'Look, it's better than the Sally Army for now, right? We're warm, we're fed, and we're safe. We can look for somewhere else if you don't like it. Let's just give it a few days, okay?'

Sophia nodded. She knew how men like this behaved. She'd seen it up close. Everything was sweetness and light until that black mood descended, and then everything turned quickly horrible. But it wasn't like they were spoilt for choice for places to stay. Could they stay out of the way until they found somewhere better? If the worst came to the worst, they could always join the queue at the homeless centre.

Every bone in her body wanted to be out of that place. But she had Kerry to consider now, and as two girls out on their own at night, they were vulnerable. It was so cold outside; they were warm here and there was food.

Cillian kept out of the way in the living room for the rest of the evening, and all that could be heard was boorish laughter and the occasional sound of something being smashed. Sophia ventured into a hot bath, an experience she hadn't enjoyed for several years. In the flat, she'd washed in the sink, using water that was seldom fully heated. Martin took the hottest water for himself, leaving everybody else to eke out what was left between themselves.

The piping-hot water was glorious, and Sophia luxuriated in there for a while, immersed in clouds of steam. Eventually, there was a knock at the door.

'Sophia! I got you some clothes—'

It was Kerry.

'Let me in. I think they'll fit you.'

Sophia climbed out of the bath and wrapped a towel around her body. She cautiously opened the door. Kerry peered through the small gap.

'Here, look, I found these in a wardrobe. You're about the same size as me. I'm sure they'll fit.'

As Sophia opened the door a little wider to allow Kerry to join her, Cillian's right-hand man, Billy, walked by on the landing and glanced in. Sophia pulled the towel tighter, horrified to have been spotted. Billy was in no such hurry. He took his time and looked her up and down.

'Nice,' he sneered. 'Very nice, too.'

Sophia pushed the door closed behind Kerry and made certain that it was properly locked.

THIRTEEN

Rose Warburton's house was bigger than Hollie had expected.

'Sheesh, we need to move up a couple of ranks!' Anderson exclaimed as they drove through the wrought-iron gates.

He'd taken the words out of her mouth. She thought about her flat. Getting a new place was going to be a priority once the case was over, even if it meant paying six months for an apartment she wasn't using.

Anderson had been well-behaved on the drive over. He'd even been conciliatory. As they'd approached the Hessle turn-off along the Clive Sullivan Way, he'd spoken up and broken the silence.

'You know, I really did forget to mention the change of location for the press conference,' he said.

They were both caught up in their thoughts. Hollie was mulling over all the information they'd gathered, and she assumed he was doing the same.

'I was pissed off at the time, I can tell you that.'

'And I was as surprised as you were when the DCC handed over to me first. She was angry with you last-minuting it, but you didn't deserve that.'

'Okay, well, thanks for telling me. I appreciate it.'

They stopped talking as they drove under the bridge.

'I can't believe he actually threw her over the side,' Hollie continued as they passed under the Humber Bridge. 'What a way to get everybody's attention. What do you think he's after?'

'Who knows?' Anderson replied. 'I stopped trying to get inside the heads of these lunatics some time ago. I leave that for the shrinks. I just try to get the little bastards before they hurt someone else.'

He took the North Ferriby slip lane.

'Can we see where the DCC was taken from?' Hollie asked. 'I'd like to get an idea of it before we see her hubby.'

'Sure,' Anderson replied. 'It's just a short diversion.'

Hollie saw the sign to Swanland ahead, but they turned off into North Ferriby, a village she'd never seen before.

'This is nice,' she said. 'It has a station, doesn't it?'

'Yes, it's a great little commuter village. I considered buying a house here, once upon a time.'

Hollie took it all in as they made their way through the village. There was a mixture of housing, and it had a school and a playing field. It was the sort of place she'd like to have come back to with Léon and the kids, for a proper look. It had a small cluster of shops, too.

'Here it is,' said Anderson as he pulled up at a small parking area at the end of the village. The Humber looked vast from that vantage point, and the area of shoreline was an obvious place to walk dogs.

'Stupid question, but I assume forensics got her car towed?' Hollie asked as they stepped out of the vehicle.

'Yes, they're giving it the once-over for the usuals, but I doubt we'll get anything.'

Hollie followed Anderson to the brick steps at the closest end of the car park and they stepped down onto the foreshore. All the time Hollie was scanning, looking for cameras or windows in nearby houses that overlooked the area where the DCC had been snatched.

'I know what you're thinking,' Anderson said. 'All the neighbours have been doorstepped by uniform and there are no cameras that cover this area. As you saw, the car park is asphalt, so we can't even get tyre prints. My guess is that he parked by these steps and bundled her into the car – or the van – when she came up off the beach. He might have been sitting on one of those benches. Nobody would have seen him, if it was quiet at the time. It's easy enough to do if you've got the nerve.'

The full span of the Humber Bridge looked spectacular in the distance. Hollie wished her relocation hadn't been screwed up by her husband. It could have been so good for the family to explore a new area and start a fresh adventure together.

'Have you seen enough?' Anderson asked.

Hollie took a slow look around and tried to absorb the scale and beauty of the estuary.

'Yes. Let's go and find out what hubby has to say.'

It was a short drive over to Swanland. Hollie took an immediate liking to the area. She'd seen a couple of letting signs outside houses, and she made a note of the estate agents in her mobile phone whenever she spotted one that looked interesting.

The doorbell at DCC Warburton's house was as grand as the property. It made a deep, resonant sound as if its sole purpose was to announce to visitors that someone important lived there. The gardens were beautifully kept, and she thought she spied a gardener wielding a hoe behind a tall shrub. The door was substantial; it took a while for the occupant to attend to the various chains and mortice locks before it finally swung open.

Rose Warburton's husband was a tall, slim man with hair that was fully grey. The colour was drained from his face, and he had a look of dread behind his eyes, as if he half expected them to be delivering terrible news. The dogs rushed to the door to see what was going on, but they didn't bark or attempt to bolt the house. They knew their boundaries and stuck to them.

'Good morning, officers. Thank you for coming,' he began, his voice weary. His wife had been missing for less than half a day, yet he sounded worn down by it already, no doubt from the endless police questioning and the relentless worry and fear.

Hollie clocked cameras and security devices all over the house; she'd expect nothing less from the DCC. It also made an anonymous kidnapping from home almost impossible.

'Hello, Mr Warburton—'

'Please, call me Timothy. Do you know anything new?'

He was clearly a man used to containing his emotions, but Hollie could tell he was struggling to keep it together. With every other word, his voice would falter.

Hollie made the introductions, and they were guided to the kitchen. It was furnished with solid wood units. A bowl of fresh fruit sat on a central worktop area. Hollie's own fruit bowl was made up of a chipped plate and a rotting banana. There were unwashed mugs piled up in the sink and splashes of milk, and grains of sugar, left unwiped on the worktop from where he'd been making drinks for the police visitors he'd been receiving all morning.

Timothy put the kettle on and led them through to the conservatory, which overlooked a beautifully planted garden.

As Hollie sank into the comfortable armchair and gazed out over the garden, she had to remind herself this was not a social call. Timothy brought in drinks, his hands trembling as he carried the tray.

'Take a seat,' Hollie motioned.

Timothy looked like a man who had enough sense to see that he was being gently handled. He looked between Hollie and DS Anderson, then took the second armchair.

'I'm afraid I have some very difficult news to give you—' Hollie began.

'Oh no, Rose hasn't been hurt, has she? She's not dead—'

'No, we've received no further news of DCC Warburton since her disappearance. This relates to her life before she met you. Do you talk much about the time before you met? Has she discussed her parents, for instance?'

Timothy shook his head.

'Both parents died before I met her. She made me promise never to speak about it after she first told me. I tried it a couple of times when we were younger, but the most I ever got from her was that she'd had a difficult relationship with her father in particular, and she wanted to look forward, not back. In time I learnt it was best to respect that.'

'How many children do you have together?'

'Just the two. Hayley is twenty-three and Marcus is twenty-five now. They're both grown up; Marcus is married. Why?'

DS Anderson shot a glance over to Hollie; she took it as a *rather you than me* kind of look.

'I've got some very sensitive information about your wife which I need to share with you.'

His face became immediately alert; had he sensed something might be up?

'I'm very sorry to have to be the one to give you this news, but your wife has another child, a son, from a time well before you met. She was the victim of rape when she was a teenager, and the baby was adopted in the seventies. We believe this is the reason Rose was abducted this morning. She had her baby at the mother and baby home which is the focus of our current investigation.'

If Timothy Warburton's face was white before, it was now ashen. His eyes reddened as he fought to contain his emotions. He stared at them, his face blank, as if overwhelmed by the enormity of what he'd just been told.

'I noticed you've got some whisky in the kitchen,' DS Anderson said. 'Would you like me to pour you a glass?'

'I think you'd better,' Timothy replied, his voice faltering like it might fail at any moment. He sat in silence, trying to process this terrible information.

'How long have you known?' he asked at last.

DS Anderson returned from the kitchen.

'We've only just figured it out,' Hollie answered as Anderson handed him the whisky.

'I couldn't find a proper glass for it, so it's in a regular tumbler. Sorry.'

Timothy took a large sip.

'Why didn't she tell me?'

'We're just piecing things together at the moment,' Hollie resumed. 'I'm so sorry that you had to find out this way; it was Rose's story to share with you, at a time of her choosing.'

Timothy looked to the floor, silent, gently shaking his head.

'Has the DCC discussed the case with you?' Anderson picked up. 'Has there been any indication that something might have been troubling her?'

'She's said very little about this case,' Timothy said. 'And now I know why. I listen to the radio, of course, and I saw her on the television. But I hadn't got a clue. It seems that everybody knows but me.'

Hollie and Anderson exchanged a look.

'It's really not as bad as that.' Hollie attempted to reassure him. 'We're handling it as a matter of delicacy at the station, and I've briefed my team to use the utmost discretion. We won't release the information to the public, but it will have to come out in court eventually, now she's been kidnapped. It's just one big mess, I'm afraid.'

Hollie and Anderson explained how they'd managed to piece together the puzzle.

'Poor Rose,' Timothy said quietly after some time. 'She's carried this terrible thing with her all her life and never felt she could share it with me. What must that be like, to hold something so dark inside you? I always felt there was something there, something I couldn't quite put my finger on. But we've been happily married for all these years. I still can't believe it.'

She could see it, lurking below the surface, but he seemed more upset that the DCC should have felt the need to hide her secret, rather than sharing it with him. Hollie couldn't begin to understand what it must have been like for her.

The three of them sat quietly. Hollie wanted to give Timothy some time to process the information before pushing him further.

The phone started to ring.

Its sound was intrusive and abrasive, shattering the silence of their thoughts.

They looked at each other, and Timothy began to speak.

'I have something that I need to tell you. I should have told you before, but you distracted me with that terrible news about Rose. I've been receiving mystery phone calls all morning.'

FOURTEEN

'What do you mean by mystery phone calls?' Anderson asked.

Hollie's heart quickened. Was this the killer?

'Each time it's a couple of rings from a withheld number. I pick it up and there's somebody there, but they don't speak. It's him, isn't it?'

'We can't know for sure, but yes, it could be him,' Hollie replied. She was certain it must be him.

The phone continued ringing.

Hollie's mind was on full alert now, her hunting instincts strong and keen. If this was their man, she'd finally know who she was dealing with.

'Shall I answer it?' Timothy asked.

'Do you have a speakerphone?' Hollie asked as they followed him into the kitchen. She rapidly considered her options; this could be her direct link to the DCC. This was a chance to save her colleague before she came to any harm. That's if he hadn't hurt her already.

'Yes, I can put it on speaker.'

He walked over and checked the caller ID.

'It's a withheld number. It's probably him. Are you ready?'

Hollie and Anderson stood close to the central worktop where the phone was placed. Her heart was pounding; she sensed the same from DS Anderson.

'Yes, answer it,' Hollie said.

Timothy let the phone ring one more time, and then he picked it up.

'Hello?'

He nodded his head.

Hollie looked at DS Anderson.

'If you're the man who's got my wife, please speak to me.'

Hollie could hear from the ambience at the end of the line that somebody was there. She held her hand out. Timothy passed the phone over.

'It's DI Turner,' she began. 'If you'll speak to me now, this doesn't have to get out of hand.'

There was more silence.

'Fuck off!' came a man's voice, and the call was ended.

Timothy was shaking.

'Was that him?' he asked.

'Probably,' Hollie replied. 'We can't rule out a crank call, but we haven't released the information to the press yet. They'll get it eventually, but for now, we can keep a lid on it.'

'It's on Twitter already,' he continued, 'or whatever it is Elon is calling it these days. Not that Rose was snatched, but speculating about all the police activity in the village. I'm guessing it won't remain private for long?'

'It's unlikely,' Anderson picked up. 'I'm sorry, that's just how it is these days.'

Timothy nodded. He'd probably had that conversation with Rose a million times before. Social media was both a blessing and a curse to policing teams. In some cases, like this one, Hollie wished it had never been invented.

'I know the uniformed officers have been through all this

with you already, but can I ask you some questions?' Hollie asked. 'Just in case we missed something?'

'Of course,' Timothy answered. 'Do whatever you need to do to find Rose.'

'Can we take the receiver back into the conservatory with us? Just in case he calls again,' Hollie asked.

'Yes, it connects to the base unit,' Timothy replied.

They walked back to the conservatory. Timothy picked up his whisky and Hollie watched as he had to place it back on the coffee table; his hand was trembling too much to hold it steady enough.

'Has anybody unusual called at the house in the past couple of days?'

Timothy thought it through.

'Not that I can think of. The gardener is in and out, but we know him. He doesn't even knock when he arrives. He just gets on with it.'

'Think laterally,' Anderson chipped in. 'Were there any salespeople or the like?'

'I'm retired now, so I would see them,' Timothy said. 'Now you mention it, we had one of those annoying men round a couple of days ago. The ones who sell bits and pieces for around the house that you never need. I was just about to take the dogs to the vet, so he caught me at a bad time. He made a big fuss of the dogs. He said he'd fallen on difficult times and was making a living going door-to-door. I asked him to come back next time he was in the area, and I'd buy something then—'

'Was that your man on the phone?' Anderson asked as they returned to their seats. 'The one who called at the door?'

'It certainly might have been,' Timothy answered. 'I can't be sure as everything sounds different on the telephone. But, if you pushed me, I'd say yes, there's a very good chance.'

'I notice you have a lot of security equipment here,' Hollie remarked. 'Do you record anything on the cameras? Is there any chance you might have caught him on camera?'

'He was wearing a red cap. He had a rucksack, too. I remember that much.'

Hollie and Anderson exchanged a glance.

'Didn't you say he had a rucksack when he snatched your son?' Anderson checked.

'Would you check for us?' Hollie asked. 'Can you access the recordings?'

'Sure, I'll go and look now. What if he calls again?'

'Is it okay if I answer the phone next time?' said Hollie. 'I'd like to get him talking if I can. We can listen for sounds in the background to see if it gives us any clues as to where he is.'

'Be my guest. I'll be back shortly, once I've examined the security files.'

Hollie waited for Timothy to leave the kitchen before speaking.

'What do you think?'

'I think we almost have our man. The red cap and rucksack did it for me. He was casing the place beforehand. He obviously realised there wasn't a chance in hell of getting to DCC Warburton via the house, so he must have watched her movements and decided to make the snatch down by the foreshore. He's not your typical psycho, that's for sure. This guy has a brain.'

'Agreed. If he's calling the house, I reckon he's working up to making a demand. I'm going to try to draw him out—'

'Don't piss him off or he'll take it out on the boss,' Anderson warned.

'Have you done the training?' Hollie asked.

'Yes, some time ago now. I've never had to deal with a kidnapping situation.'

'I'm rusty, but I think we have to try it. *Every effective nego-*

tiator uses collaboration, I remember that much. Build trust, don't wind him up, find out what's driving him.'

'That's more than I remember.' Anderson smiled. 'I'll let you do the talking.'

'I was wondering why the dogs didn't cause more fuss when the DCC was snatched,' Hollie continued. 'But they'd met him already in a friendly situation, so I'm guessing that's why they didn't bark or do anything to attract the attention of the people who live at the foreshore. As you said, he's not daft. He can plan more than one step ahead.'

The phone rang again. Hollie checked the number display. The caller's information was withheld. Timothy had been doing a crossword, so his newspaper and a pen were lying on the table in the conservatory.

'If you want to say something, scribble it on that. Don't let him know you're here.'

Hollie answered the call on speaker.

'It's DI Turner. Are you okay to talk?'

There was silence, but she could hear breathing. She listened for clues, but there was nothing distinctive in the background to work with.

'You can call me Hollie if you want. Can we talk? I'd like to help if I can.'

She waited and stopped pushing. He hadn't sworn at her yet, and the call was still active.

'Can I just check with you, is DCC Warburton safe?'

More silence.

'Take your time,' she continued.

'She's safe. For now.'

It was the same voice. He seemed uncertain whether to speak, as if testing himself for courage.

'Can I use your name?' Hollie ventured.

'No name, not yet. Who's with you?'

'It's just me—'

DS Anderson shook his head.

'—and DS Anderson. Did you see the press conference? DS Anderson was with me and DCC Warburton on the TV. So, you know all of us now.'

Anderson put his thumb up.

'Hello,' Anderson said so he would be heard by the caller.

'What can we do to help you?' Hollie asked.

There was a dismissive laugh at the end of the line.

'I don't think I'm getting any help from you bastards any time soon.'

'What do you mean by that?' Anderson interjected. 'You sound like somebody has pissed you off.'

'You might say that.'

Hollie raised her eyebrows at Anderson.

'What have they done?' she added.

'You've been investigating the home, right?'

'Yes.'

They both spoke over each other. This was good. They were getting somewhere.

'I'm just the same as all the other kids. I want to know the truth.'

'Were you born there?' Anderson asked. 'We can check the records and find out for you?'

'I don't know. I can't find out. But I think your friend the deputy chief constable might know.'

'Why's that?' said Hollie.

'Because I think I might be her son. I think she's not telling me something. She was there. She was at the home. She was a rape victim—'

He knew. How did he know that? Had the DCC been trying to forge a connection with him?

'Is that why you've taken her?' Hollie asked. 'You think she's your mother?'

DS Anderson scribbled something on the newspaper.

Careful! Don't wind him up!

Hollie suddenly felt in too deep. If she told him she knew the DCC wasn't his mother, would it make him spiral? Might he harm the DCC in frustration as he lashed out?

'She says she's not, but I don't believe her. Who wants the child of a rapist? Nobody! Nobody wants a child that came from such a hateful act. So, she ignored me. She gave me away. She wanted rid of me. She might as well have aborted me and flushed me down the toilet, for all she cares—'

'Wait—'

The phone clicked dead.

FIFTEEN

1968: SOPHIA BRENNAN'S STORY

'We should go,' Sophia urged. The girls were lying in their bunk beds, where they'd been chatting since they'd both taken a bath.

'I don't like it here,' she continued. 'I know the house is nice, but I think we're going to get into trouble. I don't like those two. Cillian reminds me of Martin. I was trying to get away from that bastard.'

'You know we can't stay with the Sally Army every night,' Kerry said. 'They won't let us. If we don't have young children, we'll take our chances with everybody else. I was out on the streets for four months, on and off, before I came here. Believe me, we're better off staying out of their way and making the most of it. We can keep an eye out for another squat, but this is fine for now.'

Sophia lay silent in the dark. The bunk bed was small but dry and warm. She hadn't felt so clean and fresh since before her dad died and they were renting the sham-four. Kerry was right. They'd stick it out for now but look for somewhere new. At least they had each other. It felt good to have a friend.

'Do you know when your mum is getting buried?' Kerry asked.

'I don't even know how to find out. The shop was closed after the fire and all the tenants moved out. I haven't a clue where they went. I don't even know who to ask. To be honest with you, I don't really know where to begin. I'm lost without my mum, and I don't have any relatives now.'

She paused a moment and realised she hadn't even asked Kerry about her life yet.

'What happened to you? You never said?'

Kerry was silent in the darkness of the small bedroom. Cillian's voice carried up the stairs. He was shouting about something or other.

'My stepfather was violent. He'd lost his leg at sea after he got caught up in one of the ropes. He just became dark and angry after that. When I was sixteen, he threw me out. When my mother protested, he hit her and strangled her. I just ran away and never went back—'

'I'm so sorry. Did he... kill her?'

'Yes. He's in prison now. I'm the same as you, completely lost. I don't know what to do to get out of it. How do you start anything if you don't even have a place to stay?'

'Do you have relatives?'

'Not locally. They live in Scotland somewhere. I wouldn't know them if I passed them on the street.'

'Perhaps you should try to make contact?' Sophia suggested.

'Perhaps—'

The door burst open. There was no knock and no shout.

'Get dressed, ladies. We're heading out.'

It was Billy.

Both girls jumped up in bed. They were mostly dressed already.

'What is it?' Kerry asked.

'You're coming with us. It's time to earn your keep.'

'Where are we going?' Sophia added. 'What do you want us to do?'

'You'll see.' Billy looked around the room. 'Once you've done this, you'll be able to stay as long as you like.'

Sophia climbed down from the top bunk and looked at Kerry.

'Get a move on!' Billy barked at them.

The girls put on the shoes and the coats they'd been wearing when they arrived. They were still grubby, but dry at least. As they stepped into the hallway, Cillian was waiting. He took one look at them and called over one of the other women.

'Sort these two out, will you? Then bring them in for a drink.'

'Come with me,' she said, leading them off into a room they hadn't been in before. It looked like it was a study, but there were assorted items of clothing strewn across the desk. The woman looked them up and down and picked out a couple of coats from the pile. 'Try those on. You'll look a lot better. Don't you ever wear make-up? You'd look much nicer.'

Sophia looked at Kerry, who shrugged.

'Come over here. Put a bit of lippy on.'

She whisked a lipstick from somewhere and applied it to Sophia's lips.

'Just move your lips like this.' The woman demonstrated. 'And whatever you do, don't make Cillian angry. It'll be all right, you'll see. You'll get used to it.'

Sophia's heart began to beat fast, and a sense of panic crept through her body. Something had always spooked her about Martin, and she was getting the same feeling now.

The woman led them back to Cillian, who looked them up and down again.

'That's better,' he said. 'Now, come in for a drink before we head out. It'll help keep you warm out there.'

Both girls were hesitant, but Cillian was insistent, and Billy was standing directly behind them, his hands at their backs, guiding them towards the living room. They stepped inside, a place they'd stayed well away from so far. It smelt of smoke, mainly, and the floor was covered with confectionery packets. There were empty beer cans all over and pictures from a *Playboy* magazine taped to the regular framed pictures that the owner had hung up around the room.

'Take a seat, girls.' Cillian smiled. 'What can I get you? A Babycham?'

Sophia had never drunk alcohol before and, seeing how it affected Martin, she had no intention of ever doing so.

'No, thank you.'

'I'll have a small sip.' Kerry made a face at Sophia.

'I insist you have something before we go out,' Cillian sneered. 'Billy, get them both a Babycham. Help the girls relax a bit.'

Billy did as he was told and brought in two open bottles.

'We don't have glasses, so you'll have to drink from the bottle,' he announced.

Sophia saw how small the drinks were and figured no harm could come from such a tiny amount.

'Drink!' Cillian said. 'And try not to look so scared. You'll frighten the customers.'

'Customers?' Sophia asked.

'Yes, you're just going to help us with a little bit of business tonight. All this has to be paid for, you know. Just think of it as housekeeping money.'

Sophia wanted to get out of there. She took tiny sips of her drink; it tasted sweet and easy to get down. Cillian and Billy chatted between themselves, urging the girls to drink up and occasionally bringing them into the conversation. Sophia's head was beginning to spin a little, and she realised it wasn't just her when Kerry laughed at one of their stupid jokes. Her body was more relaxed than it had been in months, and it sank into the sofa, allowing her thoughts to drift.

It might have been minutes or as much as an hour, but

before she realised what was happening, she and Kerry were getting into the back of a car. Kerry seemed okay with it, so Sophia followed her lead. Besides, she no longer felt as anxious as she had done beforehand, and Cillian and Billy weren't so irritable now, which was a good thing.

The beams of the streetlights made lovely patterns as Sophia's head rested against the back window, and she let her mind wander. Next thing she knew, she was being pulled out of the car and Cillian was giving instructions.

'Stand there and smile. You can use the car or that alleyway over there. Do whatever they want, but make sure they come to us with the money first. We'll be watching from over there.'

Sophia didn't understand what was going on. The whole street was gently spinning around her.

'I think they've slipped something in our drinks...' Kerry began.

'Hello, my darlings.'

Two men had walked up to them and seemed very friendly. They were looking around like they expected somebody to be there. Cillian walked up, purposefully.

'Evening, gents. Can I help you?'

'Will two pounds do it?' one of the men asked.

'Sure,' Cillian replied, holding his hand out for the cash.

The men pulled the money from their pockets and handed it over.

'Is the alleyway still good?' the other man asked, taking Kerry's hand.

'Sure,' Cillian answered. 'We'll keep an eye open for the cops. You go and enjoy yourselves.'

One of the men took Sophia's hand and gave it a tug in the direction of the alleyway.

'What's happening here? No, I don't like this,' Sophia said.

Kerry shook the second man's hand off her arm.

'One moment, gentlemen,' Cillian interjected. He put his

fingers in his mouth and gave a whistle to Billy, who was standing at a vantage point across the road. He crossed over to join them.

Billy took Sophia roughly by her arm, and Cillian tugged at Kerry's hair, then pushed her forward, towards the alley. Sophia wanted to run, but her legs were weak, and her stomach was churning. The two men led them to the dark alleyway and pushed them against the wall.

'It looks like we forgot the induction training, girls,' Cillian said as he brought up his hand and smacked Sophia across her face.

SIXTEEN

'Damn, I thought we'd got him,' Hollie cursed.

'Well done, at least we know what this is about now,' Anderson called through to her. 'It's what we thought from the get-go. He's some spurned kid from that mother and baby home come to get his revenge.'

'But it's not quite as simple as that, is it? He thinks the DCC might be his mother because she was a victim of rape. But we know otherwise—'

'We do?' Anderson asked.

She'd been careless. She had to tell him now. This couldn't stay a secret any longer.

'I know where Rose Warburton's son is.'

'I beg your pardon?'

'He's at Gilly Hodges' house right now.'

'For fuck's sake, DI Turner! When were you going to tell us this?'

'This evening,' she replied, feeling stupid.

'How did that even happen?'

'He reached out to me some time ago. It's how we got the original photo of the girls. I made certain he wasn't responsible for Sister Brennan's killing. He was trying to figure out that himself. It's why he tried to lead us to the girls.'

That wasn't quite true. Hollie had relied on her instincts; she'd taken a leap of faith. She'd been right, as it turned out, but she didn't want to dwell on it too much in case it drew further scrutiny.

'I trusted him and treated him as a confidential informant,' she continued. 'It helped the case. Without him, I don't think we'd be as far on as we are now.'

Anderson shook his head.

'This is what I meant when I said you could trust me. You can't go off like a lone wolf. I should know after what happened—'

'What do you mean?'

'It's what I did when DI MacKenzie died. I tried to fix it on my own. I messed things up. Truth be told, it's why I didn't get your job. I was stupid.'

'Look, I'm sorry, but it seemed the best thing to do at the time. He's the DCC's son. We must treat this with kid gloves. She reconnected with her son some years ago, and they meet up, in private, and unknown to Timothy. This is a powder keg for the family. But that man has got his wires crossed. Whoever his mother is, it's not Rose Warburton. The child who was born because of her rape is called Tony. He lives in Chester, and he has a wife and family there. He came to Hull to try to protect his mother. He's at Gilly's house right now, trying to contact our killer via Facebook.'

'So, this man is still around, I take it?' Timothy asked. 'Rose's son, I mean?'

He'd been listening in the kitchen. He was holding out a USB pen drive in his hand. Hollie should have been more careful. It was probably best out in the open, however hard it was for Timothy to hear.

'Yes, and I've met him,' Hollie said quietly. 'He's a good

man. He was trying to protect DCC Warburton – his mother. In fact, he's helping me – us – right now. He's trying to get a dialogue going with our kidnapper.'

'Can I meet him?'

'Later, yes, once we have Rose back and safe. I'm sure you'll all have a lot of talking to do.'

Timothy nodded.

'If you see her before I do, tell her I don't mind. Let her know that I love her and that nothing has changed. There's plenty of time to talk about this later.'

Hollie wiped away a tear forming in her eye. She noticed that Anderson was taking an extraordinary interest in the back garden suddenly, giving his own eyes a rub. Why couldn't Léon have thought that way about their marriage?

'Do you have a laptop I could borrow to look at this CCTV footage?' Hollie asked.

'Sure,' Timothy said, placing his glass on the table and getting up. He left the room and returned moments later with a sleek laptop. He placed it on the table, flipped the lid, and logged in.

'Here,' he said, handing it to Hollie. She pushed the pen drive into the USB slot and opened the video.

'It's about twenty-three minutes in.'

Hollie scrolled forward, and Anderson moved to watch it alongside her.

'Here it is,' she said, clicking on the play icon.

She watched the sequence as Timothy had described it. The video was sharp, much better than the usual crap they got from cameras, but the lighting was poor, and the man's face was in shadow. He was wearing the red cap, too, which didn't help. Its brim concealed much of his face.

'There's not a lot to work with there.' Anderson sighed. 'But the tech guys might be able to lighten it up a bit and give us a clearer shot of his face.'

'What do you reckon? Five foot ten or thereabouts? I'd place him in his fifties, wouldn't you?'

Anderson nodded at Hollie.

'Yes, fifties, I reckon. No facial hair, and he looks lean and fit. He'd have the strength to lift Sister Brennan over the side of the bridge. But why?'

'Who knows why people do what they do?' Hollie said. 'I think, for now, we work on the theory that he's one of the adopted children and, for some reason, he has an axe to grind. I'm at a complete loss as to his identity, though. We've worked through the girls who were in the home at the same time that DCC Warburton was there. But who's left? If we could only get our hands on the adoption records. I'll chase DS Patel and see if we've had any more joy on that.'

Hollie dialled the office while Anderson and Timothy made small talk.

'Hi, DS Patel, I'm sorry to lean on you when I know you're up to your ears. But we really need to be pushing hard on this adoption paperwork. The sooner we get it, the sooner we'll be able to start filling in the blanks.'

'I'm on it, boss, and no worries about loading me up at this end. We all want DCC Warburton back safe and sound.'

It was good to hear that it was heads down back at HQ. Hollie ended the call and before she had time to speak, the Warburton's home phone rang.

'Okay if I get that again?'

'Be my guest,' Timothy replied.

Hollie grabbed the phone. It was a withheld number again.

'Hollie Turner speaking.'

'I want your phone number,' the man said.

'Why?' Hollie asked, instantly regretting it. She was supposed to be building rapport, according to the training, not winding him up.

'Because I want to speak to you when the time comes. I got

this number from his wife, but I'd rather speak with you. Your copper friend said I should deal with you, too. Why do you think that is?'

Hollie hadn't got a clue, but she was grateful for the DCC's faith in her.

'Is DCC Warburton safe?' Hollie asked.

'I haven't hurt her, if that's what you mean,' the man answered. 'But she's my leverage, my safety net. You come after me and you know what I'll do. I need some time to think this through. I'll call you tomorrow. I promise I won't hurt her before then. But when I call, I'll tell you what I want. And if I don't get it, well, you'll be responsible for what happens next.'

'You're painting yourself into a bit of a corner here, you know? Why don't you give yourself up? Speak to us. Tell us what's on your mind. We can help.'

'You know I can't do that now. It's gone too far. Give me your number and I'll be in touch. Do not come looking for me, or she gets it, okay?'

Hollie gave him her mobile number and attempted to continue the conversation, but he rang off.

'Any clues?' Hollie asked.

'I couldn't hear anything in the background,' Anderson replied. 'He was speaking indoors, but there was no ambient sound. It was echoey, that's all I can say. All we can do is wait.'

'Does Rose have a home office?' Hollie looked at Timothy.

'Yes, of course, we both have our own office space.'

'I'd like to search it, with your permission, of course.'

It was a courtesy asking him, but it was always easier if he just let them go ahead and do what they needed to do; it saved a lot of paperwork.

Timothy considered it a moment. She noticed how he seemed to cope better the more he was given to do.

'I see no reason why not, under the circumstances. What do you expect to find?'

'There's a small possibility she might have tried to find out what happened to her adopted son. She may even have some crucial adoption paperwork. It might give us a clue as to the identity of this man—'

The front doorbell sounded.

'Do you want us to get that?' Anderson asked.

'No, I'm fine. I'd rather be busy. I'll get it.'

Hollie heard voices at the front door.

'It's his FLO,' Anderson said, listening to the voice. 'I took the liberty of making sure he'd been assigned one this morning while you were out of the office. She's brought a colleague with her, too. I hope you don't mind?'

'Of course not. This is exactly what I was saying to you earlier. You know the job. You're good at it. And I certainly need your help right now.'

Two detective constables walked into the room with Timothy.

'This is DC Fran Hayes,' Anderson said. 'One of the best family liaison officers we've got, Mr Warburton. You're in very good hands. DC Erica Wallace will be assisting her.'

DC Hayes smiled and asked Hollie if it was all right for her to make a start.

'Of course,' Hollie replied. 'We were just about to search through DCC Warburton's home office, but perhaps both of you can do that once you've had a moment to catch up? I'm particularly interested in locating adoption papers as a matter of priority – there's every possibility she may have these in her possession now.'

'We'll get on that straight away, ma'am,' DC Hayes confirmed.

Hollie looked at DS Anderson.

'We need to head back to the station. We've still got a killer to catch. And I've a good idea how we can trap him.'

SEVENTEEN

'Okay, everybody. Let's get started.'

It was an unusual time of day to call a briefing, but she was now ready to let everybody in on her contact. She couldn't keep Tony a secret any longer. Besides, looking at the city centre CCTV images they'd got of him, the game was up anyway.

'How are we going to deal with the issue of the DCC's son?' Hollie had asked on the drive back. This was the clincher. Would Anderson have her back for real, or would he drop her in it?

'I suggest, for everybody's sake, we describe him as a man who's recently made himself known to us. We won't tell anybody it was three days ago, mind you. That might make your life a bit difficult.'

Anderson was dead right about all that. They'd placed Tony in the vicinity of the accident, but not at the scene. When DS Patel was catching her up with events before the meeting, Hollie almost let out a gasp when she saw the images.

'There were a couple of people in the area. One of the other passers-by got a partial number plate from the motorcycle.'

'I'm going to assume that's a stolen motorcycle for now, but let's see if we can find anything from what sketchy details we've got,' Hollie added.

'I reckon it would have been easier to get the DCC out of North Ferriby in a van,' she added. 'But there's no basis for that. It's just a working theory. He can't possibly have used the motorcycle for an abduction. So there's probably another vehicle in play here.'

Hollie was about to head off.

'One more thing!' Patel stopped her.

Hollie turned around.

'Forensics got back with the check on those fibres that were found in Sister Brennan's airways. You're going to love this.'

'In a good way or a bad way?'

'In a good way. The fibres came from Father Duffy's cushions.'

'You are kidding me?'

'I told you it was good news.' Patel smiled.

Hollie was still working it all out in her mind as she called the briefing to order. The room settled; the team was as keen as her to bring the new threads together.

'Let's start by getting an update on DC Langdon,' Hollie began. 'I'd like to endorse DS Anderson's arrangement that DS Patel be our single point of contact. I know we're all desperate to hear news of our colleague, but it won't help matters if we're constantly bothering the hospital.'

DS Patel stood up and faced the room. It wasn't as full as usual, but Hollie knew several members of the team would be out of the office, knocking on doors and checking on leads.

'DC Langdon – Jenni – is in surgery as I speak. She's sustained serious head injuries. It's touch and go, I'm afraid...'

Patel's voice faltered and Hollie thanked her for the update. She paused for a moment. They all needed it; just a couple of seconds to reflect and think about their colleague. The sooner they got back to their purpose, the better. Hollie knew there was nothing worse than an idle copper.

Hollie held up one of the CCTV images of Tony, copies of which had been distributed throughout the room. Anderson gave her a nod from his seat.

'The information I'm about to tell you goes no further than these four walls. This man is called Tony, and he is the son that DCC Warburton had as a result of being raped as a teenager.'

There was a ripple of chatter across the room. Hollie let it run; it was a shock to everybody.

'We spoke to DCC Warburton's husband this morning, and we briefed his FLO before leaving the family home. I repeat, this is confidential information. It is not for use on Twitter, Facebook or TikTok, and it is not the subject of gossip. A woman who we all look up to in this workplace was the victim of a serious sexual assault as a child. For her own reasons, she chose not to share that information with her family, or her colleagues, and I expect every one of you to respect that. The DCC may be our boss, but she is also a victim. Make sure you behave accordingly.'

Hollie let that settle for a moment. There was a time in her career when she hadn't had to worry about social media. It was like a plague among the younger officers, and it pained her to have to constantly remind them about expectations of behaviour. The last thing she wanted was for the DCC's darkest secrets to be revealed via a TikTok dance sequence. And after her recent experience at the karaoke night, the threat of going viral was never closer to her mind.

'I'll be formally speaking to the DCC's son ASAP, but in the meantime, I can confirm that he has made direct contact with our prime suspect and that he is not involved in the murder in any way—'

'It's a bit of a coincidence that he should be visiting when all this kicked off, isn't it?' DC Gordon asked.

'He has said he came as soon as he found out about Sister Brennan's death. He'd spoken to DCC Warburton about it and clearly felt she might be in danger—'

'Why didn't the DCC reveal her connection to the case?' DC Gordon pushed.

For fuck's sake was what Hollie wanted to say. Instead, she took the more diplomatic route.

'I think that's up to the boss to choose how and when she reveals personal information of that nature. Besides, nothing she has done has put the case in any jeopardy.'

Hollie hadn't noticed that DCI Osmond was in the briefing room, but he raised his hand to catch her attention and gave her a small nod. She'd speak to him afterwards.

Hollie was a little taken aback at DC Gordon's insensitivity. She cut him some slack. He was young, after all, but she didn't think the DCC's situation required that much explanation.

'DS Anderson and I, after consultation with our senior officers, will determine a way ahead that will, one, keep DCC Warburton safe, and two, flush out our killer. I now have direct contact with this man, and he has my mobile number. We'll need to try to trace his calls and determine where he's holed up. We'll also need to handle him carefully so we can determine how best to proceed.'

A couple of hands shot up, and Hollie added more detail to what she'd been saying.

'We believe this man killed Sister Brennan and attempted to murder Father Duffy. He thought nothing of drugging my son and making a direct threat to me and my family. I would remind you that I saw him, with my own eyes, drive directly at DC Jenni Langdon this morning and do nothing to avoid striking her. If DC Langdon hadn't been the victim, I believe that I, or the DCC's son, may have been his target. We are dealing with a dangerous man. Whatever is on his mind, he is serious. He is also intelligent. Do not dismiss this man as your regular psychopath. He's demonstrated cunning, guile and strategy. But his motivation seems to be anger, revenge, retribution. He is a dangerous individual.'

Hollie filled the officers in on everything that had happened and assigned follow-up tasks to team members. She'd left Timothy Warburton's family liaison officer searching through the DCC's study, with strict instructions to call immediately if they found anything useful.

'DS Maxwell and DC Gordon, I'd like you to check out the mother and baby home again. It's a long shot, but he might just have returned there with the DCC. If you get any whiff that he's there, summon backup. Do not handle it on your own.'

She saved the best until the last.

'Finally, we've just had the lab report back on the fibres that were found in Sister Brennan's airways. It turns out they came from the cushions at Father Duffy's place. We think that Sister Brennan was suffocated first, and then thrown over the side of the bridge. This would mean that it's highly likely that she was suffocated in Father Duffy's flat. We know she was thought to be heading there at the time she left the convent, but this throws a new light on everything that happened that day.

'Father Duffy thought two people were in his flat, but he was unable to say who. I think the priest is lying. I think he's up to his ears in this and he's holding back information. It might be because he's scared. It could be because he's implicated. But I now want him arrested on suspicion of being an accomplice. He doesn't get to play the victim card any longer. We need to squeeze this old man for everything he knows.'

EIGHTEEN

1969: SOPHIA BRENNAN'S STORY

Much had changed since Sophia had taken up residence in the squat six months previously. For a start, they were now in a new place, another abandoned house, this time on Beverley Road, and much less salubrious.

The only way that Sophia could blank out the hell that her life had become was to disappear into the oblivion of heroin. She had come back to the squat one night, her eyes streaming with tears, her body bruised by being pushed so forcefully against the wall, and her face red from the scratching of beard stubble. Such was her sense of despair and contempt for what her body had become, she would have ended her life there and then had Cillian not hidden every sharp implement in the house. Instead, one of the girls, seeing her pain, offered her a way out.

'This will help you,' she whispered as the needle slid into the vein on Sophia's arm. Relief came in an instant; the horrors of the day evaporated like a mist in a high wind, and it enabled Sophia to make it through the night. One night became many, and soon, it was the heroin that was keeping her alive.

She'd been momentarily shaken to her senses as she sat with

Kerry in the bathroom, helping her through her morning sickness and doing her best to deflect attention from her friend's plight. They didn't know what to do. The sickness passed and the drugs made the days drift in a dull vacuum. But even in that nothingness, Sophia knew the problem would not go away.

She would return in the early hours, shoot up the moment she reached her bed, and spend much of the day out of it. She'd wake up mid-afternoon, take a shower at Cillian's insistence, smoke a couple of cigarettes with the other girls in the backyard, and then take a sedative ready for the evening. Sometimes, Cillian, Billy or one of the other men would come into her bedroom and take what they wanted. She was so far out of it now, she could barely tell the men apart. Occasionally they were gentle or apologetic. Many were rough or violent, leaving her with the marks on her body to prove it. But when Kerry died, the last flicker of light was extinguished in her life.

Sophia was there when they dumped the body, but she could barely recall it. Though she did remember that Billy had opened the car's back door and had pushed Kerry's corpse off the seat, out into the lay-by.

Kerry's death had shaken Sophia momentarily from her heroin-fuelled stupor, but for the most part, it had simply meant more clients until Cillian could ship in some new girls.

Kerry had been assaulted. A client had demanded extras and hadn't paid for them. Kerry protested and put up a fight. The client beat her up badly, with his fists, and then Billy hit her again because, he said, she was no good to anybody with a face as cut up as that.

'Next time you do what he fucking wants and then you tell us, all right? You don't handle negotiations. We'll rough the bastard up if he needs it. You just keep that lovely face of yours looking pretty. We take care of the business end.'

'I want to die,' Kerry had whispered as they returned to the squat. Sophia stroked her hair and did her best to soothe her friend.

'We'll soon get away, don't worry. We just have to get ourselves off the drugs, and then we'll be ready. One day, you'll see, we'll have our own place. We'll get away from here. We'll be happy.'

But Kerry had never recovered from a forced abortion. It had messed her up, mentally and physically.

'You're no good to us if you can't earn money. No money, no drugs, do you understand?'

Kerry understood. She'd aborted the baby using a knitting needle that same night. She'd bled for days, but they'd made her work still. Sophia saw how she sneaked out more of the sedatives, but she felt helpless to do anything. She knew only too well the bleakness of their existence.

On the day she died, Kerry shot up after Sophia. She was always first to go, desperate to obliterate the horrors of the night, eager to get out of it in case one of the men made a morning visit. But that day, she let Sophia go first.

'I love you, Sophia,' she said as she helped her prepare the syringe. 'You've made it bearable here. I don't know what I'd have done without you.'

Kerry kissed her on the forehead.

'It'll be all right,' Sophia attempted to reassure her. 'We'll be out of here soon. Hang on just a little bit longer—'

But she hadn't been able to say more. She was off to a place of oblivion where Cillian and Billy didn't exist. When she came round, Kerry was still and cold at her side.

'You should have been watching her, you stupid bitch. We're going to be short tonight now.'

'We'll dump her along the A63. Get her loaded in the car before she starts to smell,' Cillian commanded.

The rest was a haze. Sophia remembered being slapped by Billy.

'Look at the shit you've started.'

She was then forced to help carry Kerry to the car. Her friend had vomited before death and Sophia wanted to clean her up, to at least give her some dignity in death. She couldn't cry for her friend. Her emotions had long since fled, terrified to come out in case they overwhelmed her with pain.

There was no respite. Kerry was left in the car, covered by a sheet for the remainder of the day. The men waited until dark, then casually tossed the body out into the lay-by and drove off at speed. At least she'd be found there, Sophia thought. A lorry driver would pull over and notice her body at the side of the road. They might mistake her for fly-tipping, there was so little of her by the time she died. Kerry barely ate a thing; it would have been a miracle if her body could have even carried a baby to full term.

Sophia began work earlier that evening, just after it grew dark. It didn't stop the clients. It seemed that as soon as the pubs opened and work was done for the day, the customers were waiting. She shut her mind down, going through the motions, telling them what they wanted to hear, an autopilot script she'd mastered months ago. With Kerry gone, she no longer had a happy place to go to. It had been the one thing keeping her going, the thought that one day she and Kerry could get a place of their own, far away from these vile men, and just live quietly and happily. Even that had been taken away from her now. She scoured her mind for some memories of her family that she could carry with her, but they were few and far between. There had been some happy times when her father was still alive, but she couldn't picture him without seeing her mother's face. Her mother had led them to Martin and now, to this. She turned her face to the side to avoid the smell of her client's boozy breath. His stubble was scraping her cheeks, but she was too tightly pressed against the wall to move away.

The night never seemed to end. Client after client came,

and she wondered if people ever slept. Cillian made her stay until the girls had made up for the losses incurred after Kerry's death. By the time she got back to the squat, Sophia was tempted to do what Kerry had done. It would only take a moment. But Cillian was one step ahead of her and insisted he watch as she got her fix. She slipped into nothingness, wondering how she could ever get away from this man.

When Sophia woke up, there was some level of excitement out on the back step where the girls gathered to smoke. There was a new woman there, in her thirties, and she was offering tattoos. Sophia watched what she was doing. She was holding a sewing needle stuck into the eraser end of a pencil. She had some ink, which she used to create markings for the girls. She looked fresh and healthy; Sophia reckoned she was a recent arrival.

'What's your name?' she asked, still not quite with it.

'Tina,' the woman replied. 'I'm new here. I'm just relieved to have a place to stay now. Cillian said I could join you all. He seems like a nice guy.'

One of the other girls made a face at Sophia, sensing what she was about to say. Sophia wanted to tell her to run, now, while she still could. There was nothing physically stopping the girls from making an escape bid, but they were held captive by their own fear. Cillian had long ago taken up his bullying residence in their heads.

Sophia watched as the girls asked for different tattoos, usually the initials of somebody they'd lost or a person they loved.

'Do you want one?' Tina asked. 'It won't take long. Whose initials do you want?'

'KT,' Sophia replied. 'For my friend, Kerry Townsend.'

Tina made a wincing sound as she spotted the needle marks in Sophia's veins. She started to work on her upper arm. It took some time to get used to the minute stings of the needle point as Tina pushed it into her skin. She'd never had a tattoo, but they were commonplace among the dock workers and trawlermen, and she'd seen them being done this way before. Tina was gentle; it was almost as good as the drugs to feel her kindness wash over her.

'Don't stay,' Sophia whispered as Tina dabbed her arm with an ink-covered piece of cloth.

'What?' Tina replied.

'Run away from here, please, while you can.'

'But—'

Sophia grabbed Tina's free hand and held it tight.

'Please, do it tonight. Slip out and leave. Don't stay. I know you're scared of having to be homeless. I was, too. But please go.'

Tina seemed shocked. Sophia had waited until the other girls dispersed to give her a warning. She couldn't let this woman walk blindfolded into her fate.

'There you go,' Tina said. 'You're all done.'

She held up a small compact mirror so Sophia could view it in the reflection.

Tina had neatly inked the letters *KT* as she'd asked, the only reminder of her friend who nobody else would remember.

NINETEEN

'Come to my office as soon as you've deployed everybody, please.'

DCI Osmond sidled up to her as the briefing dispersed. It all seemed very cloak and dagger, but she was anxious to discover what was implied by his earlier nod.

Hollie worked through her tasks, assigning various team members to the different jobs.

'Any progress on that interview with Father Duffy?' she asked DS Patel, calling across the office.

'No, boss,' DS Patel replied. 'I think there's been a delay sorting him out with a duty solicitor. It's looking like it might be tomorrow. His doctor says he's still very fragile, too.'

Hollie pushed down her sense of frustration.

'I want this to happen sooner rather than later,' she replied, trying not to show her agitation. 'This is still a voluntary interview, so we could avoid the solicitor if need be.'

DS Anderson looked up from his desk.

'We're not arresting him?' he checked.

'No, not yet, not while he's bedbound. It's not like he's going anywhere. We may well charge him because of the interview though. If the medical advice is that he's well enough, I want us to visit him straight away.'

'Do you think he's involved, boss?' DC Gordon asked.

'He's involved all right, but there's no way he could have suffocated Sister Brennan. He doesn't have the physical strength. I suspect he's got caught up in something he can't control. The question is, what is he not telling us? I think he could lead us to the killer, but I don't think the killer is him.'

'Okay, I'll help DS Patel chase it up, boss,' Anderson said.

'Please, don't kill the old man,' Hollie warned. 'He's had a couple of days to recover among the nuns. I'm hoping you'll get the okay to bring him into the station. Let me know if you hit any snags. We'll interview him at his bedside, if we have to.'

It felt good to have a sense of momentum again. She'd need to warn Gilly and Tony. He was going to have to come in for formal questioning now, too. She couldn't protect him any further. She'd stay clear of that interview and cover her tracks. She was going to speak to Tony beforehand, though, and get uniform to pick him up ASAP.

'Chase up Theresa for me, will you?' Hollie said, turning back to face DS Patel. 'I want to know if she's any closer to getting me that adoption paperwork for her son. Oh, and I'd like to haul in McCready again once we've got it. He may be able to shed some light on it. I take it we're still no further forward with the records?'

'Excuse my language, boss, but it's a bleeding nightmare. I've been chasing around the council departments, but it's likely stored in some dusty box in a secure storage facility, who knows where? It was caught up in the county council changes and then again when they shifted to unitary authorities. It's administrative hell.'

Hollie considered that for a moment. She'd had to set up her council tax in the new flat and that had been tricky enough, what with the previous tenant having gone AWOL.

'Why don't you have a word with Gilly Hodges about that? She's a councillor, she got me into the mother and baby home, maybe she can pull a few strings.'

DS Patel looked like she'd just been handed the Holy Grail.

'That's a great idea, boss. I'll give her a call.'

'Okay, Theresa remains our best hope with laying our hands on some documentation swiftly,' Hollie continued. 'Have a word with Timothy Warburton's FLO, too. They're checking her home office, as there's a tiny possibility the DCC might have retained paperwork, though I doubt it. Is her mother still alive?'

DS Patel shrugged.

'Find out, will you? And tread lightly. Work through the FLO. I don't want Timothy Warburton any more upset than he already is. Remember, he'll be reporting everything to the DCC once we get her back. I don't want it screwing up my first performance review.'

'Yes, boss.' Patel smiled. 'Five gold stars all round. Understood.'

Hollie walked over to Osmond's office and tapped at the door.

'Come in!'

At least she knew she wasn't in line for a bollocking this time around. She looked around the office, feeling she could relax a little more. There was not much on show to give away the man's character. A photograph of him and his wife sat on the desk. It looked like an anniversary picture; it seemed to be recent. Personal development books lined the shelves, alongside all the folders and police missives she'd expect to be there. If she'd thrown all the books into a melting pot to create one generic title, it might have been called *How to Become an Influential, Powerful Leader of Teams with a Positive Outlook and*

Progressive Mindset. Hollie found strong coffee tended to be just as effective.

'Take a seat, DI Turner.'

She took a chair and settled in. The DCI looked like he'd set time aside for this conversation.

'This is not for onward communication, but the DCC had raised a potential conflict of interest on this case with the chief constable and the police and crime commissioner.'

That was good to know. So, Rose Warburton had played it by the book.

'I'm not at liberty to discuss the conversations that took place, but needless to say, she had flagged up her personal connection with the case.'

Hollie reckoned Osmond wouldn't even be in the loop regarding the confidential details of that conversation. But at least it settled her doubts that the DCC might have landed herself in a spot of difficulty once the details of Tony's existence had become known. Tony was not a suspect. DCC Warburton didn't even know he was in the city, so nothing would land her in the shit once they got her back from her kidnapper. *If* they got her back. The DCC was in a lot of danger. This man had already demonstrated his willingness to kill.

'I'd appreciate it if we took a tough line on gossip,' Osmond continued. 'This is the DCC's private life. I don't want her dirty laundry aired in public.'

'Yes, sir. As you heard in the briefing, I'm being very firm on that.'

'Are you aware there's a memorial service for the nun tomorrow? Will you be available to represent the force? It might help to level the ground after that video went viral.'

Hollie hadn't caught news of the service.

'What time is it, sir?'

'Late morning, I think. Possibly early afternoon.'

'I'll make it a priority to attend, sir.'

'Good. Right then, there's something else I want to discuss with you. Did you get that counselling session booked?'

DS Patel had apologised for not being able to fix one up for her.

'No, sir, not for a couple of days. It's been a bit frantic.'

'You must get the help you need in the job, DI Turner. I'm ESTIP trained, and I'd like to make sure we get this done today. We have targets for these things, and our officers need to be supported in their work.'

Hollie's heart sank.

'Yes, sir, of course. Thank you.'

'So, you know about the Emergency Services Trauma Intervention Programme, I take it? Did you use it in Lancaster?'

'Yes, sir, I'm familiar with it.'

'Then you know that we're supposed to have this conversation as soon as we can after a traumatic event?'

'Yes, sir.'

'This is the demobilising part of the conversation. You should make sure you book the defusing follow-up within three days.'

Jesus, more of it!

'Of course, it's a valuable resource. I think I'm okay, though.'

'Well, let's explore that, shall we? Right. DC Langdon's accident. How are you feeling about that now?'

Hollie stopped herself sighing. It was instinctive. She hated all this pop psychology. As far as she was concerned, a good cop dealt with traumatic incidents using the time-tested British technique of denial. You simply pushed it deep down and ignored it. It's a recipe that had worked for Brits for centuries. She had a file securely locked and hidden in the depths of her soul labelled *Too Difficult to Think About*. It looked like Léon was heading that way, and countless episodes from her policing career in Lancaster could be found there, too. They were all safely under lock and key. As for Jenni – she didn't know yet.

'I haven't processed it properly. It was such a shock. It was so... violent. He just drove that motorcycle directly at her. How damaged do you have to be to have that much contempt for another human being?'

'Can you think of some words to describe your emotions right now?'

Yes. Bored, pissed off, annoyed, impatient.

'Worried. Concerned. Angry. Upset. How's that?'

'It's a good start. Do you think your anger might get in the way of the work you have to do?'

This guy's been reading too many of those psycho-babble books on his shelf.

'Perhaps. I feel a rage over what he did. He threatened my son, too. But I've learnt to channel that rage and divert it to solving the case. The way to work through this is to find this chap, lock him up, and make sure he gets put behind bars for an awfully long time. It just makes me more determined to catch him. I kept my calm earlier, when I spoke to him on the phone.'

Osmond studied her face, then spoke. She could see he was getting into this. He'd clasped his hands together like a TV shrink.

'Might that anger leave your colleagues exposed? If you were confronted with the killer, and DCC Warburton's life was at risk, how certain could you be that you could separate what happened to DC Langdon and your son from that situation? Might anger cloud your judgement?'

Shit, he's getting a bit close to the bone here. He certainly read the training manual more carefully than I did.

'I trust myself to put the safety of my colleagues first, sir. I'm angry, yes. But my sole mission is to get the DCC back safely and to capture this man so that he can be subjected to the due process of the law.'

Osmond nodded. He'd been channelling too much Yoda as

far as she was concerned. He'd be wearing Jedi robes before she knew it.

'I want to explore a word you chose not to use when describing your emotions.'

'What word is that, sir?'

'Guilt. Do you feel at all guilty about what happened to DC Langdon?'

Shit! He's got me!

Hollie felt her eyes moisten. It was the terror of seeing her new friend still and bloodied on the ground after being tossed in the air from the impact of the motorcycle. She tried everything she could to stop her tears from flowing in front of the DCI, but she failed miserably.

Hollie emerged from his office half an hour later, her eyes red, grateful that she could find a quiet room to compose herself. Osmond had hit the nail directly on the head: guilty is exactly how she felt. Guilty that she hadn't been a better mentor to Jenni. Guilty that she hadn't been able to protect her.

Damn ESTIP. Maybe she should have read that manual more thoroughly, after all.

TWENTY

Hollie was grateful for the opportunity to get her head down and catch up with some paperwork after her wellbeing check-up. She'd heard Donny Osmond used to make all the girls cry, but she reckoned it must have been a first-time experience for DCI Osmond. It gave her something to consider; perhaps she'd been too hard on herself and should follow some of the advice she gave the younger officers.

Fortunately, DS Anderson had kept a firm grip on the case logbook. She'd deferred to him from the outset with the blessing of Osmond, but he'd done a professional job and it had allowed her to remain fully hands-on in her first Humberside case.

'Is everything okay, boss?' DS Patel asked as she sidled up to Hollie's desk.

Hollie sniffed and looked up, praying her eyes were no longer red.

'Yes, I think so. Thanks for managing things in the office so well, DS Patel. It's been a huge help to me while I'm running on training wheels.'

'It's no problem, boss. It's just what we do here. I hope you don't mind me saying, but you look upset.'

'You might say that,' Hollie admitted. She'd been caught red-handed; there was no escaping it now. 'I hadn't realised the toll this case is taking on me, what with Jenni, my son being snatched, and the stress of a new job—'

Hollie stopped at mentioning the bit about her failing marriage. That would have pushed her over the edge.

'It's one hell of an initiation to the Humberside force, that's for sure.'

'You can say that again,' Hollie remarked. 'Is there any joy with Father Duffy yet?'

'Yes, and no. It looks like we're going to have to interview him at the convent. How's your bedside manner?'

'Getting tetchier by the minute when it comes to the priest. Let's get a time booked in ASAP, please. This old man is holding things up now; it feels like he's trying to stall us.'

'No problem, boss. Oh, I thought you might like to know they're having a memorial event for Sister Brennan tomorrow—'

'DCI Osmond just mentioned it. Has her body been released? Surely not?'

Hollie was immediately back into work mode.

'No, but Mother Davies told me earlier about the celebration of her life when I was doing a check call on Father Duffy. I thought you might like to attend.'

'You're damn right, I would. Funerals and memorial services are great for flushing out killers. It seems to pander to their sociopathic inclinations. Buy me a ticket and save me a seat.'

'I'm not sure there'll be a queue at the door, but I'll let her know you'll be attending. You know it's not at the Church of St Mary and the Angels, don't you? They've all decamped to a different location now. Even the Catholic Church isn't immune from a bit of restructuring these days.'

'I saw it was all boarded up when we visited the old mother and baby home. Gilly Hodges said the council is tied up in knots over a legal dispute. It would be a shame to see it all bull-dozed and turned into a housing estate. Make sure DS Anderson knows about the memorial, will you? I'd like him to attend with me.'

'Will do, ma'am. And if you don't mind me saying, you should get on your way home and spend some time with those kids of yours. Everything is in order here. It won't all collapse without you.'

She was right and Hollie knew it. Besides, she needed to call in on Gilly on the way home and there was no way Jenni wasn't getting a personal call. Osmond reckoned he knew some-body who could arrange for her to visit Jenni, despite her crit-ical condition. He said he'd call her once he'd chatted to his contact. What a day it had been. No wonder she was so exhausted, with her emotions running high.

She closed the logbook and stood up.

'You're right, I'm off. Besides, this guy has my number, and the uniform patrols are all over the DCC's disappearance. Osmond authorised as much overtime as I need to get her back in safe hands, so we've got all eyes looking out for her. I hope to God this man doesn't do anything stupid.'

'What, more stupid than throwing a nun over a bridge?'

'Don't go there,' Hollie replied. 'I can't even think about what he might have planned for the DCC. The poor woman. She must be terrified.'

Hollie made her way out of the office, exchanging superfi-cial comments with members of the investigations team as she headed over to the door. They all had their heads down and were fully engaged in the case. She'd get a phone call if there were any developments.

She was grateful for the drive to Gilly's house; it gave her a private moment to think over what Osmond had said. She recognised the toll events had taken on her since she'd arrived in Hull, but it was hard paying attention to her own needs at the moment. She'd even confessed to the DCI that her marriage was on the rocks. They'd be hugging trees and chanting mantras together before she knew it.

Hollie had texted ahead that she was calling in, so Gilly spotted her parking opposite the house and was waiting at the door when she got there.

'How's your house guest?' Hollie asked. 'I'm sorry to have to do that to you.'

'It's been okay, actually,' Gilly replied in a whisper. 'I told him that I know he's Twiggy's son. He's been asking me about the home and what it was like there. He won't tell me anything about Twiggy and who she is though. It's been one-sided so far. Why won't either of you tell me who she was?'

'I can't tell you, for confidentiality reasons, but Tony is crucial to the whole investigation. He can come out into the open now. I'll run him back to wherever he's staying. We'll need to bring him in for formal questioning.'

Gilly hadn't invited Hollie in yet; she seemed keen to keep her on the doorstep.

'What is it, Gilly? You seem to have something on your mind.'

'When I was chatting to Tony, I remembered something. It's ridiculous, I don't know how I forgot it. I've remembered all sorts of little details since Sister Brennan's death, most of them minor. But I think you'll be interested in this one.'

'I'm all ears,' Hollie encouraged her.

'Before I even knew I was pregnant, my father sent me back to church after one of the services, because he'd forgotten to hand over a donation to Father Duffy. The priest was in his office, so I walked through the building, calling for him.'

'Okay. Did you see something you shouldn't have?'

'You might say that. I walked in on Father Duffy with his

trousers down. He tried to shrug it off, saying he was getting changed. But there was a nun in there with him.'

'My God. What happened?'

'Remember I was young and naive back then. It took a little while for the penny to drop. I knew it was off, but I didn't know how. I understood they were doing something that they shouldn't be, but I couldn't work out what it was. And then, when I went to the mother and baby home, Sister Brennan made threats to me, warning me to keep quiet. And Father Duffy seemed terrified that I might give the game away, but I never would have; nobody would have believed me anyway. It's ridiculous, but I only just figured it out speaking to Tony. Father Duffy was having a relationship with one of the nuns – they'd been having sex when I walked in on them. Either that or she'd been giving him a blow job under his desk. I can't believe I was so young and stupid; no wonder they were all so damn scared I might say something.'

'This is explosive stuff, Gilly. It could point to Father Duffy being blackmailed, or even trying to cover something up. Was it Sister Brennan he was having the affair with?'

Gilly shook her head.

'No, I'm sure of that. She knew about it, but she was protecting him. She owed him something and she wouldn't have him exposed. Do you think it could be connected?'

'I can't rule it out, Gilly. I'll dig a bit deeper and see where it leads. This case just gets more complex by the minute. It's taken so many dark turns.'

Gilly led Hollie through to the living room, where Tony was reading a local history book about Hull. His wound was patched up now, but it looked sore and serious.

'We should get that looked at, Tony. You can go back to wherever it is you're staying tonight.'

Hollie felt herself tense. She had to take care not to give away any crucial facts. She couldn't let Gilly know that Tony was the DCC's son before it was made public, and she'd hang onto the information as long as she could. Much as she wanted to reveal that information to Gilly, it was confidential and sensitive; it was the DCC's private life after all and she had to remain mindful of the impact this would all have on her family.

'May Tony and I chat in the dining room again?' Hollie checked.

'Of course,' Gilly answered. 'I'm going to get it bugged so I can find out what's going on.'

Hollie smiled and gave Tony his cue to follow her through. She closed the door behind her.

'Keep your voice down, please. I don't want Gilly listening in.'

Tony nodded.

'Where are you staying, by the way? I still don't know.'

'Out of town, at the Premier Inn just outside North Ferriby,' Tony replied. 'I'm in walking distance of the Humber Bridge Park. It seemed a fitting place, bearing in mind what happened.'

'I take it your vehicle is still parked somewhere in the Old Town?'

Tony nodded.

'I've heard from him. We've been messaging via Facebook.'

'You might have let me know—'

'If I thought it would help my mother, I'd let you know immediately.'

'What have you got to tell me?'

'Well, the good news is he remembers me. But he's unaware that I'm Rose Warburton's son. I maintained that secret, as you asked. It's all I could do not to swear at the guy and ask where she is.'

'Do you know why he's taken her?'

'He's trying to find out who his birth mother is. He knows he's connected with the home in some way, but he doesn't know how. He says he found out about me through a guy called Patrick McCready—'

'McCready? Really? There's a name which keeps popping up—'

'Who is this McCready? How are the two of them connected?'

'He was a social worker attached to the mother and baby unit back in the seventies when your mother was there. It's interesting that he shared information about Rose. I wonder if McCready was threatened. Did he mention your mother?'

'No, but I'm worried. He sounds like a man on the edge to me. He's convinced he's being blocked, that information is being concealed from him. He sounds paranoid. He's drawn a blank with social services. McCready doesn't seem to have been of any help. Father Duffy was no use—'

'Has he mentioned Sister Brennan?'

'No, he's said nothing.'

'Why do you think he's on the edge?'

'Here, take a look at the messages.'

Hollie examined the phone.

'Shit.'

'Exactly,' Tony replied.

'Well, it sounds like we've found our motivation for murder at last.'

'I'd say so.'

Hollie re-read the thread. Tony had done well, drawing him out without antagonising him, giving nothing away. She was almost annoyed she'd have to hand him over to her colleagues; he'd been an excellent contact. But now the DCC had been abducted and he'd been spotted on the CCTV, he had to come forward. There was no more hiding.

'How did you get him to open up like that?' Hollie asked. 'He doesn't even know you, but he's told you his whole sorry background here.'

'I volunteer on the phone with the Samaritans,' Tony replied. 'I guess the training helps.'

What this case had lacked all along was a compelling motive. Now they'd got it. She kept reading and re-reading the man's Facebook message.

My father abused me throughout my childhood. My mother was cruel to me physically when I was a kid, and mentally as a teenager. I don't know why they even wanted a child. I despised them. I want to know who was responsible for my adoption and how I ended up in an evil family like that. Why weren't they screened properly? Most of all, I want to meet my birth mother and try to understand why she would give me away like that to those horrible people. I need some closure with this. My life has been terrible. I want those who wronged me to pay the price. Something like this can't go unpunished.

TWENTY-ONE

1969: SOPHIA BRENNAN'S STORY

Sophia knew she was pregnant, even through the haze of drugs. She also saw that her time was up as soon as Cillian realised. She was on the clock. She had to look for a chance to get away.

She couldn't contemplate not taking the drugs; it was the only thing that stopped her from throwing herself in front of a car. Cillian and his men had them so locked down, the only time they got to themselves was inside the house. There were suggestions the owner might never return. Nobody had a clue what had happened to them. The house remained accessible even though it was beginning to show signs of strain inside and out. The paintwork was flaking on the window frames and a couple of roof tiles had dropped off. Inside, the house was beginning to smell of stale drink and too many human bodies in one place. The gas had been switched off two months previously, but the electricity remained connected, and that meant the hot water tank continued to operate. Sophia had been there when Cillian warned off an interfering neighbour and his threat still made her shudder.

If I see any sign of the police around this building, I will personally send three of my guys around to your house at night to rape you and your wife. Don't think I can't do that from prison. All you have to do is look the other way and everything will carry on being sweet for you and your lovely lady.

A 'For Sale' board went up next door soon after.

Sophia turned sideways and inspected her profile in the bathroom mirror, which was spattered with dried-on soap suds and splashed toothpaste. It wouldn't be long until someone noticed. She had to hatch a plan.

She couldn't reduce the drugs. She craved them like she needed air. She could no longer face the prospect of a night in the alleyway, seeing man after disgusting man, their hands all over her body, their saliva dripping on her face. Her body was no longer hers; her mind existed on a separate plain, as if it had been dumped in her physical form by mistake. She despised herself and what was happening to her, but she could not find the will to stop it.

Night after night, they'd send those men to her. Sometimes, she lost count before her mind blanked out, and the only thing between her and suicide were the drugs. The veins in her arms were useless now and she was injecting between her toes. The part of her that still survived in the wilderness of her mind knew this was the beginning of the end. If she didn't wind up overdosing like Kerry, she'd become a frantic mess, desperately trying to find a vein into which she could inject that elixir.

When Sophia came round in her bed that afternoon, she could sense something was up. The sheets were wet with sweat; they hadn't been washed in months. She'd grown accustomed to their stale odour. The two girls who now shared the room with her were still out of it. One of them was only fifteen years old, she'd learnt.

Sophia forced her eyelids open; they were fused by sleep and didn't yet want to acknowledge the new day. She could still smell the last man from the night before. He'd staggered out of the pub, drunk out of his brain, and paid Cillian's men for some time with her before returning home to his wife. He'd vomited before he could get his belt undone. She cared so little now; she'd just wiped it away and carried on. The man had protested about not getting his money's worth, even though he could barely stand, and the two lookouts had beaten him up in the alleyway, sending him on his way.

She forced herself out of bed and crept towards the door, which was wide open. The girls had long since foregone any sense of privacy. Their bodies were no longer their own and they now existed only to line Cillian's pockets. She was hungry, so she headed down the stairs. At least there was always food in the kitchen. Though, in her moments of clarity, she could see her body was wasting away, her skin clinging tight to her bones like it feared it might drop off at any time.

Cillian was sitting in the hallway, smoking. She saw him as she came downstairs, but he kept his head down. Months previously, he and his men had taken turns with her and Kerry. One day, they declared the girls had become too disgusting for them to touch, and they moved on to the newer, younger recruits. So, it was no surprise when he didn't look up. Sophia shuffled towards the kitchen.

'Turn around,' Cillian said.

She stopped.

'Pull up your T-shirt. I want to look at you.'

She did as she was told. Sophia was only wearing a pair of pants and the T-shirt encrusted with dried vomit. She lifted it up, hesitantly, because she knew he'd seen it.

'You've got yourself pregnant,' he said. 'You look like shit, Sophia. For fuck's sake, put on some clean clothes. You're no fucking use to me if you can't earn your keep.'

She pulled the T-shirt down and continued to the kitchen, taking a dirty cereal bowl out of the cupboard and not bothering to clean it. The milk in the fridge was out of date, but it didn't smell yet, so it would do. She threw a couple of wheat biscuits into the bowl and ate. What would Cillian do now he knew?

She got her answer soon enough. Her ear was drawn by voices out in the hallway. Cillian's voice was lowered, but if she strained, she could hear him. He was talking to Billy.

'How late can we sort it with a knitting needle or something like that?'

'Fuck, Cillian, she'll mess herself up if she tries that. The customers won't touch her.'

'She'll keep for a month or two at most. Some of the punters like them pregnant, but she'll get too big in the end. We might even be able to charge a bit more for her. But we can't keep her like that. She'll become a nuisance. What if she needs a doctor?'

'We can't let her walk either. She could blow the lid off the whole operation.'

'What do you suggest, Billy?'

'It's gonna have to be an OD. How far gone do you think she is?'

'It's difficult to tell. She's a bag of bones. I don't know how the punters find anything there to fuck these days. Maybe three or four months?'

'I say we overdose her and dump her with her friend. There's plenty more where she came from, and she looks bloody disgusting these days. I wouldn't wipe my arse on her, let alone shag her. She used to look so pretty when she first came in.'

'Agreed, then. Let's just bite the bullet. We do it this week, okay? And we'll dump her in the lay-by.'

Sophia waited in the kitchen until they'd gone, then peered around the corner to make sure the coast was clear. She headed back up the stairs, their words replaying in her mind, her legs shaking with fear. She darted into the bathroom, pacing the floor, formulating a plan as best as her foggy mind would allow. She thought back to her violent confrontation in the kitchen with Martin and the courage that she'd had to summon to fight him off. It made her sick just thinking about it.

Later that evening, when the other girls were shooting up, Sophia feigned sickness. Billy kicked the bathroom door down to see what was up, so she stuck her fingers down her throat to make herself throw up. He saw the evidence for himself in the toilet bowl.

'Don't think you're not going out to work tonight. It's your choice if you're not interested in the gear tonight.'

Sophia was bundled off with the other girls, but she could feel herself shaking. Her body wanted the drugs, but for just one night, she had to stay in her mind. She couldn't be swept away by oblivion.

That night was hard. As the men came, drunk, abusive, sweaty, she gritted her teeth, taking what she'd taken from them for months now and despising every second of it. When they drove her back to the squat, she played docile, like the other girls, not wanting to draw attention. She went to her room, quiet, pliant, not saying a word, and she waited.

Sophia thought they'd never shut up and go to their beds, but eventually, Cillian's pervasive voice could no longer be heard through the house. He and Billy often spent the night with one of the younger girls. It was how they got them accustomed to the abominations that lay ahead.

She lay in her bed, thinking through her plan. Her body felt frail and weak, incapable of doing what had to be done. She had to push ahead, she had to summon the last strength in her body, or they'd kill her and dump her at the roadside. All that was left of her mind was wreckage, yet somehow, she had to focus and follow through on what had to come next. She turned in her bed, her body weak and bruised, and she climbed out, catching a glimpse of herself in the mirror. She was skin on bones, her hair lank and greasy, her hands skeletal like she was some Halloween ghoul.

Leaving the lights switched off, Sophia crept down to the kitchen, her footsteps light and cautious. At every creak she paused and waited, expecting them to burst out into the hallway and finish her off there and then.

Sophia opened the cupboard in the hallway and found the can of paraffin that was used to light the open fire in the living room. She'd seen it hidden there; it was supposed to be a secret, but nothing stayed hidden for long in a cramped house like that. There were matches by the sink, surrounded by blackened stalks where cigarettes had been lit and the wooden sticks discarded. Cillian was too clever to leave kitchen knives around.

She barely had the strength to turn the cap on the paraffin can, but she eventually forced it open and caught the distinctive whiff of fumes as she walked quietly through the ground floor of the house.

She found Billy first, on the sofa in the living room and alone, wrapped in a sheet. He was out cold and drugged up. She looked at him, peaceful and silent; how could this man be such a monster? She waited, listening to his gentle snoring, making certain he was asleep. As she stood watching in the silence, her mind wandered, and a thousand nightmares came screaming at her all at once. She craved the drugs, she desperately needed to be carried away, but she had to finish this man, or she'd never escape the terror.

Sophia gently doused the bottom of the sheet with paraffin, making sure it was clear of Billy's feet so it wouldn't wake him. She pulled out a match and struck it, fearful that the igniting flame might wake him. Her mind flashed to an image of Billy raping her on that first night, telling her this was her life now and laughing as she sobbed in her bed.

As Sophia watched him, his eyes opened suddenly. She jumped, dropping the match so it landed on the sheet. There was a whoosh of ignition and Billy leapt up, immediately realising what she was doing. She dropped the matches and Billy grasped for her with his hand, just missing her as she attempted to get away. He was up on his feet; she could feel the force of his muscular body lunging towards her, primed for violence like it was instinctual. He crashed into her, her head striking the hearth and dazing her. His clenched fist was drawn back, and he was about to strike her. She was overwhelmed by his formidable strength. He had her pinned to the floor, yet still she searched with her free arm for something – anything – with which to defend herself. Her flailing hand found the handle of the fire poker and as his fist came thundering down towards her face, she grasped it, pulled it up to her right and struck him at the side of his head. He lurched sideways to avoid the blow, but Sophia knew if she wasn't fast and decisive, she would be overcome in seconds. As Billy landed at her side, Sophia rolled over and thrust the poker deep into Billy's eye. She forced it so deep into his eye socket that it reached the far side of his skull, and it sizzled from where the tip of the poker had been sitting so close to the flames. She knew what she was doing was monstrous, but she had to be sure. These men would never rest unless she killed them. For one glorious moment she saw a flash of fear as he realised what was happening. His body convulsed and twitched, yet she continued pushing down on the poker until he was still. When he was finally dead, she pulled out the poker and spat on his bloodied corpse.

She found the door keys in his pocket. She then doused his body with the remainder of the paraffin and set him alight. The flames were roaring across the sofa now and the living room filling with dense, choking fumes.

She fought the haze in her mind. She had to alert the other girls, but not before Cillian got what was coming to him.

Sophia raced upstairs, knowing the fire would soon take a deadly grip on the house. It was crackling now, the sound of burning would wake up the others. She checked in the bedrooms. Most of the doors were open, any expectation of privacy long since absent. She found Cillian in bed with the new girl, Tina, in one of the small rooms with a single bed. Tina saw Sophia creeping into the bedroom. Sophia put her finger over her lips. The girl, whose face was freshly bruised, took her cue. Tina slipped away from Cillian's side, carefully moving his hand from her waist and freezing for one moment as he stirred. Tina's body was battered; she had a cut on her lip and there was blood on the sheets where he'd forced her. From the mayhem in Sophia's mind came a rage so intense, it could only find a release in a storm of fury.

'Wake the other girls, make sure they're safe,' Sophia whispered. She handed over the keys that she'd taken from Billy, and Tina did as she was instructed.

Sophia took the fire poker and raised it high over her head. It took a force of will – it was unwieldy in her emaciated hands – but she knew there would be no second chance. As she was about to strike, Cillian opened his eyes and for a moment she was paralysed by his glare. She saw fear in his eyes, and it gave her strength. Sophia pictured his gloating face, and she thought of the times when he'd forced himself on her, just like he had with Tina.

'No, Sophia—' he commanded.

As Sophia began to swing the poker, Cillian's hand darted out and grabbed her lower arm. He stopped her dead; her attempts to get away were useless. With his spare hand, Cillian struck her at the side of her face, sending her crashing against the far wall. The poker fell on the floor as she struggled to recover.

'You stupid, fucking whore, what have you done!' he screamed at her, leaping off the bed, naked from where he'd been lying with Tina.

He was coming for her now, his eyes ignited with fury, his body language that of a predator coming in for a kill. There was screaming and frantic activity in the house and acrid, black smoke was beginning to make its way up the staircase.

For one terrible second, Sophia wondered if it was worth the fight. If she let him finish her now, it would be over, and she wouldn't have to care anymore. She was closing her eyes, readying herself for what was coming, when Cillian placed his foot on the end of the poker. It was still hot where it had been sitting so close to the dying fire in the living room and he jumped, losing his footing. With one last cast of the die, Sophia grabbed at the poker and struck Cillian's knee, to make sure he fell down. He crashed to the floor, his violent force only momentarily subdued. She had only one chance. If she didn't make this count, this was the end of her.

She struck his head with the poker; his skull made a sickening crack. It was difficult the first time, and she felt like she wanted to vomit. Sophia was no killer. Once she started striking, she could not help herself. Sophia hit Cillian's head more than twenty times before she stopped; he'd ceased struggling after the second blow. Each time, blood and flesh, and eventually the contents of his skull, spattered against the wall and onto the sheets. With each blow, she cursed each and every degradation and horror that she'd suffered at this man's hands.

Her mind was drifting; she was numb to what she'd just done. She had to make sure the other girls got out safely or it would all have been a waste.

Sophia walked around the house. The fire had taken hold now, but she checked that each of the rooms was empty. As the fierce crackle of the flames filled the house, the frantic cries of the girls subsided as they made their escape. When she was certain everybody was out, Sophia got as close as she could to the living room where she'd left Billy's body burning. It was an inferno in there; he was burning in the flames of damnation.

She walked through the front door and into the street. It was such a simple act, yet even that morning it had seemed like an impossible thing to do. The sense of freedom was liberating as the fresh, chill air of the night filled her lungs.

Sophia didn't look back. Dressed in only a T-shirt and old jeans, she walked along the footpath into the cold, inhospitable night.

TWENTY-TWO

'Has she woken up since she came in?'

'No, we've had nothing from her,' the nurse replied.

Hollie hated the ICU; she blamed that on TV shows. The beeping equipment, all the wires, the dimmed lighting. And Jenni was lying as still as when she'd left her in the alleyway, a tube in her mouth, bandages covering her entire head.

'She's suffering from cerebral hypoxia—' the nurse began. She saw Hollie's face and explained some more. 'Jenni has anoxic brain injuries because of the impact. Basically, there was a deprivation of oxygen to the brain. She's in a very serious condition.'

'Have her parents visited?' Hollie asked.

'They were taking a short holiday abroad but have got the first flight they could. They're flying back tomorrow.'

'They must be out of their minds with worry,' Hollie said. 'May I sit with her a while?'

'Yes, the sound of your voice will be helpful, if she was your colleague.'

Osmond must have pulled a few strings to get the visit organised; she wasn't above a bit of rank-pulling either when it was required. After her conversation with Osmond, she knew she had to speak to Jenni, even if she couldn't hear her. She waited for the nurse to leave and then took her friend's hand.

'Hello, Jenni, it's Hollie—'

She felt stupid. She had to get this out.

'I know you thought you were looking out for me, Jenni, but I wish you hadn't followed me. That wasn't your job—'

The tears were falling once again.

'Why didn't you just drop off the key at the flat like you'd meant to? In fact, the key wasn't important. You could have given it to me the next day. And if you thought I was being watched, you should have texted me. We could have checked it out together.'

She tried to figure out how the simple return of her key had resulted in such a terrible outcome. Something must have made Jenni behave the way she had. What had she been thinking?

'I'm taking the kids bowling when I get home,' Hollie continued, not at all sure if her colleague could hear her. 'You could have come with us and met Phoebe. I reckon you two would have got on.'

Jenni's hand was limp. There was no movement at all. The beeping of her monitor remained consistent, punctuating the silence of the room.

'I just wanted to tell you I'm determined to lay my hands on this bastard. I'm going to catch him for you, for Noah, and for Rose Warburton. I'm going to get him for Sister Brennan, too. I promise. I won't stop until we have him.'

She sat quietly for a moment, struggling to calm her emotions.

'You'd have laughed at me this afternoon, in Osmond's office. He did the post-trauma thing with me. That might have been me with the serious face, going through it with you. I'd have struggled with that after the night out we had. I think you might have doubted my credibility after seeing me sing karaoke.'

Hollie laughed through her tears, recalling the spectacle they'd made of themselves. At least things had cooled off over the viral video.

'I just wanted to let you know how sorry I am, Jenni. You were the friend I needed in Hull, and you're half my age, for God's sake. Just call it a midlife crisis. But please, please recover from this. I feel so guilty about it, about you, and what's happened to you. Make yourself better so we can have another karaoke night. We can rehearse next time. We'll blow away that old cow who stole the show.'

Hollie squeezed Jenni's hand then leant over and placed a gentle kiss on her forehead, mindful that she was only recently out of surgery. It reminded her of how careful she'd been around Izzy's fontanelle as a brand-new mother, terrified that she might harm her child in some way.

'I'll see you back in the office,' she said, walking over to the door.

'Thanks for keeping it brief,' the nurse said, seeing her leaving. 'You must know some people in high places to have got the okay for that visit.' She smiled.

Osmond knew somebody on the management team at the hospital. It was the least he could do after she'd shown him how proficient he was at delivering ESTIP.

Hollie was grateful for the drive home; it gave her some time to get her head back in the zone for family time. Phoebe and the children were heading off the next day. She was determined to enjoy at least one night out with them without the spectre of the case interfering. As she pulled up the car along the road from the flats, she wondered where Jenni had been watching and waiting the previous night. How long had she kept her vigil, ready to alert her colleagues if the man on the motorbike made a move? She wasn't so sure she wouldn't have done the same thing as a young cop. She'd been impetuous enough in her own career; it was a foible that still landed her in trouble even in her forties.

As she walked over towards the flat, she heard the crash of cymbals and the booming of a bass drum.

Not tonight, she said to herself. *He's not screwing up tonight.*

She breathed deeply and calmed herself. She was not going to get herself worked up now. But Hull's answer to Phil Collins was on borrowed time.

The next time he did this, those drumsticks were getting rammed somewhere the sun didn't shine.

Hollie made a dramatic entrance at the door, forcing a smile on her face.

'Who fancies Nando's and bowling?' she announced.

'Yes!' both the kids yelped.

As Lily and Noah got ready, Hollie caught up with Phoebe.

'How was The Deep?' she asked.

'They loved it. We had an amazing time.'

'Sorry I'm late. It's been one hell of a day.'

'You look exhausted. I don't know how you do it. All that pressure at work, then home to the kids.'

'Well, the kids help it all make sense, you know? I like to think I'm helping make the world a better place. Sometimes I wonder, though. How's Noah?'

'He didn't even mention it. That kid is like the Duracell bunny. He just keeps going.'

'Thanks though, Phoebe, really. I couldn't have done this without you. I mean it. I know I've barely been here, but it's been so good to know they've got you. I'll make it up to them, once we have this case sorted out.'

'Well, thank you for letting me stay. I love your kids. They're great fun. If you ever need a babysitter when I start uni, just let me know. I can't wait to get here. I'm ready for a place like Hull after living in Lancaster. It's so quiet there.'

The children got their trainers on and made themselves presentable, then they all headed out.

'That's a bit of a nuisance, isn't it?' Phoebe remarked as they walked out into the hallway.

'Yes, apologies for the drummer. I'm sorry if he disturbed you. I'll be somewhere new by the time you start uni. And that drummer will have taken up a quieter instrument by the time I'm finished with him.'

A night out with her children was about the only thing Hollie could think of that would keep her awake after such a long day. She was exhausted and in desperate need of her bed. But it could wait. This was proper family time, and she would not have missed it for anything.

Phoebe was right about Noah; he was in fine form during their meal and there was no sign of any lasting damage. He was full of The Deep and the creatures that he'd seen and seemed entirely undiminished by the events of the previous day.

'They had a shark there, Mum, you should have seen it. It swam right by you in the tank. It was awesome!'

'Good job it didn't eat you!' Hollie laughed, tickling him and making loud chomping noises. He wriggled and laughed; it wouldn't be long before he brushed aside this kind of tomfoolery with his mum.

The bowling at Kingswood Retail Park was boisterous and fun. She could see how fast the children were growing up by their insistence that they did not use the trainer barriers at the sides of the skittle run.

'Only old people and babies need trainer railings, Mum!' Lily teased.

'Well, this old lady won't be able to hit a single skittle if they're down,' Hollie joked, pretending to be an elderly woman.

'Don't worry, Mum, I'll show you what to do,' Noah said, touching her arm.

There he was, her beautiful, gentle boy. She hoped he'd always stay like that, even though she knew he'd soon be forced to hide his caring side when he had to survive at secondary school.

The crash of the bowling balls on the wooden floor and screams of joy whenever there was a strike made her recall happier times when they'd come out as a family. She indulged the kids with soft drinks and sweets. The health information adverts could get stuffed for one night; she was spoiling them and that was that.

Eventually, the children began to tire and the pace of bowling in the final game slowed.

'How about you get yourselves a hot drink before we go, and we can sit in one of the cubicles over there? What time is your train tomorrow, Phoebe?'

'Just before eight o'clock, if you're okay to drop us off. Mum said she'd pick us up from Lancaster station.'

'Ouch, that's a bit early for you. It works well for the morning briefing, though, so yes, no problem.'

Hollie found a seat in a spare cubicle while Phoebe took the children off to get the drinks. They were like a pack already. She had to remind herself that Lily and Noah had had a great adventure, even if she couldn't be there all the time. She sat back, took a long breath, and closed her eyes. It had been a wonderful evening and she was thankful for it.

Her phone rang. It was after ten o'clock. It had to be someone from the office. For a split second, she panicked that it might be news about Jenni.

She activated her screen. It was a withheld number. It was him.

'Find my birth mother or I'll make an example of Rose Warburton,' he said.

Hollie jumped at the sound of his voice, even though she knew who'd be on the end of the line. She was speaking to a dangerous man, a killer. That shook her.

'Please don't do anything stupid. I want to help you, but we need some more time—'

'You've had plenty of time—'

A thought struck her and sent her into a spiral of panic. Was he there? Was he watching them? She looked over at Phoebe and the children and scanned the area. She couldn't hear the sounds of the bowling alley over the phone, so he had to be somewhere else. The DCC was likely close to him.

'What do you expect me to do?' she continued, frustrated by the threats. 'We've thrown all of our resources at this. We've drawn a blank. You've got caught between two council changeovers. We'll find the paperwork, eventually, but it's going to take some time.'

'That sounds like a you problem, detective. If you want to see your colleague again, I suggest you start coming up with some new ideas.'

She couldn't afford to let this slip away. He'd already demonstrated what he was capable of. She imagined the DCC cowering nearby as he spoke to her on the phone. She had to keep him calm, so he didn't take it out on Rose Warburton.

'Do you have paperwork from your adoption?' Hollie asked. 'I'll bet there's the name of an adoption agency on it if you do. You could help us get to the bottom of all this.'

She was offering him an olive branch, and she hoped he'd take it.

'Yes, I have paperwork. I found it when my bitch of a mother finally died. She had emphysema, so it was prolonged. I hope it was frightening, too. It gave her plenty of time to think about what she'd done. I only found out I'd been adopted after she died. My life has been hell. I want those who were responsible to answer for this. At the very least, I want an apology. They sent an innocent child into a cesspit.'

Hollie reeled at his words. To hear him so hateful towards his adoptive mother was shocking, but she wondered if the scars he was carrying might be even more terrifying. He was getting worked up; she had to divert him from his anger.

'Can you remember who handled the adoption? Was it an agency?'

'Yes, it was an agency, but they don't exist now. I can't find out anything about them, it just leads to a black hole.'

Hollie thought about what McCready had told her.

'Was it Brand New Family, or something like that? It might have been Brand New Families.'

'Yeah, that was it. Have you traced them?'

'No, not yet. As you said, they don't exist anymore. Look, we'll find the answers you need eventually, but we can't do it by tomorrow night. It's impossible—'

'Well, if you don't, Rose Warburton will help to focus your minds—'

'But she's done nothing wrong!'

'You think so? There's every chance she might be my mother. She's the victim of rape. She admitted it. She gave her child away—'

'If you can get your paperwork to us, we'll be able to find out. She's a victim, too, remember. You said it yourself. You're all victims.'

That seemed to throw him, but he recovered his skewed moral compass quickly. He sounded volatile.

'She knows something about that home, but she's saying nothing. If I hear that word *confidentiality* one more time, I'm going to scream. So, it's confidential who sent an innocent child into years of neglect and abuse? It's more important to protect the names of the people who were responsible than it is to reveal the truth? Well, screw social services and our fucked-up system. If I don't get answers and accountability, I'll make sure these issues get a public airing.'

So this was it; this was a story about abuse. No wonder he was so damaged if he'd been sent out like a lamb to the slaughter. For the briefest moment Hollie felt a rush of sympathy for his plight. But he was a killer and he'd made his choices. And the DCC was in immediate and mortal peril.

'Surely you've done enough already?' Hollie suggested. 'Isn't it time to stop this now?'

'Nobody gives a shit about an old nun. But a senior police officer? I bet you'll cut through the red tape fast enough when her life is on the line.'

'Please tell me you haven't hurt her,' Hollie implored.

She pictured the DCC, bound and gagged. She was overcome with fear at the thought of it, so she tried to fix her mind on what he was saying.

'She's alive and fed—'

'What does that mean?'

The panic was rising in her now, and she could not control it.

'She wouldn't talk to me, so I had to encourage her a bit—'

'If you harm her—'

Hollie burned with anger. Whatever had happened in this man's past, he was a brute.

'What will you do if I do give her a slap? I'd say the ball is in my court, wouldn't you?'

Hollie cursed herself. She'd provoked him and that was the last thing she should be doing.

'Look, I can help, but I'll need more time—'

She hated having to reason with the man who'd abducted and drugged her son. It stuck in her craw, when all she wanted to do was punish him.

'There's no more time. Your window closes at ten o'clock tomorrow night.'

'Can you let me see your paperwork, at least? It will help us find your case files.'

There was silence at the end of the phone line.

'I'll get it to you, as soon as I can. But I can't promise, I'm not putting myself at risk. If I see an opportunity, I'll pass it over to you.'

He'd managed to leave a note with Noah, and he'd done a pretty good job of snatching the DCC in broad daylight. Thinking about Noah brought her anger back.

'Did you have to threaten my son?'

She knew she shouldn't have said it, but it just came out. It was the question she most wanted to ask him, and she'd been holding back.

'Tell me, DI Turner, do I have your full attention?'

'Yes, you know you do.'

'Would I have had your full attention if I hadn't threatened your son? Would you be promising to turn over every stone if I didn't have your boss? I've been passed from pillar to post. I started by asking nicely, but all I hit were brick walls. Nobody wants to know. But it's my life, DI Turner, and it was screwed up by my evil, psychotic adoptive parents. Somebody must care about that. Somebody has to answer for that. I don't care how many years ago it was, there should be no best-before date on guilt. You have until ten o'clock tomorrow night.'

TWENTY-THREE

By the time Phoebe had returned with the kids to the cubicle at the bowling alley, Hollie had called the overnight team in the office and set them to work with a new urgency. She'd mentioned Gilly's new revelation about Father Duffy's relationship with a nun and asked for a call to be put through to Mother Davies, to see if she might throw any light on that suggestion.

Anderson had kindly offered to update the brass so she could enjoy the rest of her time with her family. He'd given her good news, too, which made her feel slightly more positive about starting the next day.

'We've got that interview with Father Duffy sorted at last,' Anderson informed her.

'Oh, thank God for that, well done. When are we seeing him?'

'First thing tomorrow, at the convent. We can head over immediately after the morning briefing. The duty solicitor will meet us there. The doctor says it's fine, but he shouldn't come into the station; he's too frail now.'

'Good work, DS Anderson. Pass on my thanks to DS Patel, too, please. I feel like I've been on her case about it.'

'Will do, boss.'

'I'd like you with me for that interview, DS Anderson. I'd value your input.'

She had ended her call before the children rejoined her, but her mind was elsewhere, and she hated herself for it. And now she had to get out of bed, put on a brave face, and send her kids back on the train to Lancaster. And after that, she had to deliver a miracle in order to protect Rose Warburton from whatever this deranged man had planned for her. Yet a part of her felt his pain acutely. He'd been failed terribly by the system and all he was getting was closed doors and evasive responses in his quest for answers. Sometimes the lines between what was justified and what was not could get a little blurred. This was one of those cases. But whatever his sense of injustice and however justified he was in his grievances, it was her job to stop him doing crazy stuff. Once the children were safely on their way, she had every intention of throwing everything she'd got at it.

To her shame, Hollie made an early call to Anderson before leaving her bedroom. On that day of all days, she did not want Phoebe seeing her making sneak check-ins at the office.

'I read the notes on Clive Bartram, are we agreed we're releasing him without charge? I don't think there's anything to answer there. He got a soaking in the Humber for his troubles.'

'Agreed,' Anderson replied. 'If he'd just come in for questioning in the first place, he could have saved himself a short stay in hospital and a night in His Majesty's hotel on Clough Road. I think the account he gave you holds water; he panicked and made a run for it. Besides, we have bigger fish to fry.'

'Take care of that today, if you would,' she said. 'Hopefully, it'll give Mandy some peace of mind. The poor woman, she's had a lot to deal with.'

She felt terrible over breakfast with the kids, even though she kept the conversation light and informal. The three of them were laughing and chatting, and Noah seemed unaffected by his ordeal at the hands of the killer. She wished she could bounce back from life's problems like Noah did; he was irrepressible.

'You deserve a medal for what you've done,' she said to Phoebe as the children scoured the house for items to pack in their bags.

'The kids are lovely. I've really enjoyed their company. I'm so sorry about Noah—'

Hollie held up her hand.

'No, stop there. You are not to blame for what happened, Phoebe. If you hadn't been there to help, we wouldn't have found him so fast. I mean it. I want you to banish all those negative thoughts immediately.'

She heard DCI Osmond's voice ringing in her ears. This was Phoebe's well-being debrief.

'I can't wait to come to uni in Hull,' Phoebe continued after taking in what Hollie had just said.

'You're welcome to lodge with me when I get myself sorted out,' Hollie offered. 'Student accommodation costs a fortune these days. If I can help, I'm happy to do it. It also means I might get to see your mum again, too. It'll give her an excuse to visit.'

She was pleased to see how enthusiastic Phoebe was about that idea.

'I bet you'd love to see Izzy again, too. If I remember correctly, last time you two got together for a night out, I had to provide the paracetamol the next day. She's promised me she'll come and see me in Hull when she finishes her travels.'

Phobe winced at the memory of a good night out in Lancaster.

'I'd like that,' she replied. 'Not the hangover bit, though.'

The children burst into the room before they could chat any further. The flat was going to be quiet without them. Noah and Lily brought reassuring chaos into her life. She shepherded her three visitors into the car and started the engine. This was it. They were on their way home. After this, Léon might take them to France. Who knew when she might see them again? Hollie hated how stuck she was with this. Why was a solution so difficult to find?

Paragon Station was busy for that time of day; half the city seemed to be heading out for the weekend.

'Stay close to Phoebe and me,' she advised as they stepped out onto the station concourse. The train to Manchester was on time and waiting at the designated platform.

'Do you have enough time to pick up your lost phone from Piccadilly railway station?' she asked Phoebe.

'Not really, but the British Transport Police were nice and said they'd have someone wait on the platform for me, so he can hand it over while the train stops there. So long as nothing kicks off to mess up the trains, I'll be okay.'

'Come for a hug,' she said to Lily. Her daughter had tears in her eyes. She was old enough now to understand that it might be some time before she saw her mum again. She burrowed into Hollie and Noah joined them. Only Izzy was missing; she'd have loved to have had her three children with her right at that moment. Hollie pulled them both in tight. She could have stayed like that forever; it was heaven having her two babies close to her like that.

'I want to stay with you, Mum,' Lily said, crying now.

'I know, darling. We'll get it sorted, your father and I, I promise you. I can't bear being away from you two, either. I love you so much.'

The Tannoy announcement advised all travellers to get on the train, and Hollie could see that Phoebe was getting a little antsy about getting on board.

'Come on, kids, you'd better get a move on. I'll see you again soon and you can message me whenever you want.' She gave them each a final kiss.

'As soon as this case is resolved, I promise, I'll come to Lancaster, and we'll get everything sorted out. Try not to worry about things. We'll get it all organised with Dad and Veronique.'

They climbed on board the train, and Phoebe pulled the heavy door shut behind them. She followed them through the windows, along the train, until they found their table seat and got settled. The guard blew her whistle at the end of the platform and the train started to move, slowly at first, so Hollie could walk along the platform and wave. Soon, it was too fast, so she stopped and held up her hand so they could see she was still there as they pulled out of Hull. Hollie was left with a crushing feeling of loneliness and failure; she longed to stop the train and take the spare table seat and travel back to Lancaster with the kids. Her children were slipping away from her, and it was all happening too fast for her to keep up.

Hollie headed back to her car which she'd parked at the rear of the adjacent Royal Hotel. She'd been completely earnest when she'd said she and Léon would get things sorted after the case was resolved.

She pulled out her phone as she walked through the parked cars, checking the time. She felt a sudden wrench of anxiety in the pit of her stomach as she registered how little time they had to get on top of the case. They had to find their killer, figure out the identity of his mother and save the DCC from harm, all before ten o'clock that evening if he refused to move his deadline. She swallowed hard and steeled herself. She was not going to let this bastard win.

TWENTY-FOUR

1969: SOPHIA BRENNAN'S STORY

Sophia thought her body was about to give up on her; she couldn't control the shaking and nausea. She pushed on, stumbling through the dark streets, looking behind her all the time, expecting Cillian and Billy to be coming after her. Their voices filled her head, taunting her, demanding that she go back to that place, insisting that she saw one more drunken man before they finished for the night.

She stopped by a tree to throw up. She needed her fix; it felt like she would die without it.

Across the city, she could hear sirens. Were they heading for the fire that she'd started? Would they rescue those bastards and save their lives? If they were going to hell, and surely they were, at least she'd been the one to start the flames that would torment them for eternity.

'Are you all right?' came a female voice.

It was an elderly couple walking a couple of Jack Russells.

'Can we do anything to help?'

'I'm okay, thank you, I'm fine.'

The woman put her hand on Sophia's arm. It was the first

gentle and soft human touch she'd felt after the violence of the house.

'That's an interesting tattoo on your arm—'

Sophia shrugged her off. She had to get away; she couldn't afford to let these people get a close look at her; she was a murderer, after all. She staggered on, ignoring the pleas to accept their help.

'She doesn't look okay,' she heard the woman say. Would they call the police?

'My house is just around the corner,' Sophia managed to call over. 'I've had a bit too much to drink. I'll be home soon, thank you.'

She sensed the couple were still watching her stumbling along the road, but she didn't look back. Instead, Sophia attempted to make it look like she had some sense of purpose. When she reached the corner, she bolted as fast as she could.

It had only just dawned on her: she was a fugitive now, a murderer. Did it count as murder if you killed men as vile as Cillian and Billy? She thought it would, and they'd jail her and throw away the key. She'd only just escaped from one prison.

Sophia hadn't a clue where she was going. Her life had been spent around the fishing community in Hessle Road, and she had no friends to call on and nobody to help her. For a moment, she wondered if she should head for the Salvation Army hostel, but she thought better of it. They might be looking for her. Besides, she had to find drugs. She'd die without them.

It was a chilly night and she'd come unprepared. Her arms were dotted with goosebumps. She had to find somewhere to rest; she needed money.

Sophia stopped and looked around. She'd paused outside a church. And even in that desperate moment, she wondered if she'd been guided there. She looked across the graveyard to see if there was any light, but the church seemed empty. She'd lost track of what time it was. It had to be early morning by now, rather than night-time. Sophia opened the gate and walked up the gravel pathway to the church entrance.

She held her breath as she placed her frozen hands on the large iron handle. It opened; she pushed the heavy wooden door and stepped into the cold stone porch. There was a tiny glimmer of light where visitors to the church lit candles to remember loved ones. They were mostly burnt out, but in the blackness of that place, they provided a sanctuary of sorts. She headed towards the flickers of light, putting out her hands so she didn't collide with the pews. Eventually, she reached the source of the light. There were just three candles there, burning wicks in pools of molten wax.

Sophia felt for the box of candles she knew must be there. She took them out, found the taper, and lit them up. In no time at all, she'd illuminated a small area around one of the front pews. The sight of those burning flames made her feel immediately warmer, and she felt a glimmer of hope when she found an anorak hanging on a nearby chair with a small sign stuck to it saying *Is this yours?* Sophia put the coat on and rubbed her hands.

Every sound she made was swallowed by the emptiness of the building. As she lay on a pew, using a kneeler as a pillow, her entire body began to convulse, and hallucinations taunted her. The devil wore Cillian's face and he threatened to drag her with him back to the hell that had been her life in the squat. In another moment, Kerry knelt by her side and told her they were safe now. She wondered then if she was dead. If she was, it would bring blessed relief. Cillian's men had removed everything in the house that might be used to self-harm, though Sophia's arms were covered in scratches where she'd attempted to claw the poison out of her body.

She thought she might die in that place as the visions came to torment her one by one, but then she heard an unfamiliar voice.

'Bring her a blanket from the office. There's one on top of the cupboard.'

There was warmth and kindness there that she had not experienced in a long time. Her body was stiff, like her muscles had atrophied, and it was difficult to move. She heard a female voice, and a blanket was placed over her, gently, with compassion. And in that moment, it seemed like the most wonderful thing on earth.

'My lunch pack is on my desk. We can take some food out of that. She looks like she hasn't eaten properly in days. Would you fetch it for me? I daren't leave her. She needs medical attention, I think.'

Sophia drifted in and out of consciousness. She became aware of being helped to sit up, and then she was offered food and drink. She did her best to take what was offered, but all she could think of was what her body really needed, with a desperation that she was unable to contain.

'What's your name, my dear?'

It was a soft voice. Sophia thought it was Scottish. She'd heard fishermen come in from the docks with similar accents.

'Sophia. I'm Sophia Brennan.'

'Have you been taking drugs, Sophia?' the man asked.

'Yes. I've been using heroin. I need to get heroin. I'll try to stop, I promise. But I must have some now, then I'll stop—'

'Don't worry, Sophia, we can help you. Try and take some food and drink. It will help you feel stronger.'

The woman's voice was kind. It was like the way her mother spoke to her when her father was still alive.

'Sophia, we're going to call the doctor. Is that okay?'

The man was speaking again now.

'We have to get you some help. We can't do that on our own. You'll need some professional support if you're going to come off the drugs. But we can help you here. We can give you a warm bed and help you through the journey ahead.'

As Sophia took small sips of the water, her eyes focused beyond her immediate area. She saw the stations of the cross all around her, the crucified body of Christ looking down at her with tears in his eyes. It felt as if he'd called her to this place.

The man and the woman moved away from her so they could whisper, but sound bounced around the nave.

'The Church won't let her stay at the unit. She's got a drugs problem. They won't want her among the girls—'

'I'm surprised you haven't noticed already. Can you not see the bump in her stomach? The girl must be pregnant.'

Sophia was aware of the woman scrutinising her from afar.

'I'd be surprised if the baby makes it after all she's been through. It'll be affected by the drugs, too, when it's born. What on earth has this poor girl been through?'

'Do you know when the baby is due?' the man raised his voice and asked.

Sophia had forgotten about the baby. She shook her head.

'Has a doctor examined you yet?' the woman asked.

'No.'

'We're going to get the doctor to look at you,' the man repeated. 'You don't need to move yet. We'll call him out here and he can check you in the church. Then we can get you some fresh clothing over at the building next door, and we'll find a room for you. You can get cleaned up there and we'll take care of you. You'll be safe with us.'

'Do you have any family who'll be wondering where you are?' the woman asked softly.

Sophia started to cry, and it felt like the tears would never end. She'd held it all in for so long, but now, with this kindness, it had to come out.

'There, there,' the woman said. Sophia didn't think she was much older than herself. For the first time, she realised who they were. The woman was dressed in a nun's habit, and the man was a priest, a young one at that.

'I'll go and call the doctor from my office,' the priest said. 'I won't be long.'

'You'll soon be feeling better,' the woman continued. 'You're in safe hands. I'm Sister Ursula Kay, by the way, and that's Father Francis Duffy, though he prefers to be called Frank. We'll look after you and the baby, Sophia. We'll take care of everything.'

TWENTY-FIVE

There was a positive buzz when Hollie stepped into the incident room, and she picked up a keen sense of momentum and persistence as she walked through the office, checking in on the various team members. There was tension there, too, over the DCC, but they seemed intent on getting her back safely. DS Patel had a box of chocolates on her desk, next to which sat a single red rose.

'It looks like he's got it bad.' Hollie smiled.

'Can we please get this case tied up?' DS Patel replied. 'It's not every day a nice man with all his own teeth and no secret wife in tow sends you chocolates and asks you to go on a date. If I have to wait much longer, I'll have stuffed all those chocolates, put on loads of weight, and he won't fancy me anymore.'

Hollie laughed. They needed to have a joke. If they thought too hard about the danger Rose Warburton was in, they'd go mad. Everybody in that room understood the urgency of the situation.

'Any news about Jenni?' Hollie asked.

'I've called already, but they haven't done the morning

rounds yet. Her parents arrive today, though, so that's good news.'

'We'll meet at nine,' Hollie continued. 'I just need a couple of minutes to get my feet under the table.'

She made her way over to her workstation, already dreading having to return to her empty flat that night. She'd heard no more from the DCC's captor, and Léon had been conspicuous by his absence, too. She logged into her PC and then slipped into the kitchen to make herself a hot drink while it was chugging away.

Hollie took a quick swig of her tea and sat back down at her computer. A notification alerted her to an email from Theresa titled *Adoption Papers*.

She had another sip of her drink and opened it up.

Hi DI Turner, my son scanned these for you. I hope they help! Theresa.

There were four scans attached to the email and she double-clicked on the first. It was an old document; the paper was browned with age, and it had been completed by hand. It was unusual for Hollie to see official paperwork filled in using ink, but even she had experienced a small part of her life without computers. The heading indicated that the paperwork had originated in the County Borough of Hull. The very mention of county boroughs immediately felt Victorian.

DS Anderson had just walked in and was getting settled at his desk. He looked tired. Hollie guessed he'd been fretting about the DCC overnight, much like she had.

'Good morning, DS Anderson. Give me a quick history lesson, if you would. Humberside County Council was formed in 1974. That's right, isn't it?'

'Good morning, boss. Yes, 1974, that's correct. Hull had its own council before that. Why?'

'Just refresh my memory, in case I've got this wrong. The girls that we've been dealing with all had their babies in 1975, is that correct?'

DS Anderson was intrigued now. He'd not even taken off his coat but had wandered over to Hollie's desk to see what she was looking at.

'Look at this.'

Anderson peered over her shoulder. After a couple of seconds, he admitted he couldn't see it.

'Why, if Theresa's son was adopted in 1975, is his paperwork headed with the details of the old county borough? I know it was all old-fashioned and non-computerised in those days, but they wouldn't have used a bit of obsolete paperwork from the stationery cupboard to record an adoption, would they?'

DS Anderson had got it; his eyes widened.

'Damn, that was well spotted, boss. So, you think the adoption wasn't above board?'

'When our killer called me last night, I asked him if he would send me his paperwork—'

'That's a bit unlikely, isn't it? I don't want to sound negative, but if he gives you that, he gives away his identity, doesn't he?'

'I think it's a bit late for that, don't you? This is endgame stuff. We're past the point of no return now. He might get it to us. I'd love to see how it compares to this.'

The two of them examined the remaining scans. The papers had several fold lines and creases along them, the ink was faded but readable, and it was recorded in a traditional handwriting of a neatness and uniformity that Hollie hadn't seen in a long time. The scrawled Post-it notes that lined her PC put her to shame.

'I assume those are the adoptive parents?' Anderson checked.

'I reckon so,' Hollie answered. 'And look, there's McCready's signature and Father Duffy as a witness. Just let the team know I'll be delayed by five minutes, will you? I'm going to call Theresa before the briefing.'

Hollie forwarded the email to DS Patel and asked her to print out copies for the meeting.

She was ten minutes late, as it turned out. She'd had a useful conversation with Theresa, and she wanted to make sure she had as much information as possible before sharing it with the team.

'Good morning, everyone.' She called them to order. The brass was well represented in the room that morning, as well they might be. With one of their own in danger, this had to be done right.

Hollie wrote the digits 22.00 on the whiteboard to her side.

'It's 09.22 right now,' she began, 'and we have just over twelve hours to find DCC Warburton. That isn't like an academic deadline where you can last-minute it or ask for an extension. When that deadline expires, I can't say what will become of the DCC.'

She'd got their full attention. It was a little theatrical, but she went for it anyway. She filled them in on the details of her brief call with the killer the previous evening, and she also explained why she thought the man might do something extreme, referencing Tony's Facebook exchange as evidence.

'We can't assume this is a bluff,' she warned. 'He's killed already, and he has a penchant for the dramatic. He wants our attention. He feels he's been slighted, and a violent man with a grievance needs to be handled with kid gloves. Any questions so far?'

There was no reply, just a room filled with officers who looked like they were itching to get on.

'DS Anderson, you and I are going to interview Father

Duffy as soon as we're finished here. We're also going fishing at Sister Brennan's memorial immediately after.'

Hollie spotted the family liaison officer who was dealing with Timothy Warburton.

'DC Hayes, do you have anything to report from the DCC's husband? Did you find anything in your search of her office?'

'No, ma'am, the search of her office came up blank. There's no evidence of any contact with her adopted son on her mobile phone statements or the home phone records. We're assuming she must use a separate phone to make contact with him. She doesn't use her main email account to contact him either, so we think she may use a second email service, perhaps one of the paid-for subscription options. As you'd expect from someone with her experience, she knows how to cover her tracks.'

'What about Timothy?' Hollie continued questioning the DC.

'Just a lot of questions and soul-searching on his part. He's worried sick, too. I'm heading back there as soon as I know the latest. He didn't receive any further calls from our man on the home phone number.'

'Was there any evidence of our man returning to the mother and baby home?' Hollie asked, searching for DC Gordon's face among the gathered officers.

'No, ma'am,' he answered. 'The place was undisturbed. He must have moved on.'

'We need to find out where he's hiding,' Hollie reminded everybody. 'We've got vehicle descriptions. We need to be following up on all sightings and get your hands on any CCTV footage which might help. If we locate the DCC before he emerges into the open, we stand a better chance of rescuing her. He may well have stolen the vehicle he used to abduct her. Do we have any reports of missing vehicles yet?'

Silence.

Hollie fought her impatience.

'We need to be on top of all of this, people. If we can find the needle in the haystack, we stand much more chance of getting a successful outcome here.'

Hollie took a moment to steady herself. She wished all of them, including herself, could work faster, but she knew how this would play out. Either their killer would make a mistake and give himself away or they'd find him through careful, painstaking police work. She could almost hear the clock ticking away in the background now.

'Okay, I want to look at the photocopies which have been circulated by DS Patel. There are several anomalies here which point to foul play...'

Hollie talked them through her observations and confirmed the details and dates of the council changeover in 1974 as well as the rough dates when the girls had given birth. There was a consensus in the room that this appeared to be a strong lead.

'I suspect this may all relate to illegal adoptions at the mother and baby home. I also think our murderer may have been one of those illegal adoptions, which is why I think he's been unable to locate his birth mother. It seems Theresa Morgan's son may have been illegally adopted, too, but that appears to have passed without any issues. This is all conjecture at the moment, but we need to re-interview Patrick McCready and Father Duffy, under caution this time around. Even if they weren't directly involved, they may have had a suspicion about what was going on. Have we got our hands on McCready yet?'

'No, boss, he's gone AWOL. We've made repeated visits to his home, and we've got a car parked out on his street now with a 24/7 watch.'

'Thanks, DS Patel. McCready has just got himself bumped up the list now. This can't wait. Get uniform to bring him in if he's elsewhere in the country, but we need to speak to him today.'

Hollie surveyed the room. The officers in front of her were

primed, like dogs waiting to have a ball thrown along the beach. She just had to give the word.

'I need someone to chase Father Duffy's bank accounts and look for irregular payments. I'd like to see if money has been changing hands for the adoption of these babies. We should check Patrick McCready's financial records, too. It's going to be slow and difficult because the trail goes back so many years, but it may well provide some robust evidence if we can lay our hands on it.'

'One more thing, boss,' DS Patel volunteered, after noting down Hollie's last request.

'Go ahead.'

'We've unearthed an old press cutting from 1969. It might be something, it might be nothing.'

'Go on, DS Patel. This is just the sort of approach I want to encourage. The best police work often comes from hunches and gut feelings.'

'It's a report on a fire at an old squat in the city, boss. It came up in a search for the Church of St Mary and the Angels. It seems irrelevant until you read what a couple of eyewitnesses have to say. It was a couple out late at night walking their dogs. They say they spoke to a young woman who seemed agitated, as she was running from the general direction of the fire. She was heading towards the Church of St Mary and the Angels, they say. But there's one bit that caught my attention. I'll read it to you. This is a quotation from the man. "The young woman shrugged off our offer of help, but we could see she was spaced out and in distress. She told us she was on her way home, but the way she was dressed, she must have been freezing. Her clothes were filthy and her hair unwashed. She headed off in the general direction of the Church of St Mary and the Angels, but we lost her after that. My wife spotted that she had a small tattoo on her arm. It was too dark to see properly, but we were worried about her. We thought she might have been one of the residents there".'

'This is excellent work, DS Patel. Dig a little deeper on that if you can. Is that couple still alive? Are any other eyewitnesses mentioned by name? What's the address of the burned-out property and does the present-day owner have any records about what happened? Keep this up, everybody. You've got your tasks. We have just over twelve hours. DCC Warburton's life is in our hands. Let's get to work.'

TWENTY-SIX

It seemed only moments ago that Hollie had been knocking at the door of the convent with Jenni at her side. Now, Jenni was critically ill in the hospital, and Hollie had DS Anderson accompanying her.

'What do I need to know about the convent?' Anderson asked. 'I hope they'll let an old sinner like me across the threshold.'

'I had a similar thought when I drove over with DC Langdon,' Hollie replied. 'I think they're a bit like the police, these nuns, they've probably seen and heard everything.'

It felt good to have the tension between them thawed a bit since their one-to-one.

Mother Davies answered the door.

'Good morning. Do they make you do all the work around here?' Hollie smiled.

'Your colleague told me you were coming. I wanted to make sure I got the chance to speak to you first. Good morning, DS Anderson.'

Hollie recalled that the nun had met Anderson at the identification of Sister Brennan's body. Perhaps she'd been a little insensitive bringing him with her. Mother Davies had a good faculty for names for her age, that was for certain.

'Oh, I'm in my own car this morning, so if you and one of your colleagues want a lift to the memorial, it might save you a taxi fare.'

'That's very thoughtful of you, DI Turner. I'll cancel the taxi we booked. Sister Kay and I were going to get a car over. Four of the other sisters are travelling in Sister Milligan's car.'

Mother Davies showed them into the front room, where Hollie and Jenni had spoken with her earlier in the week.

'I just wanted to speak to you first, before you chat to Father Duffy.'

'Of course,' Hollie replied, taking a seat. 'I'm so sorry that you had to identify Sister Brennan.'

'DS Anderson was very supportive,' she replied. 'He made a difficult task much easier.'

Hollie had to make that concession to Anderson. He might seem like a bit of a dinosaur in some matters, but when it came to police work, he knew his stuff.

'What did you want to say to us?' Anderson encouraged her. He was right to do so. The memorial started soon, and Hollie didn't want to be late.

'The doctor has said that Father Duffy is well enough to be interviewed, but he's very agitated,' she began. 'I know he's had a fright, but the nuns watching him report very fitful sleep.'

'Has he said anything to you?' Hollie asked.

'No, he's most friendly with Sister Kay. They go way back. You'll know our religion is strong on heaven and hell, detectives, but if I had to summarise Father Duffy's behaviour, I'd say he's a man who's being tormented by the devil. He's troubled about something. He seems scared.'

'Has he mentioned any names?' Anderson asked as they all turned at a noise outside the door. Nobody came in.

'I'm very familiar with death, detectives. Many of the sisters here are old, and I've lived among many women in their final days. How they die varies. Most times, they sleep more, as if their bodies are getting ready for the final journey. But, occasionally, just occasionally, you come across an individual who's troubled. Father Duffy is one of those people. Sister Brennan was another, though that was possibly a result of her declining mental health. I just can't shake the feeling that the two of them had something on their minds.'

'I asked my colleagues to speak to you about the possibility that Father Duffy might have been having an affair with one of the nuns who was based at the mother and baby unit. Do you know anything about that?'

Mother Davies's face became immediately stern.

'You know what you're suggesting I hope, DI Turner? The mere suggestion of that is offensive to the Church; it flies in the face of everything we believe—'

'Yet, it's happened before and it's not outside the realms of possibility.'

'Let me be very clear, detective. I know nothing about any hidden relationships, and I take offence at the very suggestion. Please take great care with your allegations: lives and well-earned reputations can be ruined by malicious gossip.'

Anderson stood up while she was talking and opened the door to the room without warning or explanation. From where Hollie was sitting, she could see that Sister Kay was outside, a furtive look on her face as if she'd just been caught with her hand in the collection box.

'Can I help you?' Anderson asked.

'Oh, I was just – I thought I heard voices—' she sputtered.

'Is that Sister Kay?' Mother Davies asked.

'Yes, I thought you might have guests,' she answered as she entered the room. 'Do you need refreshments?'

'No, but I'd be grateful if you would cancel our taxi. The officers have kindly offered to give us a lift.'

'Yes, of course,' Sister Kay answered and rushed off.

'We'd best go upstairs and speak to Father Duffy,' Hollie said, standing up. 'Thank you for sharing that information, Mother Davies. That's very useful.'

She showed them up the stairs to a door at the rear of the building. It was sparsely decorated, save the occasional crucifix or picture of Jesus on the cross, though the banister along the stairs was crafted from a beautiful piece of oak, which suggested the property might once have enjoyed a more ornate past. Hollie wondered what it was like to live such a simple life; it felt devoid of colour and vibrancy.

Father Duffy was sitting up in bed, the wound around his neck looking much less fierce than when she'd last seen him. He seemed lively enough and it was a good sign that he recognised them. His solicitor was seated at his bedside, busying himself with papers.

'Really, officers, could this not have waited until Father Duffy has been given more time to recover?'

He was haughty, self-important and pompous, and Hollie took an immediate dislike to him.

'I'm afraid our investigation is at a stage where we need to speak to Father Duffy as a matter of urgency,' Hollie informed him. Hollie briefed the solicitor on the bare bones of the case and why it was so essential that they conduct the interview under caution. The solicitor agreed to it taking place, and Hollie gave Anderson the go-ahead to give him his formal warning. Anderson made sure the recording device was suitably placed to pick up their voices. He switched it on, time-stamped it, and ran through the formalities.

'You do not have to say anything, but it may harm your defence if you do not mention something when questioned that you later rely on in court. Anything you do say may be given in evidence.'

Father Duffy acknowledged that he'd heard and understood

the caution, and Hollie and DS Anderson moved in closer so the interview might be conducted as proficiently as possible, given that they were on one side of the bed, the solicitor on the other, and the priest in the middle. Hollie drew out some sheets of A4 paper from the folder she'd been carrying and passed copies to Father Duffy and his solicitor.

'These are copies of adoption papers that we obtained from one of the women whose child was taken from her in the home. I'd be grateful if you would take a close look at them, Father Duffy.'

He made a meal of putting on his reading glasses, which were perched at his side on the simple bedside table. Hollie gave him some time to study them.

'Do you recognise these papers?' Hollie asked.

The priest shook his head.

'Isn't that your signature on the bottom of the page?' Anderson pushed. 'You acted as a witness, didn't you?'

'My client has no comment,' the solicitor said.

'Maybe he'd like to say that for himself?' Hollie suggested.

Father Duffy examined the paperwork again, then sighed.

'It's all right,' he said to his solicitor.

They waited in silence as he paused for a moment.

'That is my signature, officers, yes.'

'Can you explain to us why this paperwork is not on Humberside County Council headed paper, Father?' Anderson asked.

He seemed relieved at this question, like he'd just opened an exam paper and the questions were easier than he'd expected.

'That's straightforward to explain, officers. We moved over to the new county council in 1974 when the councils changed—'

'So why was this adoption concluded in 1975, one year after the council changeover?'

Father Duffy's expression looked like he'd just turned to the second page of the examination paper and discovered the easy questions were only there to lull him into a false sense of security.

'Remember, you don't have to answer,' the solicitor said.

'It must have been a mistake,' Father Duffy blustered. 'We must have picked up the wrong paperwork.'

'In 1975?' Anderson asked.

'You'd had plenty of time to get things sorted out by then,' Hollie added. 'Why was this adoption recorded on out-of-date paperwork? Was it to fool Theresa Jacobs and her parents into thinking this was a legitimate adoption when you were, in fact, involved in some scam to handle the adoptions privately? Were you profiting from the adoptions?'

'DI Turner!' the solicitor interrupted, his voice raised. 'My client does not have to answer your questions. I'll remind you that my client has attended this interview voluntarily and he's not under arrest. Unless, of course, you have sufficient evidence to arrest him?'

Of course they didn't and this slimy solicitor knew that.

'Okay, let me ask you something else, Father Duffy. Were you having an affair with one of the nuns at the mother and baby unit?'

Hollie could see the solicitor was as shocked at that comment as Father Duffy was. The priest looked like he was about to throw up.

'I-I don't know what you're – this is completely...'

The solicitor whispered in his ear.

'This seems completely irrelevant to the case, detective.'

'Not if it gives us a motive for murder,' Hollie replied. 'Is that why Sister Brennan was killed, Father Duffy?'

He looked at his lawyer.

'I don't know what you're talking about, I don't have a comment,' he blustered.

The solicitor whispered in his ear once again.

'No comment,' Father Duffy said.

'Let's change the subject,' Anderson interjected. 'We found fibres from the cushions in your flat in Sister Brennan's airways. That suggests that Sister Brennan may well have been suffocated in your flat, Father Duffy. How do you explain that?'

Father Duffy seemed like a rabbit caught in the headlights now. He looked to his solicitor for guidance.

'Remember, it's your right to remain silent,' the solicitor advised.

Father Duffy's hand slid beneath the sheets, and when it reappeared, he was clutching a small crucifix.

'No, I want to speak,' he said. 'It's time you knew.'

'Knew what?' Hollie encouraged him.

'About Patrick McCready,' the priest continued. 'I want to tell you all about Patrick McCready.'

TWENTY-SEVEN

1969: SOPHIA BRENNAN'S STORY

Sophia could hear a baby crying, but she couldn't figure out where she was. She felt exhausted, but that wasn't a new thing. The bed linen was crisp and functional, not like her room at the mother and baby home. She was sore, too, in a way she'd never experienced before.

She lifted her hand and felt her arm. Bandages. She'd been doing it again. However hard she tried, she could not scratch the poison out of her body. Although the room was dimmed, there was a bright light in the distance and the hum of hushed conversations. She forced her eyes open, though they were heavy and unwilling. This was a hospital. It came back to her. This was Hedon Road Maternity Hospital, and she'd just had her baby. They all called it *her* baby, but it was not and never would be her baby. It belonged to some disgusting man who had raped her, giving Cillian money to do as he pleased with her in that lonely alleyway or, if he paid a little more, on the stained mattress in the back of the van.

Sophia wanted to be sick. She needed to expel every remnant of that experience and enter a state of oblivion where she would never have to remember it again. But her mind tormented her with the memories and threatened to make her lose her sanity. The only thing that helped, the only way out, seemed to be to dedicate herself to the Church. When she read the Bible, when she prayed and meditated, it helped her to detach from her past life and see a future that might not, perhaps, be so bleak. Yet, with every knock at the door of the mother and baby unit, she feared being discovered. Would the police locate her? If they worked out what Cillian was up to, would they bother much about finding his killer? She hoped not and prayed every day that they would not come for her and take her away from her new sanctuary.

She scanned the ward, looking at the other mothers. Some of them were so young, they could barely have been fifteen years old. Her resentment glimmered like a flickering coal, building up to a flame. She despised these girls, flaunting their sexuality as if it didn't matter, like it was something that could be handed out like sweets. It did matter, and she of all people knew what a deadly, terrible, revolting thing it could be. Her hand moved to her unbandaged arm and she began to scratch, digging her nails into her flesh and pulling them down to her wrist. It felt good for a moment, but then she craved something more powerful, something that would smother her pain. They'd weaned her off the drugs, and she was now using a medical substitute, but the cravings were still harsh and there were times when she would have pulled down all the walls just to forget.

'How are you, Sophia?'

The voice made her jump. She turned to see Father Duffy standing with Sister Kay. It appeared to be visiting time.

'Tired,' she replied.

'You look it,' Sister Kay picked up. 'Make sure you rest in here. Take your time. You've been on a long journey.'

Sister Kay perched at the end of the bed. She deferred to Father Duffy to take the chair at the bedside.

'We brought you some fruit,' the priest said, placing a brown paper bag on her side table, out of which a bunch of green grapes was protruding. 'I thought you might like a Bible, too.'

Father Duffy shuffled in his seat. He seemed to Sophia to be tense.

'So, you've got a baby boy. He weighed in at five and a half pounds.'

He let that hang for a moment, but it was meaningless to Sophia. She didn't have much idea how much a baby was supposed to weigh.

'That's quite light for a baby, Sophia. It's because of your – er – addiction. He's doing all right, though, and he's being looked after. He'll be able to come home with you—'

'I don't want him to come back with me—'

'He needs his mother, Sophia. You may decide that you want to keep him.'

Sophia had never been as sure of anything in her life. She was not interested in keeping this baby. She did not want to care for this baby. This child had nothing to do with her. It was a cuckoo in the nest, an abomination forced on her by men she despised.

Sister Kay moved further along the bed and spoke softly.

'The baby has some problems, Sophia. Because you're using methadone, he's had some difficulties breathing—'

'I don't care,' Sophia snapped.

'He's feeding poorly and has been vomiting, too,' Father Duffy continued. 'The nurses say that's normal with a baby born addicted to methadone, but they have to treat him for withdrawal, and they'll need to stick to formula milk while that's happening—'

'I'm not feeding him,' Sophia interrupted. 'I will not do one thing to help that baby thrive in this world.'

Sister Kay reached out to take Sophia's hand but flinched.

'You've been scratching yourself again, Sophia. I'll get a nurse to look at that. You don't want it to become infected.'

Sister Kay got off the bed and left Father Duffy to continue sharing the latest news.

'It will take a couple of weeks for the baby to be treated for withdrawal symptoms, but the nurses assure us he'll be fine. Have you thought of a name for him?'

Sophia turned to face Father Duffy directly.

'Father, I know you mean well, but I do not want anything to do with this baby. I don't want to care for it. I don't want to feed it. I don't want to give it a name. I want it taken as far away from me as possible. I feel nothing for it, except relief that it's gone. I want to get back home and start my studies to become a nun, as we discussed. The sooner I can put this behind me, the better.'

Father Duffy moved in a little closer and looked around him.

'I can help with that, Sophia, so long as you're certain. A contact of mine knows a couple who would like to adopt your baby. If you'll just agree to him coming back to the Church of St Mary and the Angels with us, I can make the arrangements. You must be certain, though. You must be sure that this is the right choice for you.'

'I'm sure,' she replied. 'I feel nothing for the child. It doesn't deserve to be brought up by me. I have only hate and resentment for it. Give him a better life. Let that couple take him. At least something good might come of all this.'

A nurse approached, holding a small metal container and a wad of cotton wool.

'Now then, Sophia, Sister Kay tells me you've been hurting yourself again.'

She shooed Father Duffy away from the chair and sat on the bed, next to Sophia, where she bathed her arm gently. She then took out a small bandage and wrapped it around her arm. Her soft touch felt glorious to Sophia, who'd grown accustomed to harsh words and violence. She loved the peacefulness and predictability of the Church. It soothed her like nothing else, even the drugs.

She was distracted by the shrill cry of a baby. Sister Kay had a tiny scrap of a child in her arms.

'I thought you might like to see him, at least—'

Father Duffy moved over to her swiftly.

'That might not be a good idea,' he said.

Sophia felt a panic rise in her that threatened to consume her completely. She saw Cillian's gloating face and smelt the stale breath of a hundred men as their drool spattered her face.

'Take it away from me!' she screamed.

'It's all right. He's just a tiny baby,' Sister Kay said, moving closer.

'I think you should take him away,' Father Duffy suggested.

'She needs to try to bond with the child,' Sister Kay protested.

'I don't want it anywhere near me!' Sophia shouted. She was burning with sweat, the poison inside her seeping out at the sight of the child.

Sister Kay moved closer, turning the baby so Sophia could see its face. Sophia began to scream, and all around her were the sounds of shock and alarm as the other mothers and visitors on the ward looked on with horror at what was going on.

At last, Sister Kay took the baby away, ushered out by the nurse, who scolded her for causing so much distress. Sophia turned her face into the pillow, willing it to swallow her up. She hadn't wanted to see the child; she wanted no connection with it. Her glimpse had been mercifully brief, and only the baby's face had protruded from the blue hospital blanket wrapped tightly around its body. She'd barely seen its face and she was grateful for that. She didn't want the image of the child haunting her dreams. The only feature she'd noticed in that short time was the tiny mole to the side of his right eye. Other than that, it might have been any baby. Either way, she didn't much care.

TWENTY-EIGHT

Hollie sighed as she ended her phone call with DS Patel.

'Any luck?' Anderson asked.

'No, no sign of McCready still,' Hollie replied. 'What did you make of Father Duffy? Was he telling us the full truth?'

Anderson shrugged.

'Who knows? Sometimes people get themselves in so deep, I think they forget what's true and what's not. I know I'd like to throw that bloody solicitor off the Humber Bridge, though. I've come across him before. He's a wily little git. Fancy shutting up the priest before he gave away enough of the story to make an arrest.'

'It's not like Father Duffy is going anywhere,' Hollie replied. 'I thought about making an arrest, but we don't have anything more to pin on him than what he's told us. I think something was going on at that place and I'm sure as hell it involves a group of people who are all covering each other's arses. I'm also certain McCready is in on it somehow, but how can we tie it all back to him? If they used unofficial paperwork, it's going to be almost impossible to track down after so many years.'

'You were right asking DS Patel to check his financial

records, that was a good call,' Anderson added. 'The same for McCready: if there's anything dodgy going on between them, we'll find it in their banking records. We might have to go way back though; it's a bugger getting your hands on information from the seventies. Did they even have computers for banks back then?'

Hollie hadn't a clue.

'We'd best get going or we'll be late for the memorial.'

Anderson nodded in the direction of the car where the two nuns were waiting for them.

'DS Patel has dispatched a team of officers to the storage facility where it's thought the old paperwork might be located, but I'm not optimistic. It's taken the council this long to even get an idea where it might be.'

'Let's get this memorial out of the way, then we can reassess where we're up to back at the office.'

He was right. But while they'd been interviewing Father Duffy, it had long since passed ten o'clock and Hollie was only too aware that their deadline was now less than twelve hours away.

On the drive over to the church, Anderson was absorbed in his own thoughts, and the nuns weren't chatty, so Hollie had a moment to reflect. She ran through what they'd learnt from Father Duffy. Patrick McCready was a bully, which came as no surprise. The priest explained to them how he would feel intimidated by the man and how much the nuns disliked him. He would always switch on the charm for the parents, so his nastiness went undetected as far as his professional conduct was concerned.

Father Duffy hadn't given a decent explanation for the cushion fibres found in Sister Brennan's airways. He fudged some answer about her taking a rest on his sofa and speculated that she might have inhaled the fibres that way. It seemed unlikely, and

Hollie caught the whiff of a solicitor's briefing in his prompt response. If Father Duffy ever made it to court, and by the state of him she doubted that prospect, the defence had to present evidence beyond reasonable doubt in the minds of the jury that that's how the fibres got there. As feeble excuses went, it wasn't a bad one if he was covering his tracks. However, she couldn't shake the feeling that Father Duffy was too scared to tell her something. She suspected she had a good idea who it was he was so scared of.

Mother Davies gave instructions as they neared the Church of the Holy Ghost in plenty of time for the memorial.

'What happened with the Church of St Mary and the Angels?' Hollie asked as she pulled up the handbrake. 'Why did the church close?'

'Well, that was a matter for the diocese, but St Mary and the Angels needed repair work, and I think it was felt, politically, that the mother and baby home was tainted and that the Catholic Church was better off distancing itself from the building. I never worked there myself. There's also the matter of declining congregations. The Church is very much like any other business, DI Turner. It undergoes reorganisations and restructuring just like everywhere else.'

A small group of people were gathered outside the church. There were several other members of the religious community present. There appeared to be more representatives from the local press, and Hollie recognised a number of faces from the press conference they'd held at the beginning of the week. One of the BBC reporters spotted her and headed her off before she could escape.

'Are there any developments in the case that you can share with us?' the reporter asked. She was holding out her phone, so Hollie had to assume her words were being recorded. It only seemed five minutes ago that reporters were all plugged into cabled microphones. It was so difficult to spot if she was being recorded these days, as the viral video of her karaoke session confirmed.

'Aren't you supposed to tell me if I'm being recorded?' she asked. 'You have guidelines, don't you?'

'You're being recorded,' the reporter replied.

'There is one thing the local media can do to help,' she replied, wondering if it might be worth taking a chance. 'We're particularly interested in speaking to anybody who had a baby adopted at the mother and baby home between 1974 and 1975, and who might have retained paperwork from that time. Please let Humberside Police know as soon as possible if you can help with that matter.'

The reporter asked a couple of harmless follow-up questions, and Hollie was feeling smug that she'd managed to turn the encounter to her advantage. The reporter then made a show of turning off the recording app on her phone.

'Thanks for that, detective. I'm not recording anymore. I want to ask you something off the record. We've heard a rumour that the deputy chief constable has gone AWOL. What can you tell me about that?'

Hollie was caught off-guard. She knew she was showing it in her face, but she couldn't help it.

'What's your source?' she asked.

'You know I can't tell you that,' the reporter replied.

'You should be sure of your facts before you report anything on the radio,' Hollie said, desperately trying to think of a decent response. How had this journalist caught wind of Rose Warburton's abduction? She'd specifically instructed her team not to say anything. She trusted the BBC and the independent stations to play by the rules. It was social media and the amateur sleuths she was most concerned about. But if there was a leak in the office, she needed to find it and sort it out fast.

'Don't worry, we won't run a story that we can't substantiate,' the reporter reassured her. 'I just wondered if you could let me know if I'm barking up the wrong tree.'

'There's nothing I can say about that,' Hollie asserted. 'On or off the record. The police press office will tell you the same thing. If we have any further information about the case, we'll be sure to let you know.'

Hollie continued up the narrow path to the church entrance. Anderson spotted her and broke away from his conversation with the priest who was taking the memorial service.

'You look flustered,' he said. 'Did the press pack get you?'

'We may have a leak in the office,' Hollie replied, suppressing her fury that one of her team must have opened their big mouth. 'Who might it be?'

'That's anybody's guess. Cops often drink with the press. It only takes a slip of the tongue to a sharp-witted reporter and the cat's out of the bag.'

'Well, I shall be clamping down on that. I don't expect to be hijacked by the media like that. Have you found anything useful?'

'Not really. It seems that Sister Brennan was clearly losing her marbles at the time of her death. Anybody who knew her reports her memory becoming inconsistent due to her dementia. They all say the same thing – that she appeared to want to make amends for something, but it was not clear what was troubling her.'

Hollie checked her phone. It was time for the memorial service to begin and people were filing into the church. The priest led the way, and Hollie and Anderson held back while the religious representatives and the journalists filed in.

'Right,' said Hollie as she led the way through the wooden door, 'we're officially here to pay our respects. But unofficially, let's see if we can learn anything new about our murder victim while we're here.'

TWENTY-NINE

It was some time since Hollie had been in a church and she preferred to avoid them. She'd reached an age where funerals now outnumbered weddings and christenings, and the fun and celebration had long since been knocked out of religious ceremonies. The next time there was any prospect of a positive church experience was when her kids got married, if that was even a thing people did by the time they grew up. For all she knew, they'd be exchanging partners on Tinder every week by that time, or they'd get hitched with someone they'd only just met on TV on the promise of a Z-list celebrity career and a front-page splash on *Hello!* magazine.

She shuddered for the future that awaited her children, yet who was she to speak? The entire case reflected the changing moral outlook of the country. Young girls who were once ostracised for daring to get caught in pregnancy before marriage had now been replaced by youngsters who were queueing up to have sex with new partners on screen in reality TV shows and using that as a launchpad for their successful OnlyFans careers. She was not immune either. Her mother and father would never have contemplated the separation that Léon had just instigated, and she had been relaxed about sleeping with men in her younger years. And there was Izzy, too, beautiful Izzy who she couldn't bear to imagine not being a part of her life. The Church would have condemned that pregnancy at one time; moral standards were forever shifting, and one person's sin was another's normality.

The nuns' lives seemed to promise a wonderful simplicity, yet they cut themselves off from so much opportunity and joy in their dedication and commitment. Hollie was in her mid-forties, and she still didn't have any answers. Her life was just like the case: a growing pile of problems to which she could offer no solutions. She gave up thinking about it and tuned in to what the priest was saying.

He was young for a priest, and for the first time she considered that must have been the age of Father Duffy at the time he was dealing with Gilly, Mandy and the other girls. It was difficult to imagine people who were so old as their younger selves, but it gave her pause for thought. They were all viewing Sister Brennan, Father Duffy and even Patrick McCready as old people, thinking them to be harmless in their advanced years. But they'd been young once, and if they'd done bad things, their aged bodies only served to hide the sins of their past. She resolved not to be caught off-guard by that. Even murderers grew old and needed to pick up their pension from the post office.

The priest said lots of cordial things about Sister Brennan, but it appeared to Hollie that they knew little about her, other than a bland procession of key dates and events. She'd first encountered the Church as a troubled teenager from Hull's fishing community in 1969. She'd gone through a period of discernment and grown increasingly involved in the Church, eventually becoming a novice, and finally taking her vows. The various stages of becoming a nun were alien to Hollie, and if she'd been pushed, she would have admitted that most of her knowledge came from *The Sound of Music*. However, the suggestion of a troubled past confirmed her instincts about the self-harming scars and the small tattoo on the nun's arms. DS Patel's newspaper cutting was interesting, too; surely the young woman thought to be fleeing a house fire all those years ago couldn't have been Sophia Brennan?

Hollie's thoughts returned to the service as a hymn began. She was too embarrassed to attempt a tune with DS Anderson sitting next to her in the pews. She opted for half-miming and sang so quietly that he gave her a look. Anderson had a reasonable singing voice, to her surprise. The remainder of those gathered sounded like they could barely be bothered to knock out a tune. It was reassuring to see that even those who'd dedicated their lives to their religious beliefs didn't seem overenthusiastic when it came to a singsong.

As this was only a memorial service, an old black-and-white photograph of Sister Brennan was on display at the front, supported by what looked like an artist's easel. She was young in the picture; her face seemed gaunt and haunted. Hollie wished she could step into that image to find out more about her.

The priest was speaking again, and he concluded the service by inviting the attendees into an anteroom where there were sandwiches and refreshments.

'I didn't expect food,' Hollie said, her voice now lost in the hubbub of movement and chatter. 'Look at those reporters. They'd happily crush those nuns in the rush to get their hands on the best sandwiches.'

As Hollie stood up, she noticed that flowers had been placed around the base of Sister Brennan's photograph.

'I'm going to take a snoop at those floral displays before I get a sandwich. Make sure you have a word with the priest and Mother Davies, will you? The tattoo and marks on her arms are troubling me. It suggests a past life that nobody is able to give us any information about. And the newspaper article that DS Patel found, it fits our timeline neatly, so there may well be something in it. I'm just concerned that a bit of information is going to come at us left of field here. There may be something in her past we're overlooking. I can't shake that feeling. We should dig into those two guys who died in that house fire, too. There'll be a coroner's report somewhere on file, I'd like to see what it says.'

'I'll chase it, boss. What sandwiches do you want me to keep back for you? Egg and cress, or cheese?'

'Oh, please let there be a decent selection. I'll take my chances, thanks. I'd forgotten how basic church sandwiches can be.'

They went their separate ways, and Hollie joined Mother Davies in looking at the flowers. She was struggling to kneel, and Hollie offered her a hand.

'Old age is a terrible tyrant,' she said to Hollie, and she accepted the offer of help. 'At least I have my sharp mind still, even if my body is falling apart. It was sad to see what it took away from Sister Brennan. What was worse is she knew she was losing her mind. She seemed like a woman in a rush to make things right before she became consumed by her dementia.'

'What do we know of her past?' Hollie asked.

'She's always been a bit of an unopened book, that one, but it's not for me to judge. Sister Brennan dedicated her life to God and the Church, and I've never had any cause for complaint or redress.'

It was well over forty years since Sister Brennan had worked at the home and encountered Gilly and the others. All sorts might have changed for her in that time. Hollie thought of how much she'd changed since her twenties; it was a lifetime for Sister Brennan.

'I'd best go and get some sandwiches before those journal-

ists gobble them all up. You'd think that nobody feeds them at
home.'

Hollie smiled and watched as the old lady made her way to
the adjacent room. Hollie knelt to examine the flowers. There
were four arrangements there: two of them simple bunches of
flowers and two arrangements. One bunch had been sent on
behalf of Father Duffy. The message was printed out, like it had
come from a florist.

*To a good friend. What a life we've had. You're in God's care
now, Frank.*

She was going to pass by the final arrangement, as her knees
were getting sore on the church's cold stone floor, but something
caught her eye. The card that was attached to the flowers was
handwritten, in ink. Under normal circumstances, that would
have been unusual, but this was an elderly person's funeral, and
the use of a fountain pen was not that out of place. It was the
style of writing that stopped her in her tracks. She'd seen it
before – and recently.

She put her hand in her coat pocket and found the folded
papers she'd shown Father Duffy earlier. She unfolded them
and held the scanned document printout next to the tag on the
flowers. The writing on the adoption paperwork was the same
as that on the tag. And the tag gave her exactly the information
she needed.

Such a needless death. Patrick McCready.

THIRTY

1973: SOPHIA BRENNAN'S STORY

Sophia ran her hands under the mattress and searched for the shard of glass she'd procured from the kitchen bin. The sisters would miss a kitchen knife, so she'd secreted the small fragment in her handkerchief. She rolled up her sleeve and pushed it into her lower arm, the flow of blood giving her an immediate sense of release. She forced it deep, hating herself, praying that the darkness might lift one day so she could be set free from her mental prison. Without the drugs, this was the only option available to her. She wanted to live, and she desperately yearned to keep going, but the dogged wretchedness of her depression and self-loathing dragged her down every day, and she could not find the energy to pull herself up.

She scraped the roughest edge down her lower arm to just above her wrist. The feeling of her skin being torn made her wince, but it was the only way she knew how to let the bile out. Every day, she was haunted by the faces of those men. Cillian and Billy would torment her in her dreams, and although she knew they were dead, their evil spirits lived on in her mind, never releasing her from their grip. She lived in fear of the police arriving at the doors of the mother and baby home, looking for their killer. Would that couple who were walking their dogs lead them to her? That old woman had seen her tattoo; at least it was covered under her habit now.

Sophia despised her weakness; she had everything to live for and so much to be thankful for. Her new life among the sisters at the Church of St Mary and the Angels was a blessing and it had given her everything she needed. Her newly found devotion to God was exceeded only by her loyalty to Father Duffy. The morning he'd found her shaking on that church pew, desperate for a fix, wondering if she should end her life, had to have been divine intervention. She could find no other explanation for it.

He'd made sure she had all the help she needed to kick her drug habit. It had been hard – a living hell – but she'd done it, in memory of her father, who'd unwillingly given his life at sea. How could she end her life early when he'd had his snatched away from him like that?

Sophia wiped the glass clean on some tissue and placed it back under the mattress. She dabbed her skin and pressed on the wound to stop the bleeding. She never cut where they'd see it. At least as a novice, she'd gained her privacy. When she'd been in the squat, she'd lost ownership of her body. Now, she could be alone, her secrets safe with her until she went to the grave.

She made sure the bleeding had stopped, then in the porcelain sink in the corner of her small room, she bathed her arm. It was raw and red. The anger and resentment would not release itself from her body.

Sophia pulled down her sleeves, checked her hair, and made sure there were no giveaway signs. She picked up her Bible from her bedside table and left her room, making her way into the dining room where the sisters were gathering for breakfast and morning prayer. They ate separately from the girls, and she thought that was a good thing, though she kept that to herself. How could they flaunt their bodies like that, getting pregnant out of wedlock, choosing to place themselves at the mercy of men when they had control over their lives and destiny? She resented their choices when she'd had none. She'd been forced to do what she did. They'd given themselves willingly, and she hated them for it.

Sophia navigated breakfast and morning prayers with only superficial conversation, then went off for study and reflection. She had her final appointment with the psychologist that day, and she hoped she'd get the all-clear on her mental health state so she could progress to taking her vows.

'It's been a long journey for you, Sophia. You've come a long way.'

Sophia only tolerated this woman, but she understood that engaging in the recovery process was essential if she was going to put her past life behind her. All it had taught her was how to lie about what she was thinking, to fool the psychologist into believing that everything was all right.

'You were terribly angry when I first met you, Sophia. It's been wonderful to see how calm you've become here. Do you mind if we speak as friends today, rather than as professionals and clients?'

'Of course, I'd like that,' Sophia replied. *Just give her what she wants, and she'll go away.*

'Father Duffy tells me you're making excellent progress and you've committed to progressing to your full vows. Congratulations, you've really turned your life around.'

'I owe Father Duffy my life. I feel like I've been given a second chance.'

'Do you ever feel like you might want to marry and start a family?'

This again. Sophia had only touched on the terrible things that had happened in her past. But she would never go near a man again, that was for sure. And as for having a family, that choice had been taken from her.

'I think that when God decided I couldn't have any more children, he was guiding me. That was his will. For me, it was like a rebirth.'

She knew where this was heading. This woman couldn't let it go.

'I know we've discussed this before, Sophia, but I only worry that one day you might want to be reunited with your son. I know you've had so much to deal with, what with your drugs habit, your hysterectomy, and your child, but one day I think your anger and defensiveness will subside and you'll want to meet him.'

Sophia knew she had to bat this away one last time. If she was going to get a clean bill of health, this woman had to be clear that she was no longer a danger to herself. Sophia would struggle alone with the rest; it was her burden to carry.

'You know my child was born as the result of rape. I hated him and wanted him out of my body. He was an abomination to me. I could never have loved him. I didn't want a child back then and I still don't want one now. God led me here so that my child could go to loving parents who would look after him. I wish him no harm, but he's brought joy to a married couple somewhere and I consider that something good came of something horrible. I'm happy like that, I really am.'

The psychologist looked Sophia up and down. It didn't seem like she believed her, but Sophia knew she'd given her no grounds to take further action. Her arm felt raw still and the pain distracted her from confronting any real truths. If she went down that path, she'd destroy herself with drugs.

'Well, Sophia, I'm pleased to say that I'll be giving the Church a clean bill of health for you. I wish all my patients were as successful at turning their lives around after such misfortune.'

She didn't know the half of it. None of them knew about her life. She told them she'd been raped after her mother had died in a house fire. She omitted to mention the months spent working for Cillian in the squat. If they'd known the truth and the darkness she carried with her, they would have locked her up in De la Pole Hospital and thrown away the key.

She shook the psychologist's hand, thanked her for her help, and rushed to the office to find Father Duffy. He was not there, but the nun on duty directed her to the church, where she thought he was busy with some church administration.

Sophia walked across the narrow gravel path which linked the church with the home and entered via the side door. She heard voices from along the corridor and she hesitated. They seemed conspiratorial and hushed, not the normal tone she'd expect to be used in church. The door at the far end of the corridor clicked open and she panicked, not at all sure that she should be there, anxious about angering Father Duffy and finding herself out of favour.

She ducked into the side, taking refuge in a small cupboard, but leaving the door ajar so she could see what was going on. She heard light footsteps, a woman. A swish of crinoline, too: the sure sound of a nun. The woman was furtive, checking her clothing and making sure she was alone before exiting via the side door. It was Sister Ursula Kay.

Sophia was silent for several minutes, processing what she'd just seen. She didn't like Sister Kay; she was weak with the girls and Father Duffy gave her too much status. She'd been spiteful with her baby, trying to push the wretched thing on her. For a moment, she saw an opportunity, but she stopped it dead in its tracks. She owed Father Duffy her life and she would protect him from this secret for as long as she could draw breath.

THIRTY-ONE

Hollie was on her phone straight away. It was time to haul McCready over the coals; the man had to be in it up to his neck.

'DS Patel, we need to ramp it up on McCready. I'd like to issue an appeal through the media, with a photo if we can get one. Oh, and speak to DCI Osmond about securing permission to get his bank information. I know that's likely to come in too late for today, but I want to see the whites of that man's eyes ASAP.'

'Will do, boss. We've drawn a complete blank on him so far. Uniform had a suspected sighting in town, but they lost him in the crowds at St Stephen's Shopping Centre—'

'Did you get a look at the CCTV?'

'Not yet, but I can see if we can get it pulled if you want?'

'Yes, please. I want to know if it was him, and if he was with anyone. Let's see if they can tell us where he's gone to ground. Even the coppers stationed outside his house haven't spotted him. I'm sure he's hiding from us; it's like he's got a second home or a hideout—'

'We made some small progress on that newspaper article, boss. The house that burned down was on Beverley Road. It was an unsolved crime at the time. There were two bodies found in the aftermath, both of which were identified via dental records. They had been violently assaulted; one had had something rammed through his eye. It was thought to be a turf war or act of revenge at the time, as the victims were well-known local bad guys, thought to be involved in drugs and a local prostitution ring. It was never cleared up and there's no mention of Sister Brennan, I'm afraid. The dog walkers are long since dead. Sorry.'

'That's great digging, DS Patel, thank you. I'd love to know if the woman who was spotted walking away from there was Sophia. It would be useful if we could match the dates when she arrived at the home with that house fire. It would help fill in a bit of background at least.'

'I'll keep chasing it, boss, I've got the bit between my teeth now.'

Hollie was aware of a movement behind her. It was Sister Ursula Kay, a plate of sandwiches in her hands, sitting on one of the pews nearby.

'Look, I've got to go. Keep me in the loop. Let's flush this bugger out!'

Hollie ended the call and walked over to Sister Kay.

Sister Kay finished chewing her last bite from what looked to be a lacklustre egg sandwich.

'I wanted to speak to you. While I'm out of earshot of the other sisters.'

'Oh?' Hollie replied. This was a conversation she wasn't expecting.

'I should have mentioned it to you earlier. I've been wrestling with my conscience, if truth be told. You must know that Father Duffy, Sister Brennan and I go back many years?'

DS Anderson walked up, holding a paper plate full of sandwiches with a pile of crisps heaped on the side.

'Sorry to disturb you, boss. I thought you might be hungry.'

He'd avoided the egg. Thank goodness for that. Maybe it was the prospect of having to share a car with her on the way back to HQ that had made him cautious; he was right to be so nervous.

'Thanks, DS Anderson. That was very considerate of you.'

He looked like he was going to hover, or even attempt to join the conversation, but Hollie was delighted when he seemed to pick up on her vibes and returned to the room where the refreshments were being served.

'I've served God for three-quarters of my life—' Sister Kay began.

'It's a very admirable choice to make—' Hollie offered.

'—but there are things I've done that I will be judged for.'

It was time for Hollie to shut up and let Sister Kay say what she had to say in her own time.

'I want to confess something to you that I've never told another soul.'

Hollie studied her face. This was a struggle of faith for Sister Kay, and the battle she was fighting did not seem an easy one.

'Can this remain private? Between me and you?'

Much as she wanted to promise the earth to get the information that was on offer, Hollie knew in all good conscience that she could not.

'I can't promise that, Sister Kay. If what you tell me has legal implications, or becomes essential evidence in the case, I can't keep it to myself. When you confess to me, I'm afraid it comes with small print and clauses. I'm sorry. It's not like making a confession in church.'

'It's all right, I know that. It's just that I'm nervous.'

'If you have something to tell me that pertains to Sister Brennan's murder, now would be an excellent time to share it.'

'I'm not sure if this will help you to solve your case, but it might make you understand things better. I heard you speaking to Mother Davies earlier. I know I can't hide this any longer, so I'll tell you on my own terms and in my own way.'

'Go on,' Hollie encouraged. 'Take your time.'

'Father Duffy and I had a personal relationship that spanned almost a decade.'

Hollie felt her mouth opening, and she had to make a conscious effort to draw it closed again. So was this the nun who'd Gilly spotted all those years before?

'I'm sorry to be blunt about it, but do you mean a relationship of a sexual nature?' she whispered.

Sister Kay nodded gently.

'We should have left the Church years ago when we were young and could have had a life, but Frank wouldn't do it. He couldn't face the shame of it. A life of Catholicism creates deep, deep roots, detective. They do not pull out of the ground easily.'

'I don't wish to state the obvious, but doesn't that mean you broke all sorts of rules from the Church's point of view? I mean, not using contraception is an important rule in your faith, isn't it?'

Sister Kay gave another gentle nod.

'Father Duffy is a complex man, detective. I met him as a young woman and was immediately in awe of him. I'd taken my vows and never even considered another way of life. But, with Frank, the devil tempted me, and I succumbed.'

Hollie had nothing to say. In all her years of policing, she thought she'd seen and heard everything. This was unfamiliar territory for her.

'Frank was always conflicted about what we were doing. But if the Church is all you've ever known, it provides everything for you, your food, your shelter, your purpose in life. We always knew what the right thing was to do, and I urged him to do it when we were younger, but the conflict for him was insurmountable. We ended our relationship, eventually, but that was not my wish. It was Frank's. We have retained our working relationship and I have never stopped loving him, but he couldn't find the courage for us to have a normal life.'

Hollie sat in silence with Sister Kay, thinking over this added information.

'Did anybody know?' she asked at last.

'That's why I'm telling you this. If you can protect Father Duffy, please do so. But Sister Brennan knew of our relationship and Gilly, the girl who's now a councillor, once walked in on us many years ago. I don't think she saw me, but she knew something was going on. Now, there was no love lost between Sister Brennan and me—'

'Tell me about your relationship. You suggested there were issues when I was helping you with the washing up the other day.'

'Sister Brennan was a damaged, spiteful woman. She came to us in a terrible state. She was on drugs, pregnant—'

'Pregnant? Sister Brennan?'

This was perhaps the past life that the tattoo and the scars on her arms had suggested.

'When most people see old folk, they only think of them as frail and harmless. But they were young once upon a time, and they may have been vastly different people then. Sister Brennan was like that. She was a bully to many of the girls in the mother and baby home. We never knew what had happened to her before she arrived at the church, but Frank – Father Duffy – thought she'd been involved in prostitution and that it was forced upon her.'

'Oh, the poor woman,' Hollie said, and she meant it. Whatever Sister Brennan's faults, she didn't wish that fate on anybody.

'She could not shake her demons,' Sister Kay continued. 'She resented the girls for their pregnancies, because I think she hated them for having choices over their bodies, and then – as she saw it – squandering them. Where she'd had no choice in her life, the girls had every choice and still ended up having illegitimate children. When she became involved with the Church, I think she struggled to align her old life with a new moral code. You'd say she was screwed up, nowadays.'

'What happened to her baby?' Hollie said.

'The baby was adopted out. She was in no state to care for it and it was dependent on drugs when it was born.'

'Was she in touch with her child?'

'No, not that I'm aware of.'

'Why not?'

'She didn't want to know. The child was the product of rape—'

'While she was being forced to work as a prostitute?'

'I assume so. The father was unknown. When she finally came off the drugs and could see sense, she was pleased the choice had been made for her. She never wanted to see that child again. It was a hateful thing to her.'

'And did she continue to think that way, even in her older years?'

'That's why I wanted to speak to you. She changed her mind as she got older, and when dementia began to set in. She became determined to set things right.'

'In what way?'

'She wanted to find her child and make amends. But that meant exposing what Frank – Father Duffy – had been involved with. And he couldn't let that happen.'

THIRTY-TWO

Hollie knew she was in the wrong, but this was the first time she'd thought of Sister Brennan as a woman rather than as a nun. She'd wondered about her other life when she'd spotted the tattoo and long-healed scars along the nun's arm, but she'd been too tunnel-visioned, thinking only of her bullying nature and religious status. The clues that would help to solve this case most likely came from her life before the Church. Sister Kay was correct. Thinking that Sister Brennan had only ever been elderly had clouded her judgement. It had distracted the entire team.

'I need to understand what Father Duffy has been up to. He described himself as a weak man when we spoke to him earlier today.'

Hollie was fully immersed now; her cop's instincts were running on overdrive.

'Yes, he's both a weak and a strong man,' Sister Kay continued. 'When Sister Brennan came to us, he showed ferocious strength in supporting and rehabilitating her, and then in encouraging her through to taking her vows. She, in turn, was fiercely loyal to him. She knew all his foibles but would not hear a bad word said against him. The one positive thing I heard her say, repeatedly, was that she owed him her life. But when she began to lose her mind, she became a loose cannon.'

'What was Father Duffy so worried about her revealing? Was it worth killing her for?'

Sister Kay sighed.

'I'm not sure Father Duffy has the strength to kill. You've seen how weak he is. I don't know everything, but I do know that Frank was in terrible financial trouble when I first met him. He'd had gambling problems and had run up huge debts. He never spoke to me about it, but I saw the signs. Betting slips torn up and thrown into bins, hushed visits from menacing characters. You know better than I do how these things work. Then, one day, it was all over. A weight lifted from his shoulders and the debts were paid.'

'He's a priest. He has extremely limited opportunity to boost his income. How did he manage that?'

'I don't know, but that's why I'm speaking to you now. I can't keep it to myself any longer, and with Frank so nearly dying, I don't think he'd want to leave us without a clear conscience.'

Hollie suddenly became aware of movement over at the far side of the church. It appeared the attendees had eaten their fill of sandwiches and were ready to move on. She didn't want Sister Kay to clam up, so she encouraged her to get to her point.

'What was Frank's secret? Why do you think it's so important?'

'Because Frank's money worries disappeared as soon as Patrick McCready was assigned to work with us. And it happened just after Sister Brennan arrived—'

'You think it's connected?'

'I'm certain it is. I was never a party to it, I promise. Patrick

McCready was – is – a nasty man. I think he bullied Frank into doing something he didn't want to do. But it also solved Frank's financial problems, so in many ways, he probably had to do it. And I think it all began with Sister Brennan's child.'

Hollie was pleased she'd set DS Patel on the financial trail; if they could link payments between the two men, that would be a major breakthrough. But as far back as the 1970s? That would be a challenge.

'Do you reckon some of the adoptions might have been off the books?'

'I do, but I can't prove it. There was a steady flow of couples wanting to adopt babies. Some of them would have done anything to get their hands on a child.'

'So, you suspect it all started with Sister Brennan? Is there a reason for that?'

'I think she gave them an easy opportunity. She was an addict. She had no family and no advocates, except for Frank. I think he supped with the devil. Sister Brennan didn't want her baby. She was pleased to be rid of it. She didn't particularly care where it went, either. And I don't think they only did it once. Frank exchanged one set of bullies for another.'

Hollie needed a moment to take all this in, but people were heading their way now and her time with Sister Kay was limited. She lowered her voice.

'How do you think Sister Brennan is involved?'

'If you asked me to guess, I think she knew what was going on but said nothing because of her loyalty to Father Duffy. I also think that as dementia took a firmer hold over her, she wanted to tell the truth, to unburden her soul before she was unable to remember her sins—'

'And you think someone – Father Duffy, Patrick McCready, perhaps even somebody else – you think they wouldn't allow that to happen?'

Sister Kay nodded and looked up to smile at some of the other nuns, who were now approaching.

'I'm going to have to get this on the record, I'm afraid, and we can't protect Father Duffy, even if he's nothing to do with Sister Brennan's death. If I had to advise you, I might recommend you encourage him to make his confession. And, you know, I'm sorry.'

'What for?'

'I'm sorry that you were unable to have the relationship you deserved. I know it's very complicated for both of you, and that the course would never have been easy, but I'm sorry you never got to live your relationship out in the open.'

Sister Kay placed her hand on Hollie's and gave it a squeeze.

'Not all good people answer directly to God.' She smiled.

Sister Kay stood up. Their conversation was over. Hollie observed the confessional box tucked away to the far side of the church and considered that they'd been talking in the wrong place. Sister Kay seemed like a woman unburdened. DS Anderson rejoined her.

'You haven't eaten your sandwiches,' he observed. 'You must be starving.'

'I've got some brilliant background info for you, but we'd best drop the nuns off first before I tell you. Is it rude if I take this plate as a doggy bag? I don't know what the etiquette is at a memorial service.'

Anderson laughed and advised her to take it. They found Mother Davies, who was still chatting over sandwiches.

On the journey back, Sister Kay was silent, but Mother Davies seemed buoyed at having done something so positive to celebrate the life of their friend.

With their passengers safely back in the convent, Hollie and Anderson returned to the car. She put her finger on the ignition key, and then she removed it, deciding against setting off immediately.

'I made some good progress in there,' Hollie began. 'I didn't get to eat my lunch, but I've found some new information I need to share with you. I'm just trying to get it straight in my head.'

'Did Sister Kay have something for you? I sensed you didn't want me hanging around when I brought that food over for you. I'm empathetic like that, you know.'

Hollie smiled. At least this man could send himself up.

'Sister Kay and Father Duffy had a relationship—'

Anderson looked at her with his mouth wide open.

'Of the carnal variety?'

'Yes.'

'Fuck.'

'Exactly.'

'Bloody hell, that's going to require a rosary a mile long. Does anybody else know?'

'Maybe. Gilly thought something odd was going on, so I'll bet that was it. She says Father Duffy was a weak man and he had money worries. It sounds like Sister Brennan may have been protecting him all these years, but that she wanted to confess about it before she lost her memory.'

'I feel guilty,' Anderson said, after giving it some thought. 'All I learnt from the afternoon is that I quite like cheese and onion crisps and that sandwiches made with white bread and butter may be bad for you, but they're much tastier than brown bread or granary.'

'Great detective work,' Hollie replied. 'You're right about butter. Why were we ever fooled by margarine?'

They sat in silence for a while, considering what they'd learnt.

'I think the most logical explanation for all this is that our killer is Sister Brennan's son,' Hollie said at last. 'But why would he murder his own mother? It just doesn't add up. We're into Oedipus and all that crap. Matricide is incredibly rare. I just can't see it.'

'What if he didn't know it was his mother?' Anderson said, deep in thought.

'How could that happen?'

'I don't know. But just assume it's true for a minute. That would explain things, wouldn't it?'

'But that takes us right back to where we started. Who the hell wants to kill a nun?'

'Father Duffy? Patrick McCready?'

'The motive seems unclear, that's for sure. But Father Duffy? I still don't think so. And Patrick McCready? He's a retired social worker, for heaven's sake. That's not the best starting point for becoming a killer.'

Anderson was silent as he thought it over.

'He left flowers in memory of Sister Brennan,' Hollie added. She fumbled for her phone and found the photo she'd taken of McCready's message.

'That's the mark of a sociopath, if he did kill her.'

'What is?'

'Leaving flowers for Sister Brennan with his name on like that. That's sociopathic, isn't it? If he killed her, it is.'

Hollie thought for a moment.

'I guess so. So, you think McCready's a sociopath?'

'I think he's a tosser. I'm still not certain about the sociopath bit.'

'You do agree that's the same handwriting as Theresa's adoption papers?' she checked. 'Or, at least, it's uncannily similar.'

The phone rang in her hands.

'Talk about divine intervention,' she quipped.

'Good afternoon, ma'am, it's DC Hayes.'

'It's Timothy Warburton's FLO,' Hollie whispered.

'I thought you might like to know that we've found something while we were searching the DCC's home office.'

'What is it?' Hollie asked.

'We found some of her parents' old belongings in an unlabelled box file. It contains the adoption paperwork for Rose Warburton's son.'

THIRTY-THREE

1976: SOPHIA BRENNAN'S STORY

Sophia woke with a start. Something had been troubling her for several weeks, and at that moment she finally saw what it was with a clarity and intensity that had been lacking previously. This was her conscience speaking, and she could no longer ignore it. The more she studied and prayed and talked, the greater her understanding became. And she knew what they were doing was wrong.

She'd struggled with many issues since being given sanctuary at the Church of St Mary and the Angels. Her former life gave rise to the blackest spectre, and it was always with her, dragging her down and goading her whenever she dared to enjoy a moment of happiness or hope. But Sophia was conflicted, and she saw it now. What Father Duffy and Patrick McCready were doing with the babies was wrong, but there was no way on earth she was going to play Judas to the priest. She owed him everything. He'd shown her kindness where she'd known none, and he'd helped her to rebuild her life again. She would not betray him. Yet, she saw what they were doing. Whenever a baby was born out of rape or violence, or the girl's parents were simply unable to accept the shame of a daughter's pregnancy and wanted the child taken away as fast as possible, that's where opportunity lay.

Father Duffy was a weak man, driven by his addiction to gambling. Sophia knew the curse of addiction; she'd fought her own battle and understood only too well the strength and determination that was required. She'd also seen how Father Duffy would make an anonymous donation to the Church whenever he received money from private adoptions. He was doing his best to reconcile his conscience, and she still believed he was a good man. But Patrick McCready was the devil. It was he who'd sown the idea in the priest's mind. McCready thought nothing of the Church and used the money only for his own glorification. Sophia knew men like him of old and she wanted him to fall.

That morning, her mind had worried about the dilemma long enough to provide her with a solution. She needed to confess, but she dared not offer the truth to any person in case they betrayed her, and Father Duffy was thrown to the wolves.

The seed was sown the day before. She'd been in the office, alone, with McCready. He'd been preparing paperwork. That's how the two of them worked. Father Duffy gave his witness signature to forms that were not yet completed, leaving McCready to finish them in his absence. That way, he could convince himself he'd done nothing wrong. The private adoptions were unknown to him, a consequence of McCready's deceit. As Sophia had moved around the building and through the office, she'd quietly observed it all. They thought she didn't know, but she'd pieced it all together.

Father Duffy would receive his cut in cash, and McCready would place it in the priest's Bible, which was kept in the office. Father Duffy would disappear that afternoon, no doubt to pay his debts, and the next day he'd announce how another anonymous financial contribution had been made by a wealthy donor. McCready would arrive the next time with a new, expensive watch or a flashy car, perhaps boasting about his boat or a foreign holiday, and she'd despise him even more. Father Duffy was not the same as Patrick McCready. McCready was evil, and Father Duffy was a flawed man who was wrestling his demons.

As Sophia had placed an item of paperwork into the filing cabinet at the back of the office, she had become aware of McCready moving towards her. Before she could turn, he was pressing himself against her, his hand running up and down her clothing.

'I know what you are,' he whispered into her ear, venom dripping from his words. 'You may act like a nun and dress like a nun, but I know what you want, you filthy bitch—'

He pulled away sharply as the door opened and Father Duffy walked in.

'Is everything sorted out now?' the priest asked, oblivious to what had just happened.

Sophia darted out of the office, heading directly to the nearest cloakroom, where she threw up in disgust, both at herself and at the attack. She could hear McCready's voice along the corridor, chatting away like nothing had happened.

She'd be ready for him next time. She would protect Father Duffy, but she would not allow a man like that to take advantage of her ever again.

Now, Sophia got out of bed and headed directly for her small desk. She pulled out her writing pad and fountain pen and began to write it all down: everything she'd seen and everything McCready had done. But she needed more. She had to get the names. There had to be a record of what that man had done. And one day if, God forbid, Father Duffy was to come to any harm, she would reveal everything then.

After prayers and breakfast, Sophia knew what had to be done. McCready was back that day to complete the adoption. She'd do it then.

It was her turn to clean that morning, so the opportunity was perfect. She hovered in the hallway, running her duster along the stair rails, waiting for her moment. McCready was in there, doing whatever it was he did when he was alone. Father Duffy had made himself scarce, turning his blind eye, busying himself elsewhere.

McCready stepped out of the office and walked towards the front door. He was going for a cigarette. The moment the door closed behind him, Sophia darted into the office. His paperwork was spread out on the desk, turned upside down, should anybody enter. She drew out the notepad and pencil she'd brought with her and turned the papers over, taking great care to replace them exactly as she'd found them. Then she found it: the record of everything they'd done. There were seven in all. Seven babies passed on through illegal, private adoptions. Sophia jotted down the names as fast as she was able to, then checked everything was as McCready had left it. She slipped out of the room just as his hand struck the handle of the front door. She had to dart into the donation cupboard to steady herself, she'd been so tense and nervous.

The next evening, having written up everything she'd gleaned, Sophia slipped off along the gravel path at the side of the mother and baby unit to make a private visit to the adjacent church. Secreting a small, metal biscuit tin under her coat, in which were placed her notes, she sought a safe place where she could conceal the truth. If ever the time was right to reveal everything, if ever she could give that horrible man what he deserved, it was all there, just waiting for her to hand over to the police. She found a small recess in the church's walls, behind one of the stations of the cross. She hid it there, safe from discovery, just in case it was ever needed. She would never betray Father Duffy while he was alive: he'd saved her life. But if he were to pass away before her, or if ever any harm came to him, she would tear down the walls and make sure McCready was buried in the rubble.

THIRTY-FOUR

'Call into the office and see if we're any further forward, will you?' Hollie said to DS Anderson as she balanced what was left of her sandwiches on the car's front console. 'I want to know where we're up to with locating the records for that adoption agency. Also, was Gilly Hodges able to move things along with locating the county's old adoption archives? And we need to haul Patrick McCready back in for questioning.'

It was quite a list, and the clock was ticking relentlessly towards ten o'clock. Meanwhile, Anderson had eaten the crisps to spare her from having to clean them up off the car floor. She started up the car.

'How far is it to Swanland from here? Twenty minutes?'

'On a good day,' Anderson responded, taking out his phone.

Hollie put the car in gear and drove off, listening to Anderson as he caught up with DS Patel in the office.

'Put her on speaker, will you?' she asked.

Anderson touched his screen and Patel's voice came on, mid-sentence.

'We've had the BBC on,' she began, as Hollie tuned in to what she was saying. 'Our man has been onto them—'

'What, on the radio?' Anderson checked.

'No, he called the newsroom number, and they let us know immediately. He's asked them to have a satellite truck ready to go live for the evening bulletins—'

'Did he give a location?' Hollie shouted across the car.

'No, ma'am, he said he'll give half an hour's notice. He's planning some kind of spectacle. He told them if they leave the engine running outside Queen's Gardens, they'll have time to get there.'

'Damn, did they confirm it's him and not a crank call?'

'He knew about DCC Warburton.'

Hollie cursed herself for not noting the name of the reporter she'd spoken to at the memorial. She'd promised not to run the story unless they could substantiate it.

'Are they running with the story?'

'No, boss, we wouldn't verify it with them, but it confirms to us it wasn't a crank call.'

'Are they intending to send out the satellite truck?'

'Unless we request a news blackout, they're going to be there.'

'Bollocks! Okay, DS Patel, we need as many officers as possible within a half-hour radius of Queen's Gardens. Find out what time their live news updates run. I haven't got a clue. And, at the risk of repeating myself, can we please get our hands on Patrick McCready? I know everybody's doing their best, DS Patel, but we're up against the clock here.'

'I'm on it, ma'am,' Patel reassured her. They ended the call.

'Sorry, I hijacked your call there,' Hollie apologised.

They drove on in silence for a couple of minutes, both mulling over the implications of what might come next.

'This is the stage in the investigation where I'm pleased you're the case lead and I'm just one of the troops,' Anderson said at last. 'I don't envy your stress, particularly with him having the DCC. If this guy lays a finger on Rose Warburton, the shit's really going to hit the fan.'

'Thanks for the reassurance, detective,' Hollie teased him.

Hollie felt her car speed increase in line with the amount of adrenaline that was flowing. By early evening, she'd be driving at over one hundred miles per hour if they hadn't seen a breakthrough by then.

'Fuck!' Anderson said.

'What?' Hollie asked, chewing on a ham sandwich. It was crushed and ugly from its arduous journey, but it still tasted great.

'What if Sister Brennan's son killed her because he was pissed off with her?'

'What would piss you off that you'd kill your own mother though? I mean, I know Noah gets stroppy if I overcook his oven chips, but don't expect to see me dangling from a bridge because of it.'

'If you were placed in an abusive home, you'd blame your mother, wouldn't you?'

'So, you're reunited with your mum after several decades and the first thing you do is kill her? That doesn't sound likely to me. Wouldn't you shout and scream and take it out on her? You wouldn't want her dead.'

Anderson thought on that and the expression on his face told Hollie he probably agreed.

'Who the hell is he, then?' he said at last.

'What about Father Duffy killing Sister Brennan?' Hollie wondered aloud. 'I still think it's unlikely. He may have owed money and been scared, but Father Duffy strikes me as being at the shitty end of the criminal spectrum. He's the sort of guy that does nothing unless he absolutely must. If he's cornered, he'll strike, but only under duress.'

'I agree, but what if he was cornered? What if the snake was forced to bite?'

'We need to speak to Patrick McCready. That bloody man, where the hell is he?'

They'd arrived at Warburton's house.

'Keep those gears whirring,' Hollie said as she secured the handbrake. 'Let's see what DCC Warburton's documents look like.'

DC Fran Hayes was waiting at the door for them.

'He's been going out of his mind,' she told them in a lowered voice. 'He's turned out all the drawers and cupboards and been up in the loft. He's got it into his head that she's been hiding all sorts from him.'

'That's all we need, a spouse on the rampage,' Anderson remarked.

Timothy Warburton was sitting in the conservatory, sorting through a box of documents. Like all good FLOs, DC Hayes had succeeded in winning his trust and confidence and was able to come and go in the house as she pleased.

Timothy stood up when he saw them.

'Ah, detectives, have you made any progress? Is Rose still alive?'

His eyes had a haunted quality about them now, but he was channelling his anxiety into searching through DCC Warburton's things. The conservatory looked like it had been ransacked; there were papers strewn all over the place.

'We've still nothing new to report,' Anderson updated him, 'but I want to assure you that every police officer in the city is working on this. There's a team of detectives who won't leave any stone unturned to make sure the DCC is returned safely to you, you have my word on that. Where are these papers? We need to get a look at them.'

Timothy handed them over in an envelope, then began to cry. Hollie encouraged him to sit, checking that Anderson was examining the adoption papers while she dealt with him. She took a place next to him, offering what reassurance she could.

'I feel like a traitor,' he sobbed. 'On the one hand, I'm scared out of my mind about what might happen to Rose. But I'm also angry with her for not sharing this with me. Not only did she not share it, but she also proactively hid it. I found this box file in the small loft space over her closet, after DC Hayes and her colleague had turned out all the cupboards and drawers in Rose's office. I didn't even think she knew there was a storage space there. I feel angry and betrayed by her, but I also can't stop shaking with fear. This is unbearable. I don't know how you keep your wits about you in your line of work.'

Hollie thought back to Noah's abduction. She'd been lucky; that was just a warning shot. But the simple truth was, she'd been out of her mind in a panic, too, and what Timothy was experiencing was completely normal.

She took a few moments to reassure him as best she could, then leaned over to take the adoption documents from DS Anderson. The paper was faded and creased, the typewriter print blurred by age.

'Look at the adoption agency,' Anderson said.

Hollie scanned the paperwork.

'Brand New Family again,' she observed. 'Can I just confirm with you that both of DCC Warburton's parents are dead?'

'Yes, long before I knew her. That part of her life was a closed book. It's easy to see why now.'

Hollie was keen to steer him away from his wallowing; he appeared of late to be that way inclined. She hoped DCC Warburton was made of sterner stuff. She'd need a strong presence of mind for what lay ahead.

'So, she must have had these papers for some years?'

'I assume so. Who knows with Rose? She seems to be a law unto herself.'

'It's the same handwriting, yes?' Hollie checked with

Anderson. She handed over her phone with the photo of the flower tag on the screen.

'I'd say so,' Anderson confirmed. 'Though we'll have to get a graphologist on the case if we're going to use it in court.'

'Would you excuse us a moment, Mr Warburton?'

Timothy stood up.

'Of course, officers. Can I get you a drink?'

He took their orders and left them to it.

'So that's Theresa Morgan, Rose Warburton and Sister Brennan now. We know of two adoptions around that time that have McCready's handwriting on them. I'll bet that Sister Brennan's was the first, just like Sister Kay suggested. That would have been easy enough to pull off in those days.'

'Yes, boss, but wouldn't Sister Brennan's child have been adopted in the sixties? Theresa's and DCC Warburton's babies were adopted in 1975. Why the gap?'

'Perhaps they got bold? Maybe they spotted an opportunity when the councils changed over? This paperwork is not on Humberside County Council headed paper. In 1975, it should have been. This is how I think they kept the private adoptions off the books.'

'At her interview, Theresa Morgan told me her parents were very caught up in the life of the Church. They were close to Father Duffy. She said they just wanted the baby taken care of. From what she said, it's unlikely they'd have been too fussy about how that was achieved.'

Hollie shook her head. She couldn't see a path through the tangle of deception, lies and falsehoods.

'I'm beginning to suspect this agency – Brand New Family – might never have existed. What if it was just made up to fill that section of the paperwork? The parents and the girls wouldn't have known, they'd have just trusted McCready—'

Hollie's phone rang at the same time as DS Anderson's. They looked at each other.

'It's the office,' Hollie said.

'Mine, too,' Anderson replied.

DCI Osmond spoke on Hollie's phone. She could hear from the pitch of the voice that it was DS Patel on Anderson's line.

'Are you sitting down, Hollie? You're not driving?'

He'd used her first name; that was worrying.

'No, I'm sitting down.'

Osmond's voice sounded strained.

'I'm sorry to have to inform you that our colleague DC Jenni Langdon was just rushed in for emergency surgery. She's got a blood clot. It's touch and go if she's going to make it.'

THIRTY-FIVE

'May I step outside into the garden for a moment?' Hollie asked, after ending the call.

'Of course, the door's unlocked,' Timothy called through from the kitchen.

Hollie's chest felt tight, she couldn't breathe. If she didn't get out of there, she'd lose it in front of all of them.

'Are you all right, boss?' Anderson asked.

'Just give me a moment—' Hollie snapped, more abruptly than she would have wished.

She slid the conservatory door open and took in a long, deep breath of fresh air. There was a tree to the side of the structure, and she walked in front of it so she couldn't be seen. Her mind was a whirlwind of what-ifs; if she loosened her hold on the reins, she'd buckle.

She'd been ignoring the possibility that Jenni might not make it, but now? She had to face that very real prospect. And it was because of her; it was because she'd been sneaking off to meet with Tony instead of involving her colleagues. For a moment she thought her feelings of guilt might crush her, but she couldn't allow that. The DCC was relying on her and her team: she had to keep her head in the game. They were so close now, it was imperative that she keep her shit together. She took a long, deep breath and returned to the conservatory, her face straight.

'Is everything okay in here?' Timothy Warburton said as she slid the door shut. 'I could feel the mood changing from in the kitchen.'

DS Anderson walked him through it. Hollie could hear the voices, but nothing was sinking in. How could Jenni's condition have deteriorated so fast? She'd only recently been at her bedside, and it had all looked fine then.

'Here, have something to drink,' Timothy offered, passing Hollie's cup of tea via DS Anderson. The four of them were silent for several minutes as the three officers took in the enormity of the news and Timothy had the good sense to leave them to it.

'I can't believe what he's done to her,' Hollie said, at last.

'We've got to get this bastard,' Anderson added, then remembered he was with a member of the public, the DCC's husband at that.

'Cuss all you want,' Timothy said. 'That same bastard has my wife. The angrier you feel, the more likely I am to get my wife back in one piece. I'm so sorry to hear about your colleague. Rose will be distraught to have an officer so badly injured in the line of duty.'

'She's barely out of university,' Hollie added, not entirely sure where she was going with the statement. Her head was swirling with random thoughts. Jenni was so young. They'd had so much fun together when they hit the town. She'd been great to work with. She showed so much promise as a detective. And now – now she was in mortal danger. And it was because she'd been looking out for Hollie that she'd placed herself directly in the path of such peril.

DC Hayes encouraged her to drink her tea, and as she did

so, the heat of the liquid, the taste, and the sensation of swallowing brought her out of her mind and back into the room. It was as if she'd collapsed in on herself for a short time, and DC Hayes had pulled her out of the hole. No wonder she was a family liaison officer; she had exactly the right temperament.

'How are you feeling?' Anderson asked.

'Numb. Absolutely numb,' Hollie replied. 'I can't believe it. I assumed they'd patch her up and she'd be on her way. I knew it was bad, but you just think they can fix everything these days. That poor girl. And her parents, too. They'll be distraught.'

'I think DCI Osmond is concerned about you staying on the case,' Anderson said. 'He thinks it might impair your capacity to focus on the matter in hand.'

'Did he say that to you?' Hollie asked, alert once more.

'Don't worry, I put him right on your behalf. But just so you know. He probably thinks the shock will be too much for you to work with a clear mind. It's just a heads up in case he suggests it to you.'

'Screw Osmond!' she snapped. 'I'm so sorry, Mr Warburton. That was unprofessional of me.'

Timothy smiled.

'I'll let you know a secret, but I'll deny I told you if I'm ever asked. I've heard Rose say those very words about that man on more than one occasion.'

It was the right thing to say at the right time and it gave them all a moment of relief that they desperately needed. They all had a laugh at Osmond's expense, and it blew away some of the tension. Hollie took a long, deep breath.

'I thought I was having a heart attack,' she explained.

'It's anxiety,' DC Hayes said. 'You'd be surprised how common it is when people hear shocking news.'

She took Hollie's hand and gave it a squeeze.

'Will you step aside if Osmond asks you to?' Anderson asked.

'Only if he orders me to do it,' Hollie added. 'If he tries to take me off this case, I'm going to be furious. How dare he deny me the chance to catch Jenni's assailant? He might now be her killer—'

It was so difficult to say the words.

'I agree,' Anderson continued. 'It would be crazy to remove you at this late stage. If it's any help, I told him as much.'

'Thank you, DS Anderson, I appreciate that.'

Despite the tensions between her and Anderson, she felt they respected each other now, and that was, at least, a good start.

'May I have a few moments with Hollie?' Anderson asked. He'd used her first name. She didn't pick him up on it. Sometimes, in police work, moments of humanity were required. Rank could be superfluous then.

Timothy and DC Hayes took their cue and removed themselves to the adjoining kitchen.

'What is it?' Hollie asked.

'I just wanted you to know that I know how you feel.'

Hollie looked at him, wondering where he was going with this.

'I was first on the scene when DI MacKenzie's body was found. You're feeling raging anger and overwhelming guilt right now, I'm guessing?'

'You can read my mind.'

'I know, it's a horrible thing. You blame yourself for not being able to save them, you want to beat the shit out of the person who hurt them, and you feel a crushing shame that you failed in your duty as a police officer.'

'That's just about it,' Hollie said quietly.

'I told you a lie before.'

Hollie looked up at him.

'About my son and my wife. I screwed things up with them because I couldn't carry my anger. My wife asked me to leave. It was like I couldn't be around regular people because they didn't understand what I'd been through. It was just copper's bravado, what I said about my son. I don't care about his bloody pronouns. I'd really just like to be back in their lives.'

She'd not seen Anderson so earnest since she'd met him.

'This fucking job' – she half laughed, half cried – 'it really screws you up sometimes. Osmond did a number on me earlier. He insisted I have a debrief after Jenni's accident. The bastard made me cry.'

'I promise I won't tell.' Anderson smiled at her. 'Though that prick frequently makes me cry, only for a different reason.'

Hollie laughed again; it felt good and helped to push away the tears.

'We never found MacKenzie's killer,' Anderson picked up, deadly serious again. 'There's not a day goes by when I don't think about it or open up the case records on my PC and see if I've missed anything. It gnaws at me. The boss – the old one – was far from perfect, but we'd worked together for a long time, and he knew the job. I never got the chance to put his killer – or killers – behind bars, but we can get justice for Jenni. If we work fast and keep our wits about us, we can have this bastard locked up in a police cell by the end of the day. And I think you and I can do it between us, what with my good looks and your policing skills.'

Hollie smiled, then took a deep breath and looked directly at her colleague.

'Okay, my head's back where it needs to be now. Let's get going, we've got a killer to catch.'

THIRTY-SIX

2022: SOPHIA BRENNAN'S STORY

The horn sounded impatiently, and Sophia jumped at the screech of the tyres.

'I don't care if you're a bloody nun. You could be the Pope himself, I'd still tell you to watch where you're fucking going!'

Sophia looked around her. The black Range Rover was less than a metre away from her. It was more of an assault vehicle than a family car. Had it hit her, she'd have been like a splattered bug on a windscreen.

To her left side was a small Fiat, driven by a woman who'd also had to brake hard to miss her. She was climbing out of the driver's seat, a look of concern on her face.

'Is everything all right, Sister?' she asked patiently. 'You seem a little confused.'

This wasn't the first time it had happened. Sophia knew what was going on. She'd been trying to ignore it and pretend everything was fine. But she was forgetting things and losing track of time.

The woman helped her across the road and sat her on a nearby bench. Angry drivers were sounding their horns because the woman's car was in the middle of the road, the hazards flashing as if they'd created some magical traffic force field.

'Just stay there. I'll pull my car over then I'll be back with you.'

Sophia watched as the woman started up her car and moved it to the side of the road, out of the way. She rushed back over to Sophia as soon as she was done.

'Now then, sorry about that. Are you okay? That must have given you quite a fright.'

Sophia wasn't quite sure where she was. She looked around, seeking landmarks to help her identify her location. She clutched a piece of paper in her hand, which she unfurled and examined.

Post Office. Buy stamp and envelope. Convent of the Sacred Heart of Mary. Holderness Road.

'Is that where you live? The Convent of the Sacred Heart of Mary?' the woman asked.

Sophia wasn't entirely certain at that moment, but she figured it must be. Why else would she have written it down?

'Well, there's a paper bag in your coat pocket, so it looks like you've been to the post office already,' the woman said kindly. Her calm voice helped Sophia to gather her wits. It was all so confusing.

'Do you mind if I check?'

Sophia gave the woman the go-ahead, and she removed the white paper bag from her coat pocket.

'Yes, it's an envelope and stamp,' she confirmed. 'At least you've done what you set out to do. Are you struggling with your memory, Sister? It's just that my mum has dementia and I recognised that look on your face when you were standing in the road. Do you have anyone to help you?'

That brought it all back. Yes, she did have dementia. She

recalled the doctor giving her the news. She hadn't yet told Mother Davies, though she was sure she suspected. There was something she had to do before she raised the matter. Sophia couldn't recall what was so important at that moment, but she knew it was the reason for her buying the stamp and the envelope.

'Now, is there anybody I can call to come and collect you? Or do you want me to drive you back to the convent?'

'If it's not too much trouble, I think I might like you to drive me.'

'Of course, Sister.'

The woman held out her arm and she escorted Sophia to her car. She hadn't wandered far; they were back on Holderness Road in no time and the woman stayed with Sophia while she rang the doorbell and waited.

'We'd better let the other sisters know what's been going on,' she said.

Sister Kay answered the door. She looked at the woman and then at Sophia.

'Oh, is everything all right?' she asked.

'Your friend just got herself in a little bit of trouble,' the woman said, making a face at Sister Kay. She took the hint.

'Go and sit in the lounge, Sister Brennan. I'll bring you a nice warm drink as soon as I've had a chat with this lady.'

Sophia shuffled along the hallway to the lounge, the voices of the two women fading behind her. Her secret was out now. Sister Kay would, no doubt, have been fully briefed by the woman about what had happened.

Sophia waited for the voices to stop. She heard the heavy front door close, then the sound of Sister Kay making her way to the kitchen. Sophia closed her eyes and attempted to shepherd her mind back to sharpness. It was much like an amateur sheepdog herding an unruly flock. After a couple of minutes, the door opened, and Sister Kay entered, holding a mug by the handle.

'I made you some hot milk. I thought that might be best.'

Sophia hated hot milk but took it anyway.

'I'm pleased it was you who answered the door,' Sophia said.

'Why?' Sister Kay replied.

'Because this concerns you.'

She watched as Sister Kay took a seat.

'I've got dementia,' Sophia began.

'I think we've all noticed,' Sister Kay replied. 'This isn't the first time you've got confused.'

Sophia tried to remember. Did they know already? Had she told them? It was impossible to recall.

'I've written a letter,' Sophia continued. 'About what happened. I can't lose my memory and let it die with me. Someone has to know.'

Sister Kay's tone changed.

'Nobody has to know,' she said, her words sharp and taut.

'I won't tell anybody about you and... you and—'

'Father Duffy,' Sister Kay reminded her. 'That's been over for years. You know he couldn't go through with it.'

'But that girl Gilly knew, the cocky one. She knew, and I warned her off. She never spoke up, but she knows. One day, she might tell.'

'It's been years. I'll bet she doesn't even remember now. What's in your letter?' Sister Kay asked.

'About the babies. And about my baby. He's out there somewhere. I hated him when he was born. I despised him growing inside me. If I'd had the courage to, I would have torn him out of my stomach. But I think about him now. Does he wonder who his mother was? I did such terrible things. And I was so horrible to those girls.'

'It's water under the bridge, Sophia. It all happened years

ago. If your son wanted to reach out to you, he'd have found you by now. He must have a happy life, or you'd have heard from him. It's best to let it lie now.'

'But what about the girls and the babies? That wasn't right. I know Father Duffy was having money difficulties, but he should never have agreed to do those things with that monster. Patrick McCready, that man is evil itself. If Father Duffy hadn't helped me like that – if you hadn't helped save my life that day – I'd have told them everything. But I can't go to my grave with that on my conscience. I'm forgetting things. I must tell somebody before I forget. I've written it all down. I've bought a stamp and envelope to send it off. I'm posting it to the local paper and then everybody will know the truth.'

Sister Kay stood up and walked over to Sophia. She bent down so that she was directly in front of her.

'You really shouldn't do that, Sophia. Some secrets should follow us to the grave. What's done is done. God will know you meant no harm.'

'But I did do harm, didn't I? I turned a blind eye. I need to make this right now.'

'But what about Father Duffy?'

'Father Duffy died last month—'

'Sophia, no he didn't. He's alive and well. You're getting confused again.'

Sophia thought it over. She was certain Father Duffy was dead. That's why it was time to tell the truth. She owed Patrick McCready nothing at all.

'Look, Sophia, please don't do anything just yet. Is that the stamp and envelope in your pocket? Let me take it for safekeeping so you don't lose it. I'll arrange it so you can pay Father Duffy a visit, then you'll see for yourself, he's very much alive.'

Reluctantly, Sophia let Sister Kay take the paper bag with the envelope in it.

'Are you sure Father Duffy is still alive?'

'I'll prove it to you, Sophia. I'll make plans for you to go there for tea. I'll accompany you to the bus myself to make sure you don't get lost. And if you still want to send that letter when you get back, you can have this stamp and envelope and I'll walk you to the post box so we can make sure it gets sent off.'

THIRTY-SEVEN

'Do you mind if I call in via my house on the way back to the office? I forgot my bank card in the rush to get the kids off to the station on time. I think I'm going to need it to buy food, it's going to be a long day.'

'Of course,' Anderson answered. 'Take the turn-off up ahead and it'll be faster.'

He was looking over the paperwork Timothy Warburton had supplied and seemed engrossed. Hollie was happy to stay in her own head. It was a relief to do something routine and mundane like driving, and she was still relieved that Osmond hadn't called her bluff over the job.

When she'd made the threat, she'd half meant it. If Osmond sent her packing, she'd return to Lancaster, apply to re-enter the Lancashire Constabulary, and even try to sort things out around the kids. The devil in her knew that it would be harder for Léon to take them to France if she could trump him by being able to keep them in their regular school.

Hollie was almost disappointed when Osmond caved immediately, though she did get a ticking off.

'I don't appreciate your tone or manner, DI Turner,' he'd

said sternly. 'Don't think this won't be discussed at some length when the DCC returns to her desk.'

She wasn't sure whether to take it as a threat or a compliment; after all, Osmond was assuming the DCC would soon be back at work.

'Jesus, look at the state of him!'

Anderson's voice pulled her away from her thoughts and she looked around to see what he was referring to. An overweight man was walking along the path. His behind was hanging out of his jogging bottoms, which were twinned with a baggy, well-worn T-shirt flapping in the breeze, emblazoned with the phrase: *Choose Life.*

'I'd rather he chose stronger elastic for his trousers,' Anderson remarked, and Hollie burst out laughing at the ridiculousness of it.

'See, all you need is a few bad dad jokes and you'll soon be back to full fighting form.'

Hollie was grateful for the chatter. She was on the brink of complete collapse and knew Osmond was right to try to take her off duty. She wasn't entirely certain she'd be able to make it through the day without a breakdown, but if she was going to end up a wreck, she might as well finish strong and do what she could to get the case wrapped up and DCC Warburton back to safety. She was beginning to feel anxious about the lack of a phone call from the DCC's kidnapper. He'd got in touch with the BBC, but if this variety of psycho was going to stay true to form, she knew there would be a threat or ultimatum on its way soon. When he did call, she still had sweet fuck all to offer him. But then, there was the possibility that the agency mentioned on the paperwork never existed. That would explain why he'd hit a dead end trying to find out what had happened in his past.

'This is my place,' she said as she pulled up directly outside the flats.

Anderson scanned the building. He looked like he was

about to say something, stopped himself, and then said it anyway.

'I see you've spared no expense in your relocation to Humberside Police. This area of the city is quite a hot spot for crime. Talk about taking the job home with you.'

'Needs must, I'm afraid.' Hollie grimaced.

'Is that thunder?'

She listened.

'No, it's the arsehole drummer who lives in the flat above me. I've asked him to keep the noise down. Look, I won't be long. Stay in the car, would you? I don't want you to see my flat. I'm embarrassed now.'

'Hey, no judgement from me,' Anderson replied, holding up his hands in a gesture of peace. 'I'm living in the saddest bedsit in Beverley while I pay for my wife and son to live a life of luxury. I'm the archetypal miserable, middle-aged bloke. All I need is a girlie calendar on the kitchen wall and a home bar in the corner of the living area and my tragic life will be complete.'

Hollie got out of the car and walked over to the flat. The drummer sounded like he was attempting to play three songs at one time; it was like an assault of sound violating her ears. As she stepped inside the shared hallway, an older couple were approaching the door.

'That's a bit much, isn't it?' Hollie said. 'Hi, I'm Hollie from Flat 2,' she continued.

'We're getting out of the building until he stops. It's too much for us at our age. We just want to watch *Countdown*, but we can't hear ourselves think in there.'

Hollie held the door open for them and felt a sudden rage come over her. All it took was one fuckwit to mess up an entire building. He had all the residents on tenterhooks, living in perpetual fear that he might start his brain-numbing sounds at any moment, day or night. As the front door clicked shut and she felt for her flat key in her pocket, she thought of Jenni again. Something snapped inside Hollie.

Fuck it! she thought as she stormed up the stairs. *This is the perfect time to tackle neighbourly relations.*

She knocked at the door, giving it her best police officer technique. The drumming continued. He was going crazy for the cymbals now; she'd need the paracetamol at this rate. She knocked again.

'Hey, answer the door!' she called.

The drumming continued. That was enough. She twisted the handle, but it was locked, probably using the same flimsy mechanism as her own flat. Her rage took a firm hold, and she pushed her shoulder against the door. It resisted her force, so she gave it a second shove, much harder this time. She heard the split of wood as the door frame gave way and she burst into the room.

He didn't see her for a moment. He was completely absorbed in what he was doing, oblivious to the outside world and everything around him. Then she spotted something which fuelled her anger even more: he was wearing earplugs.

The drummer looked up and was shocked to see her.

'Hey, you can't just come bursting in here—'

'And you get to wear earplugs!' Hollie exclaimed.

'Sorry, I can't hear you,' he said, picking the plugs out of his ears.

'Who the hell are you? I didn't hear anything just then—'

'I'm your downstairs neighbour who asked you very politely to keep the noise down—'

'Hey, it's my flat—'

'—and while you shatter the peace and quiet for everybody, you wear earplugs to deafen out the sound.'

'Well, it's a health and safety issue, isn't it? I don't want to lose my hearing—'

'What about health and safety for the rest of us? Are you

aware of how this annoying hobby of yours impacts the lives of everybody else? Is there not a rehearsal room you can use where you won't disturb anyone? Don't you have a job to get up for? You're playing these damn things at all hours!'

'No, I'm currently receiving disability benefits. I get anxious—'

'*You* get anxious! I've just spoken to an elderly couple in the hallway, and they've had to leave the building because you're shattering their nerves.'

Hollie was shouting at him now. She knew she shouldn't; she knew it was stupid; she knew it would come back to bite her on the arse. But it felt so good to let it all out. It was flowing so fast now she couldn't rebuild the dam to hold it all in. Then he made the remark which finally pushed her over the edge.

'It's a free world. I don't know why you're getting your knickers in a twist.'

The *free world* defence was like a match to lighter fuel, a red rag to a bull and jam to wasps. It was the go-to comment of tossers throughout the country, and she'd heard it too many times in her policing career.

Hollie stormed over to him, snatched the drumsticks out of his hands, and then used them to stab holes through his drum skins. Even as she was doing it, she pictured the knife scenes in *Psycho*, the murder weapon striking repeatedly until the victim was dead. In this case, the guy's drum kit looked like it had just been dropped from a plane from a very great height.

'You're a bloody nutter,' he shouted at her. 'I'm calling the police. You can't do that!'

'I am the police!' Hollie screamed at him. 'I'm also a middle-aged woman who forgot to grab a new oestrogen patch this morning, so you'd better be very afraid!'

She was enjoying herself now, even though she knew she'd have to pay for her outburst later.

'I'm the police, too,' came a man's voice from the flat door. It was Anderson. 'An old couple let me in. They'd forgotten their umbrella,' he continued, looking around the room.

'I want to press charges,' the drummer blustered, half sitting and half standing at his stool.

Anderson had spotted something on the table at the far side of the room. He walked over and picked up a small bottle and a syringe.

'Diamorphine,' he said. 'That's a Class A drug. I reckon that'll be four years in prison. The only drumming sound you'll get in jail is the bang, bang, bang of the other inmates fucking you up the arse. So, I'll give you one chance. Hand your notice in on the flat today and take these drums to the tip. Then fuck off somewhere else and stop screwing up your life and the lives of everybody else. Understood?'

The drummer hung his head; he was beaten.

'Understood.'

'Come on,' Anderson said to Hollie, 'let's get back to the office.' Over his shoulder, he said, 'I'm coming back here first thing on Monday morning. If these drugs haven't been handed into a safe disposal centre, I'm nicking you anyway.'

Hollie and Anderson walked out of the flat and made their way down the stairs.

'I didn't know you felt so strongly about drummers,' Anderson remarked.

'I always did prefer acoustic guitar,' she replied.

THIRTY-EIGHT

'I feel exhausted already,' Hollie said as she stepped back into the car.

'I should think so,' Anderson replied as he settled into the passenger seat. 'You just got your invitation rescinded to this year's drumming convention.'

'Look, I'm sorry about that—'

'It's okay, I know that prick. He's got form as far as drug use is concerned. You tend to see the same old faces once you've policed a place like Hull for a while.'

'Tell me about it. Lancaster was a smaller place. Some of the idiots there were like bad pennies.'

Hollie started the engine. 'I wish this bloke would call. It's unnerving me. I'm scared he's going to do something stupid, and we won't get time to stop him. We can't lose another officer to this case. DCC Warburton has to get out of this alive.'

Anderson's phone sounded; he picked it up before it got to a second ring.

'I'll put you on speaker,' he said. 'It's DS Patel—'

'Sorry to trouble you with more bad news, boss—'

'It's all right. Go ahead, DS Patel. We're heading back to the office right now.'

'You might want to take a diversion,' Patel continued. 'We're getting reports of a fire at the Church of St Mary and the Angels—'

'Oh, for Christ's sake, didn't we check that out?'

There was silence.

'He's been hiding in the bloody church all this time, hasn't he? Who checked out the damn church?'

Hollie could hear DS Patel checking her notes on her PC.

'A couple of uniformed officers checked it over, boss. It's pretty well sealed up, apparently. He must have found a way in.'

'The mother and baby home was surrounded by fences and all boarded up, but he got in there all right—'

'It might not be him, boss—' DS Patel suggested.

'It's him,' Hollie interrupted. 'I'll bet you a bashed-up drum set that it's him.'

'What?' DS Patel asked.

'It's a long story,' Anderson interjected, 'and one which can wait for the pub when we're celebrating DCC Warburton's safe return. Do we have anybody else over there?'

'Yes, uniform is there already. I thought you'd like to get over there, too.'

'Good call, DS Patel, thank you. We're on our way now.'

Anderson ended the call.

Hollie was rough on the clutch in her hurry to get off. The car lurched forward.

'You think this is it?' Anderson asked.

'Yes. He's burning his bridges now. This is misdirection. We'll all go piling over to the church while he's setting up whatever the sick bastard has planned—'

'If he calls again, you have to stay calm,' Anderson remarked.

'I know. I want to scream at him, but I promise, I'll control myself, for Jenni and the DCC. That drummer back there will never know what a valuable public service he just provided. I'm feeling a lot calmer now. It did me the world of good, assaulting his drum kit.'

Anderson directed her through the back streets to avoid the traffic and they were parking along the road from the church within ten minutes. Black smoke billowed over the trees, and two fire engines were parked directly outside on the road, their hoses drawing water from a nearby hydrant, the teams already deployed to their tasks of limiting the damage. Members of the public were gathered, but the uniformed officers had set up a cordon to keep them out of the way of the firefighters and at a safe distance. They got out of the car, not bothering to close the doors in their rush.

'Who's in charge here?' Hollie asked one of the uniformed officers, holding out her ID for examination. Anderson followed suit. Hollie had to raise her voice to be heard; the engine was making too much noise for her to speak at a normal level. The officer pointed to the lead fire officer and lifted the barrier tape so they could pass. They walked up to the crew manager and made the introductions.

'Is there anybody in there?' Hollie asked.

'We don't believe so. The church is near derelict,' the fire officer replied. 'We think it's probably vandals.'

'There's a small chance there may be a woman in there. You should make your teams aware.'

Hollie briefed him on the bare bones of the case and explained why they might need to be more cautious in their approach. The fire officer got on the radio straight away and updated his teams.

'We're worried about the roof caving in,' he explained. 'It's always a risk with these old structures.'

'How long has it been burning?' Anderson asked.

'Half an hour, tops.'

From that distance, Hollie could see the flames beginning to swirl around the chipboard panels that had been put up around the windows. The ferocity was startling, even from the safety of the road, and her respect for the firefighters soared as she watched their well-rehearsed response from afar.

'Call Timothy Warburton, would you?' Hollie suggested. 'I'm a bit jittery in case the DCC is in there.'

'He wouldn't, would he?' Anderson asked, with a look of surprise that suggested he hadn't seriously considered the possibility.

'I don't think so. God, I hope she's not in there. There's no way they're getting her out alive if she is.'

A TV satellite truck had pulled up outside the cordon and the driver was asking a uniformed officer for a safe place to park.

'Is that a BBC vehicle?' she asked nobody in particular. 'Please tell me he didn't make his call early.'

Hollie ducked under the tape and caught the truck driver before he wound up his window. She showed him her ID. It was a relief to step away from the noise of the fire engine and the sound of a motorcycle revving further along the road.

'Did he call you and tell you to come here?' she asked. The reporter was sitting in the passenger seat. She thought he looked familiar; he had probably been at the press conference.

'No, we didn't get his call yet. We're on standby for later this evening, but we thought this would make some decent establishing shots for our report tonight.'

'You're sure?' Hollie checked.

'I'll call the office now and double-check for you,' the reporter replied. 'We'll get parked up, then I'll let you know.'

The truck reversed down the street and the driver manoeuvred into the tightest parking space Hollie had ever seen. She took a moment to admire the man's driving skills. The two-man crew set to work immediately, the reporter prioritising Hollie first.

'You're all-clear. He hasn't called us yet,' the reporter confirmed. Hollie felt a wave of relief sweeping over her. The chances of DCC Warburton's burnt body being dragged out of there had just decreased significantly. She knew how men like this worked: they liked a show, and they craved attention. Sister Brennan's death was a public display. Whatever he'd got planned for the DCC would most likely follow the same pattern.

The fire crew manager was trying to get Hollie's attention, so she thanked the TV reporter and ducked back under the cordon tape.

'I've got an update from my guys,' he started, raising his voice to be heard over the noise. 'Whoever set the fire gained access via the back door. The chipboard had been wrenched off the door frame. It was wet and rotten. It wouldn't have been too difficult. The door looks like it was smashed in using an old stone vase from one of the graves. That's just an early guess, of course, but there was one discarded nearby—'

'Was anybody in there?' Hollie asked. At that moment, she didn't care much about the church.

'It's too early to say. I need to clear my teams to go inside. If there is somebody in there, they're not coming out, I'm afraid.'

'How soon until you can get in?' Anderson shouted.

The fire officer shrugged.

'I'm not sending anybody in until I can be sure that roof's not coming down. We're getting a specialist guy over ASAP. Things are tight, so it's going to take a bit more time than usual.'

'Is someone's phone ringing?' Anderson asked.

Hollie listened. He was right. Somebody's smartphone was sounding. There was such a racket, it was difficult to hear anything. She pulled her phone out of her pocket.

'Damn, it's mine,' she said, ducking under the cordon tape

so she could hear the call. She tapped the answer button before she'd gained sufficient distance to be able to hear the caller.

'It's DI Hollie Turner. Who's speaking?'

'Have I got your attention yet?'

It was him.

THIRTY-NINE

2022: SOPHIA BRENNAN'S STORY

Sophia stepped off the bus and surveyed the area. She'd written it all down again, in case she forgot. There it was, a little way along the street. Stanstead House, just like her notes told her. She'd made this journey to Father Duffy's flat so many times over the years, but she knew her mind was going. It wouldn't be long now before it would be too hazardous to make a journey like this.

She remembered the fields that ran along the side of Noddle Hill Way. It always struck her as incongruous: a housing estate on one side and open fields on the other. At least she couldn't pass by the high-rise; there was no missing that. Sophia walked along the path, past the houses and into the garth that led to the flats. She was pleased she'd got a room at the convent; it wasn't so easy for Father Duffy in the flats. After all those years of service to the Church and they made him spend the last of his days in that place. She knew some residents would never leave them, but the estate had its problems, everybody knew that, and it could be scary for those who were frail and more vulnerable.

Sophia reached the high-rise and made her way to the entrance. She took out her piece of paper again and reminded herself of the details. Flat 4, Floor 15. She hated the lifts in that place. They scared her. Fancy housing an old man so high up. She pressed the bell. It sounded dead to her. She tried again. There was no response. A man had been smoking a cigarette in the car park and he walked up to her.

'Do you need any assistance, Sister?' he asked.

'Would you be able to help me get inside?'

'Of course.'

He let her in using his key.

'Can I help you with the lift?'

He accompanied her across the entrance hall and checked which floor she needed. He rode with her up to the seventh floor, then wished her a good day as she continued her journey upwards.

Father Duffy's front door was slightly ajar when she stepped out onto the landing, and she heard male voices coming from inside.

'Father?' she called, pushing the door open a little more. There was some movement, then a familiar voice.

'Come in, Sophia! The kettle's on.'

Sophia pulled the door closed behind her. Father Duffy was too old to be taking risks with open doors.

'It's lovely to see you, Sophia,' he said, joining her in the short corridor and encouraging her into the living room.

'I thought I heard voices,' she said, seeing he was alone.

'Oh, er, it was probably just me talking to myself. You know how it is. It's living alone that does it.'

Father Duffy escorted her to the sofa and gave her a cushion to support her back. He then shuffled off to the kitchen to fetch the tea. She recalled how young he'd been when she first met him in the church. He'd been like a guardian angel to her. Now they were so old, their lives behind them. It was funny how she could recall the old memories; it was the recent ones which troubled her more.

Father Duffy brought in her tea and sat in the opposite armchair. She saw how stiff his movements were now and what an effort such a simple task was for him.

'Now, Sophia, what's on your mind?'

She took out her slip of paper once again. All she had to do was to stay sharp long enough to say what she had to say. She owed him that much, at least. If her memory went completely and devoured her past, she'd go to her grave with her sins. She had to put things right, for all of them.

'You know I've loved you for so many years now, Father Duffy. As a sister, I mean. You were so good to me when you found me in the church that day. I was going to end my life, you know. It's only because I fell asleep on that pew before I could go through with it that I'm here today. And you found me there and you helped me. It was God's will. I don't know why He chose to help a wretched thing like me, but He did, and He sent you to save me. I know I'm losing my mind now, but before I disappear, I must tell you how grateful I am.'

'I know, Sophia, I know. It's been a long journey for all of us. You know how much I cherish your loyalty to me.'

'I'm going to die soon, Father. When my mind goes, I might as well be dead. But I need to put some things right before I do.'

'I know, Sophia. You said last time we spoke that this day was coming. Tell me what you want to do.'

'I hid your relationship with Sister Kay as I always promised I would. I won't tell anybody about that. That is a matter for your own conscience and reconciliation.'

'I was a weak man, Sister Brennan, and I led Ursula – Sister Kay – along a path of darkness, for which I will forever be repentant. But I appreciate your discretion, thank you.'

'I have to tell them about the babies, Father.'

'I thought you might say that.'

'I turned the other cheek for so many years, even though I knew it was wrong. But I must confess it, Father. We have to tell the truth. I was wrong to punish those girls for what they'd done. I was confused and angry and hateful. I have to make amends. I can't leave things that way.'

He was crying. She knew Father Duffy had shown weakness in his life, but she didn't know why he was so upset now. There was a movement to her side, then the blur of something approaching her face. She was struggling to breathe. Someone had launched at her with force and was pushing her down, a cushion pressed into her face. As she struggled for breath, she heard the protests and tears of Father Duffy and a cursing voice that she hadn't heard for some years. It was older now, slightly reedier than it had once been. It was the social worker, McCready.

'You're not telling anyone about anything, you old bitch.'

Sophia heard him seething as she fought for air.

'Shut the fuck up, Frank. You took some of the cash. This is saving your snivelling arse, too.'

Sophia's lungs felt like they were about to collapse. Her head was ready to explode. She was fading and she let go, happy to sink into the oblivion of death.

She woke, dazed, in pain, and cold. She was unable to move, but her mind was sharp. She was sitting down, in a wheelchair, moving. It was dark. They were outdoors. There were voices. It was McCready and another man, a voice she didn't recognise.

'You do this, and you get your revenge on the bitch that kept you in the dark all these years. It was she who destroyed the records; you'd know who your mother is if it wasn't for this woman.'

That was McCready. How had the man stayed so hateful?

Even she'd mellowed as she'd grown older, despite everything that still haunted her. Sophia kept her eyes shut, playing dead, waiting to see what was planned.

'But she's a fucking nun! Even I know not to go hurling nuns off the side of bridges.'

'Believe me, get this done and there'll be such a commotion, you'll soon find out who your mother is. Once I take care of the old man, the way is clear. Now, get this sorted and we're good. If the old hag shoots her mouth off, you'll never get your answer. Hang this sign around her neck when she goes over. The press will love it.'

Sophia felt the wheelchair handles being gripped and she lurched forward.

'Just follow the path. It'll take you to the bridge. You can avoid the steps. I'll meet you with the car on the other side. Oh, and throw the chair over the barrier into the water. Wear your hat low and keep your head down, just like I told you. I'll pay you the second five hundred pounds in cash as soon as we meet at the Barton side.'

Sophia remained still. The person pushing the chair was shoving it aggressively. A man on a mission. She could feel they were heading up a rise in the path, and she dared to open her eyes for a moment. She knew that sight. The Humber Bridge. Where were they taking her? A panic gripped her: they thought she was dead. Were they going to leave her on the bridge? If she stayed still, would she escape with her life? The choice was taken away from her. The wheelchair struck a stone and jarred, throwing her out onto the ground. She let out a scream and her head struck the pavement hard.

'For fuck's sake,' came the man's voice.

Sophia attempted to speak, to beg for help, but the words would not come.

He spun her around on the path and his strong, gloved

hands grasped her around the waist. As Sophia faded from consciousness, she caught a momentary glimpse of her killer from the small area of his face that was in view. The tiny mole to the left of his right eye brought a final memory back to her, sharp and real.

FORTY

'I've taken the papers from your car and left you a little treat.'

'What?' Hollie said, partly outraged but mostly unnerved. 'Was that your motorcycle I heard a few moments ago?'

'It was. I brushed right past you. You were too busy chatting with that firefighter. You could have caught me.'

Hollie's mind raced. She'd had him in her grasp, and she'd missed him. If she'd been more attentive, she might have stopped this before it went too far. He was playing with fire now and taking risks. He was becoming more reckless, and that meant he posed a greater threat to DCC Warburton.

'What papers did you take?' she asked, walking over to the car. She knew the answer already, but she asked him anyway. She needed him to talk to her and make his boast. That way he would feel in control and assume he had more power.

'It's your boss, isn't it?'

'What do you mean?'

'Even you think she's my mother.'

'What?'

Hollie was confused and uncertain about where this was coming from.

'I just looked at the papers. They have the name Rose written all over them. The surname is different – of course it is. She was a child back then. But the copper I've got is called Rose. She told me that almost immediately. I assume they teach you police officers to build relationships with people like me by giving us your first names. Well, McCready told me she was caught up in all this—'

'You know Patrick McCready?'

'Of course I do. He was the social worker at the mother and baby unit around the time I was adopted. He was one of my first contacts. You cops are not the only ones who can do a bit of research, you know.'

Hollie's mind was racing now. He knew McCready. Interesting that McCready hadn't thought to mention that to her in his interview. And this man now believed Rose Warburton might be his mother. Should she tell him the truth?

She scanned the area for DS Anderson. She watched him making his way up the path to the church, accompanied by a fire officer. It looked like he was trying to confirm there were no bodies in there. That was certainly a priority, so it was good he was onto it. She could have done with a second opinion right at that moment, though.

In a split second, she decided it was best not to tell him about the DCC. While he thought there was a chance Rose Warburton might be his birth mother, there was no way he would harm her. But what might happen when he discovered the truth? Would he be angry and take it out on her? She had to buy time. That was the only option. If she told him the truth at that moment, it might accelerate whatever he'd got planned. She wished to God she'd been paying attention when the motorcycle drove by.

'Have you left me your adoption papers?' Hollie asked.

'I have. Tick-tock, tick-tock, you've not got long to figure it out now.'

Hollie struggled to control her anger. She wanted to see those papers, too.

'Why did you kill Sister Brennan?' she asked. It seemed the best way to deflect him, and he seemed to be in a conversational mood.

'That's not what happened.' He was defensive, almost offended by the suggestion.

'I beg your pardon?'

She'd just assumed this was their man. And now he was denying she'd died at his hands.

'It's true. I didn't kill her.'

'But you tried to kill Father Duffy?'

'No, that was not me.'

Hollie was stunned. He was not what they'd regard as a reliable witness, but he'd not hesitated in giving his answers.

'I did not kill the nun, and I did not kill the priest. I did hurt your police pal and I'm sorry about that. I was trying to scare you. I wanted to know what you were up to. I expected her to jump out of the way. There wasn't much room down that alley.'

Anger raged through Hollie's body as she thought of her colleague – her new friend – and she wanted to scream at this man and tear his eyes out. She forced it back down, thinking of DCC Warburton and knowing that, if she messed up this conversation, she might well be losing a colleague that day.

'I also slapped your pal, that mouthy woman, but she deserved it.'

Hollie was about to challenge him, but she kept her mouth shut. She knew from experience that when this type of monster felt like they had all the power, they'd often shoot off at the mouth. He was being true to type.

'Are you intending to hurt DCC Warburton?'

'Not if she's my birth mother, I'm not.'

'So where do you go from here? What if she is your mother? What happens next?'

He hesitated for the first time since he'd made the phone call.

'That's enough now. You'll hear from me later.'

The line was dead. Hollie took a couple of deep breaths; a rush of anxiety threatened to engulf her. For a moment, she considered alerting uniform about the motorcycle, but what information did she have? He was far away now, to wherever he was hiding.

'I called 999 and they didn't want to know—'

Somebody was speaking at her side, snapping Hollie out of her self-absorption. She turned to see an elderly lady with three neatly groomed poodles at the end of three thin red leads.

'I beg your pardon?'

'There's been a white van coming and going along this road all week. I used to oversee Neighbourhood Watch, you know, but nobody seems to care much about that these days. I think the police have completely given up. If you check your call logs, you'll see I telephoned in. I can tell you're a police officer by the way you're standing.'

'I'm sorry, you'll have to explain,' Hollie replied over the yaps of the dogs, which didn't seem to like her much.

'My house is just along the road there. Number 21. My name is Constance Smith. I've lived on this road for over twenty years, so I know all the comings and goings.'

Hollie had met people like this before. Sometimes they could be a godsend. At other times they could be a bloody nuisance. She was as yet uncertain which category Constance fell into.

'I've been involved in Neighbourhood Watch for fifteen of those years. There was a time when the police valued what we told them. Fifteen years ago, if I called the local police station with a concern, they'd send a couple of officers around and take it seriously. Nowadays, I'm lucky if someone picks up the phone.'

PAUL J. TEAGUE

All Hollie could do was apologise for the level of service. She was about to defend her colleagues by reminding Constance about the cuts, limited resources and budget restrictions, but she sensed the public knew what the problem was and had become resigned to a crumbling system. She just gave an affirmative nod and waited for Constance to continue; she needed little encouragement.

'That van has been coming and going for the past couple of weeks. He parks it in various places, so nobody notices, but I do. I see everything when I walk the children.'

Hollie didn't say anything. The hand-sewn coats that each dog wore told her everything. Trixie, Pixie and Dixie. The names were embroidered on the jackets; they were clearly a particularly important part of this woman's life.

'When I saw him taking a motorcycle down a ramp at the back of the van, that's when I knew it was suspicious. I mean, that seems strange, doesn't it? And he doesn't live here, I'm sure.'

'When did you call the police?' Hollie asked. She didn't really want to hear the answer. She could guess what had happened. In a busy investigation, it was easy for scraps of information to slip through the net, especially when they came from people like Constance. They were easy to dismiss and shrug off, but they were usually the backbone of local communities.

'I called them twice. Nobody came around, and nobody followed it up. And now look what's happened. That lovely old church has been burnt down and the van is nowhere to be seen. You don't need to wear a police uniform to see how it all adds up. And now he's got away, hasn't he?'

Hollie felt ashamed of the force she represented, even though she knew how deeply dedicated most of her colleagues were. It wasn't just Humberside Police; she'd increasingly felt it in Lancaster, too. They were so pressed for resources that they were barely able to do their jobs properly. Crime didn't give a shit about funding. It carried on regardless.

'Did you ever get a good look at him?' Hollie asked. 'Could you give us a description?'

'I can tell you he was in his fifties with grey hair. It was completely white, but the face underneath is much younger than it should be. There's nothing extraordinary about him, but he's strong. He had no trouble moving that motorcycle up and down the ramp at the back of the van.'

'Did you see him with anybody?' Hollie asked.

'Only the other night, when I was out walking the children. I thought I saw him with somebody else, but it was dark, and the council don't replace the bulbs in the streetlights like they used to, so I couldn't see very clearly.'

Hollie sighed silently, wishing she'd had this information passed on to her earlier. One of the civilian officers or, perhaps, a detective constable would have filtered that out, thinking the information was too inconsequential to make its way to the desk of a senior officer.

'Is there anything else that might be useful?' Hollie asked, scouring the area for a police constable to take this woman's contact details and make some detailed notes about her experiences.

'Oh, yes.' Constance smiled, reaching into her coat pocket. 'That's why I came out of the house when I saw all the commotion. I'll bet I've got your full attention now. I jotted down the number plates of both vehicles, as well as the makes and models. They used to train us well in Neighbourhood Watch, you know. I've got everything you need right here.'

FORTY-ONE

'There's a note here that says she's a bit of a nuisance,' DS Patel confirmed.

'Get that information updated, will you? But only after you've got all units on the lookout for those vehicles. If we can head him off before he even gets to the DCC, we're in with a chance of ending this thing without anybody getting hurt.'

'The alert went out as soon as you gave me the number plate details. And that record is updated—'

Hollie heard Patel clicking her keyboard deliberately at the end of the line.

'—right now!'

'That woman deserves a medal. Follow the paper trail, would you? I'm curious to know who took those calls and why they didn't make their way to the investigations team.'

'Will do, boss. Those pictures of the adoption paperwork have just come through—'

Hollie could hear Patel clicking on her mouse on the other end of the call.

'Damn, same again. Old council paperwork. There's McCready's signature, Father Duffy's and Sister Brennan as witness. And there's his name, too: Doug. Family name is Maybury. And the adoption agency – bloody hell, it's all there – excuse my language. Even a home address. I'll get in touch with the Met and get it checked over. I'll see if I can pull up a file on the man as well. This is a great breakthrough, boss.'

'I'm sure as hell now that this is a racket,' Hollie picked up. 'It doesn't help us much right now knowing who he is. We need to know where he is.'

'Where are you heading next, boss?' DS Patel checked.

'I'm waiting for this call to come in from our man. Doug. I want to know what he's got planned.'

Hollie considered sharing her doubts about what she'd done with her junior colleague, but as she was about to launch into her confessional, she saw DS Anderson approaching with a couple of evidence bags in his hand.

'I've got to go,' Hollie said. 'Call me immediately if anything comes up.'

Anderson looked like he had something to tell her, so Hollie let him share his news first.

'They're as sure as they can be that there are no bodies in there,' he began. 'But look what they found.'

He held out the evidence bags. Inside were two dog leads wrapped around in loops.

'Looks like he used these as restraints,' Anderson said. 'There are signs of blood along the edges. It looks like he was rough when he pulled them off.'

'I take it they belong to the DCC?' Hollie checked.

'I'm just waiting for the FLO to confirm that now,' he replied. 'She's with Timothy Warburton. I sent some photos over. Don't worry, you can't see the blood from the angle I took them.'

'I'm pleased to hear it.'

Anderson's phone vibrated and he checked it.

'Yes, DC Hayes has confirmed they're the leads from their

dogs. So, we know she was in there and the fire team are ninety-five per cent certain there was nobody in there at the time of the fire.'

Hollie shared her news as they made their way back to her car.

'We've got to get this guy now. The number plates were the missing piece of the jigsaw. Did Patel run them through the system?'

'I'm just waiting for her to get back to me on that. Let's hope they're not stolen, shall we? We might get a name at last.'

Hollie checked in with the BBC reporter, who'd just finished an interview with the senior fire officer on the scene.

'Anything yet?' she asked. He shook his head.

'How about we exchange phone numbers, then we can do each other a favour if there are any developments?'

That seemed to please the reporter. They exchanged contact details.

'What next, boss?' Anderson asked. 'I'm dying from the tension—'

Hollie's phone rang, just as she'd saved the reporter's details.

'Is it our man again?' Anderson asked.

'No, I don't know who it is.'

Hollie picked up. It was Osbourne Street police station. The fire engine was still too noisy to be able to put the call on speaker. She listened intently and noted the details.

'It's McCready,' she said, ending the call. 'He's been spotted on Dagger Lane. Uniform are scouring the area now.'

They got out of the car on Dagger Lane and rushed up the street towards a man slouched against a wall. It was McCready. He was nursing a wound to his face. He seemed dazed and shocked.

'Well, you're a difficult man to find, Mr McCready,' Hollie began. 'You must know we've been trying to speak to you. Where the hell have you been?'

'He's crazy. I'm telling you, the man is out of control—'

'Who's out of control?' Anderson asked.

'He said he's going to kill me.'

'What's his name, Mr McCready?' Hollie pushed. 'That would help, for starters. And what's your connection with him?'

'He's called Doug, Doug Maybury. He's been looking for his birth mother. I don't know how he found me. He must have somehow got in touch with one of the staff at St Mary and the Angels. He's convinced I can reunite him with his birth mother.'

At least he was telling the truth. Doug Maybury, he was their man.

'Can you reunite him with his mother?'

'No, I can't. It's a long time since I worked there, detective, and as you know, the paperwork is difficult to find after the council changes—'

'About that, Mr McCready. We've come across some forms which suggest that old council paperwork may have been used for fraudulent adoptions. Would you know anything about that?'

'Am I being interviewed under caution?' McCready asked after a silence. 'Besides, can't you see I've been assaulted here? I only came to meet him in the pub, and he did this to me. I need medical assistance, I'm hurt.'

'Why were you even meeting with him?' Hollie challenged. 'He's a wanted man.'

McCready's face told her he'd realised the implications of what he'd just said. He blustered.

'I was trying to shake him off and get him off my case. I'd have told you afterwards, of course I would.'

Now she knew he was lying. She wanted him patched up and delivered to her in an interview room ASAP.

'Best call an ambulance,' Hollie whispered to Anderson. 'He does look a bit pale.'

She turned back to McCready, who was still slumped against the wall.

'You're not under caution at this moment, but you will be the moment I can get you to an interview room.'

'I'm not saying anything further. Here's what I want from you.'

'I'm not sure you're in any position to make demands—'

'I think I am, detective. I can tell you who was responsible for Sister Brennan's death and exactly what happened, because I was there.'

It was Hollie's turn to remain silent this time. She despised this man, but he sure as hell was up to his eyeballs in whatever had been going on. Was he bluffing?

'What is it you want?'

'Police protection, for starters.'

'Well, there's a nice, warm custody cell at Clough Road with your name on it,' Anderson said, his call now finished. 'There's a car already on its way. Maybe somebody leaving the pub spotted him.'

'I want to make a deal—'

'This isn't the USA, you know,' Hollie replied.

'I know that, but I can help you out here. You get me an assurance that certain matters will be overlooked, and I'll help you solve this case.'

'You know I can't do that—'

'If you don't, I've a feeling you're going to lose a senior police officer. Yes, I do know about that. I'm still well-connected locally, you know.'

Hollie thought it over. It was possible to offer McCready

some kind of deal, but it wasn't the sort of result that could be rustled up at five minutes' notice.

'What do you want?'

'Immunity from a charge of obstructing a police officer or perverting the course of justice.'

'Have you done those things?'

'I haven't been entirely forthcoming.'

'In what way?'

'You get me immunity from prosecution, I'll give you your explanation and hand you your man.'

'Okay, I'll do my best, but I can't promise anything.'

'You've got half an hour.'

'Dammit, Mr McCready, you know I can't do that.'

'A senior police officer's life is on the line. You'll manage something.'

An ambulance siren sounded up the street.

'Give them a wave in, will you, DS Anderson? We're a bit out of the way over here.'

He walked back towards The Mission to guide in the medics.

'Why don't you make that call right now?' McCready asked. 'There's no time like the present.'

Hollie took a look at him. For all his mouth and bravado, he looked like he'd received quite a beating. She took out her phone and scrolled for DCI Osmond's number. As she did so, DS Anderson walked around the corner, leading the ambulance in. Hollie held up her hand to give him a wave and they drove slowly up the cobbles and parked up in front of Hollie.

'Right, let's get this bastard checked over and cleared for questioning—' Anderson began.

Hollie noticed his eyes widen.

'Where the fuck is he?'

Hollie turned around. She'd only had her back turned for two minutes, but McCready had gone.

'Oh, for fuck's sake!' she shouted. 'The man was claiming to be half-dead five minutes ago, now he's done a runner.'

'I'll go ahead, you take the street behind us, we'll try to head him off.'

'Where can he go from here?'

'If he knows these side streets, he can lose himself quickly. Where the fuck are uniform when you need them? I thought they were supposed to be scouring these streets.'

They ran off, leaving the ambulance crew to figure out what was going on. Around the corner, Hollie spotted a patrol car and flagged it down, flashing her ID.

'Get out the car and help us look for him on foot; he's done a runner.'

The officers got out of the vehicle.

'You take that street, and you take the other one. He's hurt, you can't miss him.'

Hollie walked the length of Robinson Row, meeting with an out of breath Anderson at its junction with Fish Street.

'The bastard's got away, hasn't he?' Hollie said.

Anderson's face said it all.

'Let's see if those uniformed officers come up with anything,' she suggested.

Hollie's phone rang, and she answered it immediately.

'Call the plods off—'

'It's Lazarus,' Hollie informed DS Anderson. 'Where are you, Mr McCready? You know this doesn't help your case, don't you?'

'Call the plods off and get me immunity from prosecution, then I'll give you your explanation and hand you your murderer.'

'Look—'

'You're wasting time, DI Turner. Get me what I want, and I'll give you what you want.'

Anderson looked like he was dying to know what was going on.

'Okay, how do we work this? I expect you to give me something in return.'

'Of course. Meet me by the bridge between the railway dock and the marina. Come alone and enter from the Holiday Inn side. I won't show myself until I see you there. I'll call you, then we'll speak. But only if you've kept your end of the deal. Understood?'

'I've got it. I can't promise anything, but I'll do my best. I'll be there in half an hour.'

'Make sure you are.'

He ended the call.

FORTY-TWO

'What did you think about his list of demands?' Hollie asked.

'Call it in to Osmond. He's a shitty little man, but if he can't pull this off, nobody can. I'm pretty sure he'll know someone who knows someone else who can scratch somebody's back. You know how this stuff works with the brass.'

Unfortunately, Hollie understood very well how things worked.

'You're going alone?' Anderson asked.

'What choice do we have?'

'We could station officers in the area.'

'I think that's a good idea bearing in mind his recent disappearing act. If he's there, I can get him; once bitten, twice shy. Let's just have a couple of cars in the wider area. I daren't risk spooking him at such a delicate state in the operation.'

'And if our man – Doug – calls?'

'Uniform can arrest McCready and we'll attend to the DCC as a priority. In the meantime, you'd best get those dog leads checked into evidence. Can you hitch a ride back?'

Anderson nodded.

'You know where you're going?' he queried. 'Park at the

Holiday Inn and walk past the flats. You'll see the bridge at the end of the residents' car park. There are roadworks in the area. Don't miss your turn.'

'Got it, thank you.'

Hollie watched as Anderson walked over to a uniformed officer, who'd just returned out of breath and empty-handed. They exchanged a few words and he put his thumb up; he was getting them organised and he'd alert more patrols via the radio in their car.

Her phone was ringing again. Every call seemed to be inching them one step closer to a resolution. She'd need to eat again soon. She was burning off energy like an exploding planet. She made her way back to the car as DS Patel brought her up to speed.

'I've got you that number plate info, boss.'

'Great, what did you find?'

'Do you want the good news or the bad news first?'

'Lead with the bad news, please.'

'The van was stolen. It's got false plates on. They were stolen from a scrapyard in Southwark.'

'Shit, that's a bad start. What's the good news?'

'The motorbike is registered to him. He's Douglas Geoffrey Maybury, age fifty-four, who once lived in his parents' former house in Southwark but is currently registered at some shitty ex-offenders' bedsit in London. That's where I've got more bad news.'

'I don't think I want to hear it.'

'You don't. Please don't shoot the messenger. This guy has form and lots of it. Juvenile detention, a history of violence, burglary. You name it, he's done it.'

'What has he been in prison for?'

'Assault. GBH to be precise. He once bludgeoned an old lady so he could steal her purse.'

Hollie briefed her colleague on the latest developments and

instructed her to liaise with Anderson to make sure they'd got McCready's exits covered. As she drove off in her car, leaving Anderson to deal with the ambulance crew and the uniformed officers, she pulled over by a coffee shop which was at the end of Dagger Lane. Hollie wanted to kiss the corner shop assistant. Not only did they have a decent sandwich in the fridge, but there was also a Scotch egg just within its sell-by date. There was something about the Scotch egg that could give a copper who'd been on duty far too long the energy to keep going. With one hand on the steering wheel and the other rapidly funnelling food into her mouth, she made her way across the city centre to the Holiday Inn.

She thought about the events to come and how they might play out. All their necks were on the line now – DCC Warburton's most of all. Whatever happened, this case would be concluded by the end of the day. Whether it had a successful conclusion was yet to be determined.

Hollie's mind focused better on a full stomach. Her legs had started to shake when she'd been on the scene of the fire, and she'd been relieved to get back into the car. A chocolate bar and a can of Coke finished off the snatched meal, and she felt fortified and ready for whatever was ahead.

She pulled off the A63 into Commercial Road and parked the car just before the turn-off to the Holiday Inn to figure out where she was. She was running tight on time. He'd said half an hour. She took a moment to get her bearings, but she didn't know this area at all well and thought it had probably changed since she'd been a student, anyway. It was a mix of new and old, with The Whittington & Cat pub and The Boathouse keeping the flag flying for the city's heritage, while the expensive boats and executive flats brought a slick and modern feel to the area. McCready had the advantage over her, but she was certain she could outrun him if he made a dash for it. Besides, DS Patel and

DS Anderson had patrol cars parked up in locations where they could deliver a backup response within minutes. They were far enough away not to be spotted by McCready, but close enough to be there swiftly if called.

Hollie followed the road around in front of the hotel and then to the furthest parking space just before the bollards that marked the start of the marina. This was perfect. The small bridge that McCready had mentioned was directly in front of her. She stepped out of the car and began to walk towards the narrow footbridge, scanning the area to see if McCready was already there. To her right was the Railway Dock Marina, and to her left was the main marina, each with yachts and motor vessels moored to their sides. She walked up to the footbridge and read the sign: *Welcome to Hull Marina.* There was an automatic gate sign as well as a *Gates Closing* alert. She looked across at the far side. McCready was nowhere to be seen.

For a moment, she wondered if she'd been duped. Had he sent her on a wild goose chase in some sort of sick power play? Her answer came when her phone rang. It was him.

'Okay, I'm here,' she answered.

'I know you are. I can see you.'

'Where are you?' Hollie asked, looking all around her. A family was walking with a dog and there were a couple of other people milling around, but it was getting late, and the area was quiet.

'Did you get what I asked for?'

'I've requested it at a senior level, but you know I can't give you that guarantee. I'm waiting for a call back from the senior officer who's attending to the matter.'

'Then I'm not sure we have anything to discuss.'

'You said he's coming after you. Why? What will he do to you?'

McCready paused. She could hear the wind catching the

speaker on his phone and she could also hear an engine revving nearby. He was outdoors and remarkably close. But where the hell was he hiding?

'He came to me because he thought I could solve his problem. But I can't—'

'Can't or won't?'

'I told you, there's no paperwork left that I know of. This all happened a long time ago. I can't remember the names of every baby we dealt with back then. I vaguely remember some of the cases, but not the adoptive parents. Why would I? Do you remember all the ne'er-do-wells and scumbags that you deal with in your line of work?'

He had a good point there. She remembered the persistent offenders and the big or memorable cases. But ask her about the minor crimes she'd dealt with in Lancaster as a police constable, and there was no way she could recall those names. She decided to push him while she attempted to figure out where he was hiding.

'Paperwork has come into my possession which suggests that you – or somebody whose handwriting has an uncanny resemblance to yours – used old social services paperwork at a time when the adoptions would have been recorded on Humberside County Council headed paper. Were you running an adoption racket, Mr McCready? And were Father Duffy and Sister Brennan involved?'

'I'll call you back in five minutes. If you don't have a guarantee of immunity for me, this is the last you'll hear from me.'

The call ended.

Fuck!

She'd pushed too hard. She had Osmond's number in her speed dial. She called him.

'Sorry to disturb you at home, sir—'

'You've got it. I was just about to call DS Patel to get the information over to you. If it secures the safe release of DCC Warburton, we can consider lesser charges. If he's killed anybody, though, there's no free pass.'

'What if he's been involved in illegal adoptions?'

'Can we prove it?'

'I think it's possible.'

'Damn. We'll have to cross that bridge when we come to it. See if you can tempt him with what I've given you. It's all we've got, I'm afraid. Oh, and DI Turner?'

'Yes, sir?'

'Good luck tonight, however this plays out. I'm in constant touch with the team. Do your best.'

'Will do, sir.'

Hollie ended the call. As soon as she did, her phone rang. How had he done that? He had to be close enough to see her, but where was he hiding?

'Was that the call?' McCready asked.

'You know that if you killed Sister Brennan or you conspired to kill her, we can't ignore that?'

'Yes, of course. Can you make me an offer?'

'Yes, I've got the go-ahead. Now, speak to me. Tell me about this Doug Maybury.'

'It's straightforward. Maybury got it into his head that I could tell him who his birth mother was. I told him I couldn't and that he'd have to go through the official channels.'

'How did he react?'

The wind blew up and she heard it brush across the speaker on his phone. It was killing her trying to figure out where he was. She searched the windows of the Holiday Inn behind her. Was he watching from one of the rooms?

'He got angry. The one thing I may have done is to lead him to Sister Brennan and Father Duffy. If I did, that was in error. I thought I was helping him. They were the only people I still knew from back then. He seemed harmless at that stage, so I referred him on.'

'And what about the suspicious paperwork?'

'What about it? It could easily have been forged by somebody else. It wouldn't have been difficult for somebody to get their hands on the paperwork for the old council and pull the wool over the eyes of the parents. The parents of the girls just wanted rid of the babies. The adoptive parents didn't give a damn where the babies came from. They were so desperate. Things were different back then. We didn't have the same safeguarding mechanisms in place that we do now. Maybe it was Sister Brennan and Father Duffy. I don't know. Perhaps it's divine retribution—'

The lights on the *Gates Closing* alert began to flash and two automatic gates blocked the small metal bridge. *No access when closed,* the sign read. A boat from the Railway Dock Marina side had left its mooring and was now wanting to cross into the main marina. She could hear the siren sounding through his phone. He had to be within spitting distance.

As the bridge began to lift, she finally figured it out.

'I think you're not telling me the truth,' she said, looking along the boat as it neared the bridge, which jolted and started to lift.

'Either way, I don't much care,' McCready said. 'That's the situation, and I'm telling you the truth.'

Something in Hollie's gut told her he was on that boat. She couldn't see him, and he wasn't driving it, but in an instant, she saw what was happening there. McCready was leaving the city, and he was selling her his version of events. If he made it out of the marina and into the Humber, he might be gone – forever, if he was clever enough. He only had to make it to somewhere like the Netherlands and he could disappear himself with the right connections.

Hollie took one more look around to make sure she hadn't grabbed the wrong end of the stick. Then she slipped her phone into her pocket, ran towards the low barrier, jumped over it, and ran at the footbridge, which had just begun to lift.

FORTY-THREE

He was not getting away. She was determined about that. In the instant she decided to make the leap, she considered all the options. There was a possibility that McCready could be blocked before he reached the Humber or, if he made it that far, while he was on the Humber. There was also the possibility she was just about to make a fool of herself and attempt to stop a boat belonging to a completely innocent person. For all she knew, McCready might be parked on the opposite road, hiding on another boat or in one of the Holiday Inn rooms, as she'd initially suspected. But the sound of the siren coming through his phone was much closer than that and he just had to be on that boat. Besides, he had all the makings of a sociopath and sailing out right under her nose would be exactly the sort of move a man like him would make.

As her feet thudded along the walkway, she wished she'd thought it through a little more thoroughly. It was one thing acting on a hunch and another thing entirely having a well-thought-out plan. As the bridge jolted upwards, she climbed over the side of the waist-high railing and leapt towards the bow. It was a ridiculous angle to leap from but, turning sideways, she just had enough time to jump before the angle became too steep. She looked at the water below and recalled Clive Bartram's fall into the estuary. If she messed this up, she'd look like a complete idiot.

It was now or never. Hollie leant into the drop, hoping she'd make it onto the front deck.

Her right foot landed on the lip of the bow, just ahead of the boat's front rail, and her left foot veered towards the starboard hull. She forced herself forward, her hands outstretched. She grasped the railing and hauled her left foot over the top rail and onto the deck, followed by her right. She held on tight for a moment, not quite believing she'd made it.

Behind her, the footbridge was now almost fully raised, and the boat's engines were being revved in anticipation of passing through. Hollie steadied herself on the bow, feeling in her pocket for her ID card.

Certain she was now steady on her feet, Hollie grasped the rope that was fastened to the cleats and moved around to where the ship's operator was sitting. When she appeared at his side, he looked like he was about to leap overboard.

'Police, stop this boat, please.'

'What the fuck—?'

She repeated herself, and he put the boat into a neutral gear. Hollie let him examine her ID.

'Is Patrick McCready on this vessel?' she asked.

She got her answer. McCready was already coming up from below decks, his phone still to his ear.

'For Christ's sake!' he cursed. He looked in a bad way from his beating. She wondered if he'd been heading for the boat when they apprehended him on Dagger Lane.

'The game's up, McCready. You don't have anywhere to go. I'm guessing your captain here doesn't know what's going on?'

'I haven't a fucking clue what's going on,' the man

confirmed. 'What's happening, Patrick? You paid me to get you to Rotterdam. I thought it was just a routine trip.'

'It's okay, Olaf. You can moor us up.'

'Is this your boat?' Hollie asked.

'It is,' McCready replied.

'It must have cost a pretty penny. Social services pensions must pay out well.'

McCready scowled.

'So, what happens now?' he asked. 'You can't arrest me for taking a perfectly legitimate sea trip on a legally registered vessel. And you've already told me you don't appear to have any credible evidence about the alleged illegal adoptions. Neither can you link me to the murder. So, what's your beef here, DI Turner?'

'I can bring you in for questioning under caution in connection with the murder of Sister Brennan and on suspicion of involvement in fraudulent adoptions. You can make this difficult if you want to. I suggest you come with me, and we get this all cleared up.'

'You're not putting me in handcuffs?'

'How much room do you think I have in these pockets? I have handcuffs in the car, and I should warn you, we do have police vehicles stationed in the area. I suggest you play nice, and if everything is as you claim it is, you'll be able to walk out of the police station and continue your little boat trip.'

Hollie turned to Olaf. 'Is this something he does regularly?'

'Yes, from time to time. Patrick owns the boat. I sail it for him. It suits both of us. We've done it for years. But I don't know what's going on here, I assure you.'

'So long as you reverse this boat up and let me take Patrick on a short trip to the police station, I'm sure you have nothing to worry about.'

Olaf looked terrified; he did not strike her as a criminal mastermind. He did as he was told and returned the boat to its mooring. Hollie escorted McCready to her car and phoned in her progress to the office. As she briefed DS Patel, she suddenly sensed a change of atmosphere at the end of the line; it was almost tangible, even through her phone.

'What just happened?' she asked.

Somebody had turned up the volume on one of the office TV sets.

'Jesus!' Patel exclaimed. Hollie's phone vibrated with a second call.

'Get in the car,' she instructed McCready. He looked like he was about to say something but decided – wisely – to keep his mouth shut.

'Come on, DS Patel, don't keep me waiting.'

She looked at the number of the incoming call. It was the BBC reporter she'd spoken to at the fire.

'He's at the bridge,' DS Patel began. 'He's got DCC Warburton at knifepoint at the side of the Humber Bridge. He's hung some shitty sign over the side saying, "Justice for Hull's adopted children". The TV crew have got a live feed of it—'

'Okay, hold your nerve, DS Patel. Get uniform to halt the traffic around the bridge, if they haven't done it already. Alert Humber Rescue and let's get some manpower over there, but do not engage. See if we have a negotiator available, and let Osmond know what's going on, if he hasn't seen it for himself already.'

'What are you going to do?'

'I'm driving over there. I've got McCready. We can get this thing thrashed out. If anything changes, call me. This is the endgame, DS Patel. What we do next determines what happens to DCC Warburton. Let's keep our focus, yes? And wherever Anderson is, make sure he's somewhere close where he can advise. I want him on this.'

Hollie finished with DS Patel, then climbed into the car alongside McCready. Seeing she'd missed the second call, she dialled into her messages to see what the BBC had to say. It was a brief message, but it confirmed what was going on.

'He's at the Humber Bridge,' the reporter's voice informed her. 'The bastard called the Calendar TV team before he called us. We're heading over there now.'

'You want to get treated more leniently when we finally figure out your involvement in all this?' Hollie said, curt and impatient.

'I told you already, I didn't—'

'I don't want to hear it.'

'What do you want?' McCready asked.

'I want my DCC safely off the side of that bridge,' she snapped. 'And I'm as sure as hell that you're the man who can help me to do it. You help me with this thing, and I'll do what I can for you.'

'Okay. I think he's deranged, though, so take no notice of anything he says.'

'We'll handle this when the time comes,' Hollie replied. 'Do you have 5G on that phone?'

'Yes, why?'

'Get the live feed up of what's going on at the bridge. I want to know what we're walking into when we get there.'

She started the car, and she screeched through the Holiday Inn car park, slamming through the gears out onto the A63.

'This traffic is going to grind to a halt as we get closer to the bridge. Can you guide me round?'

McCready was distracted, looking at his phone.

'I never thought he'd go that far—'

'What?' Hollie pushed, half watching the road and half trying to see what he was looking at on his phone.

'He's got your boss on the Humber Bridge at the spot where Sister Brennan was thrown over. She looks scared. They need to black this out. It looks like he's going to shove her off the side.'

FORTY-FOUR

'Which way? If they shut down the road around the bridge, this traffic is backing up soon. I'm turning off at St Andrew's Quay. Can you navigate me from there?'

'Yes, make your way up to Hessle Road. We should be able to avoid it.'

Hollie's phone sounded again. It was Anderson. Things were moving too fast to pull over, so she took the call while driving.

'Are you on your way over?' he asked.

'Yes, driving there now.'

'Is McCready with you?'

'Yes.'

'Is he playing ball?'

'Not really.'

'Can you put this call on speaker so he can hear?'

'You're sure? You're not going to say anything confidential, are you?'

'Nothing that McCready can't hear.'

'Turn here,' McCready said.

Hollie pressed a button on her car radio. She knew she had

Bluetooth and had got it working once but didn't really know what she was doing. To her surprise, after pressing a couple of buttons, Anderson's voice came out through the car speaker. She placed the phone in her cup holder and put both hands on the wheel.

'Are you hearing this, Mr McCready?'

'Ah, that sounds like DC Anderson—'

'DS Anderson,' came the reply. 'You might want to remember that rank. You and I are going to be speaking together shortly.'

McCready snorted.

'And why is that, detective?'

'I got the patrol vehicle to run me by the Church of St Mary and the Angels after you'd led us on a wild goose chase, McCready. They'd damped down the fire by the time I got there. The senior firefighter handed me something which he believed might be of interest to the police.'

'Oh, yes, and what was that? The collection trays? A Bible, perhaps?'

'No, it was a document which was found hidden in a small recess behind one of the stations of the cross. Ironically, it was the station where Jesus is condemned to death. The painting had burnt, but the document was protected in a small metal biscuit tin.'

'And why should I care about that?'

Hollie would have thrown him out at the roadside if she'd had a choice.

'Because you're named in the document. It appears to have been written by Sister Sophia Brennan sometime in the seventies. It outlines a series of adoptions, which she notes as having been off the record. Interestingly, we know about a couple of them already. Do you have anything to say about that?'

Hollie took her eyes off the road for a moment to look at his face. All colour had drained from it; McCready was a man who knew his time was up.

'Now would be a good time to help us out,' Hollie said.

'That stupid, fucking bitch—'

'Just shut your mouth, will you?' Hollie said. 'The number of times I hear men using the word bitch like that. What you mean is that you're fucked, and you've just been screwed by a nun who was one step ahead of you. If ever there was a brilliant example of divine retribution, this is it.'

Anderson chuckled at the other end of the phone line.

'Hey, I know where we are now,' Hollie said. 'That must be Tony's Premier Inn up ahead. DS Anderson, would you give him a call? We have his number now, I think.'

She heard Anderson tapping his keyboard.

'Stay on the line,' he said.

Anderson muted the call, and Hollie pulled up at the road-side just before the turn-off to the Country Park. There was a click at the end of the line.

'He's walking over there now. He was watching it on the television. He'll join you as soon as he gets there.'

'Brief him on the situation, please. Doug Maybury thought DCC Warburton might be his birth mother. I suspect she'll have put him right on that now, bearing in mind he's got her with him at the side of the bridge. I think Tony might be useful. Has anybody spoken directly to Doug Maybury yet?'

'No, he's told uniform to keep well away. He's waiting for the BBC guys to get set up. Fuck knows what he's got planned. He's certainly got our attention, that's for sure.'

'Okay, I'm going in,' Hollie announced, putting the car back in gear. 'This will be a suitable time to pray for the DCC, if you're religious. I can't begin to imagine what that poor woman is thinking right now.'

'Good luck and be careful.' Anderson signed off.

Hollie drew into the car park. The uniformed officers had it cordoned off already and there were numerous police vehicles there. She wound down the window to show her ID and was waved through. As she got out of the car, she heard a helicopter far off in the distance, and she realised they were pulling out all the stops for the DCC. An officer with a gun got out of a van several metres away from her.

'Is he armed?' she shouted over to one of the uniformed officers.

'Not that we know of,' came the answer, 'but they're not taking any chances.'

They were expecting her, and the way had been cleared for her to go up to the bridge and begin the negotiations.

'This is your big chance to make things right,' she said to McCready. 'Whatever you do to help now will swing things more in your favour. But you must know that the game's over now, surely?'

'It kind of looks that way,' McCready replied, his wings finally clipped. 'If I play ball now, what do you think might happen?'

'I can't say. You certainly can't screw things up any more. If the DCC gets out of this and we bring Doug Maybury in safely, you may be able to present things more favourably in court.'

Hollie received a hasty briefing from the assembled police team. There were guns on them in case Maybury was armed. They were required to jacket up. Humber Rescue was out in the estuary. The police helicopter and air ambulance were on standby. They were all set.

'When Tony arrives, get him suited up and make sure he's allowed to follow me over. I've a feeling he's going to play an important part in what happens next.'

Hollie paused a moment and steadied her mind. She had to stay sharp now. This was not only for DCC Warburton but for Jenni, too – and Sophia Brennan, if she was an innocent party, as recent developments seemed to suggest.

'Okay, Mr McCready, it's showtime. Follow my lead, keep your mouth shut unless I say otherwise, and let's see if we can resolve this mess between us.'

She led the way, following the side path up towards the bridge. As they made their way towards the looming concrete pillars, Hollie looked over the side at the queues of static traffic below. They'd got a ringside seat, just like for Sister Brennan's horrible end. Maybury had set this up so it would all play out in the open.

She could see him up ahead now; he'd spotted them, too.

The DCC saw her. She looked terrified.

Hollie swallowed hard and headed towards them.

FORTY-FIVE

'Don't do it, Doug. Your story doesn't have to end this way. McCready will tell you what you want to know. Rose Warburton has nothing to do with this.'

He could barely hear her from that distance, Hollie knew that, but she had to do something. The traffic was still thundering across the bridge, the wind cutting through the cables and creating a sharp, whistling sound. The traffic on the Clive Sullivan Way directly below them was still, at least. If Warburton fell right now, there was no way she could survive from that height.

Hollie was thankful Sister Brennan was dead already when she was hurled over the edge. She couldn't imagine how scared the DCC must be at that moment. Doug had a knife at her throat.

'You know him better than I do.' She turned to McCready. 'What do you suggest we do? Will he respond to reason?'

'He's out of his mind,' McCready replied.

'You know it's over for you now, right? All you can play for now is leniency with your sentence. You help me save the DCC and it's likely to go considerably in your favour.'

'I'm not stupid, detective. I won't be alive when I leave prison, and if I ever outlive my sentence and probation, I'll likely be geriatric by that time.'

'Why the hell did you do it?' Hollie seethed at him. 'You had an excellent job, great career prospects. Why screw it up by cheating the system?'

She could never figure out why people like McCready did the things they did. She could understand Doug Maybury. The child of a rape, thinking his mother never wanted to know him. She got how that might drive a man insane. But not McCready, who had everything most people would wish for.

'Because I could,' he replied. Even with the short distance between them, he had to shout to make himself heard. 'A situation presented itself. I was hard up at the time and a social worker doesn't make that much money. When I'd got away with it once, with Sophia Brennan's child, I left it for a while. Then, with all those vulnerable people and desperate parents, it was easy, and I got greedy. I won't apologise for it. It was rich pickings. And I did most of them a favour. The parents wanted rid of the babies. Did it really hurt anybody in the long run? The babies still went to parents who were desperate to receive them. And Frank was a soft touch. He was so shit scared that his creditors might hurt him, he was like putty in my hand. I spotted an opportunity, and I took it.'

Hollie restrained herself from passing comment. McCready was compliant now, and she had a crisis on her hands. It looked like he was going to make himself useful. A scumbag right to the end. If he knew his time was up, he'd have the good sense to make things look as positive as possible for his inevitable court appearance.

Doug Maybury looked like a man cornered. There was nowhere for him to run now. The bridge was so long they'd have him at either the Barton end or the Hessle side. He was coming with her, one way or another. The only question now was if DCC Warburton would be accompanying them.

'We must get closer to him. This is your chance to redeem yourself. Do not mess this up or I'll make a point of begging the judge to throw the key away when they bang you up.'

Hollie started to move closer to Doug.

'Back off!' he screamed at them.

Hollie held her hands up but continued to edge a little closer. If she couldn't even talk to him, there was no getting out of this situation.

'It's okay, Doug. I just want to talk, I promise—'

She cursed the noise. It was so exposed up there with the wind blowing off the estuary.

Without warning, Doug pushed the knife to Warburton's throat and took her arm. She could hear the DCC screaming at him, and just for a moment Hollie considered rushing him. But he sensed it and turned to face her.

'No further!' he shouted. 'This is just a bit of insurance—'

Still holding the knife, Doug forced DCC Warburton to climb over the edge of the barrier. She did it entirely by feel; her eyes were closed, and she looked like her body might freeze, such was the terror on her face. One slip and she'd be dead.

'Now, come closer, but no sudden moves. You make a wrong step and I push her, okay?'

'Okay, Doug, we're moving over—'

A blue light flashed along the bridge.

'Oh, for fuck's sake!' Hollie yelled, directing her voice away from Doug. That's all she needed to calm down the situation.

Doug panicked immediately. He looked like he was about to push the DCC.

'Wait, Doug, I'll call them off.'

She took out her phone and dialled Anderson.

'Boss?'

'I'm on the Humber Bridge—'

'I can't hear you. It's too windy—'

'Anderson, it's Hollie Turner. I'm on the bridge. Tell uniform to back off, I've got this—'

'You're where?'

'Call Control and tell them to back off!'

'Got it, okay, will do!'

She ended the call.

She heard the faint sound of helicopter blades.

'For fuck's sake, isn't it too windy to send out the bloody chopper?'

Hollie turned to McCready.

'Right, Patrick, we're going in. Don't mess this up.'

Hollie and McCready inched steadily forward, Doug getting into a defensive position and holding out the knife.

'Time's up, McCready. I want to know who my real mother is. It's certainly not this bitch, that's for sure!'

McCready held his hands out to show he meant no harm. Hollie was aware of movement at her side. At first, she thought it was one of the uniforms, but they seemed to have got the message already. They appeared to be staying well back. It was Tony. They'd given him a stab vest and sent him up after them as she'd asked.

'Keep back for now, Tony, I've got this—' Hollie began.

'Not a chance,' he replied. 'I've come this far. I'm not stopping now.'

McCready looked like he'd seen a ghost. He'd spotted Tony's birthmark; he remembered all right.

'I want to speak to McCready!' Doug shouted.

Warburton opened her eyes momentarily and she caught Hollie's gaze. Hollie's hands were cold from the wind. She didn't know how Warburton was managing to hang on so tight at the side. DCC Warburton spotted Tony. Hollie saw it in her eyes; at least she knew her son was standing by.

'I'll tell you who your real mother is,' McCready said, inching nearer with every word.

They were close now, so close that with a lunge, Doug could have reached McCready with his knife. Hollie was pleased they'd suited him up in a protective jacket.

'Stop stalling, McCready! I want her name.'

'I'll tell you,' he promised. 'I need to come closer. I don't want the others to hear.'

Doug seemed uncertain, but such was his desperation to know, he let McCready get closer. As he neared, McCready made a sudden grab for the knife.

'For Christ's sake!' Hollie cursed as Doug blocked his attack, spun him around, and held the knife to his throat.

'That's my mother you've got there,' Tony shouted, running over. 'I don't want her to die, Doug. Will you let her climb over? She's innocent in all this.'

Doug hesitated.

'She's not innocent. She hid the truth about you, just like the truth was hidden about me. We were a dirty little secret. They were ashamed of us.'

The knife's edge had drawn a line of blood from McCready's neck.

'Who is she? Who is my mother?'

'Okay, okay.' McCready tried to calm him.

'It was Sister Brennan—' Hollie began.

Doug's face said it all. This was enough messing around. She had to get the DCC off the side of that bridge.

'You got me to throw my own mother off the bridge?'

'I can explain,' McCready began to plead. 'It was all a mistake—'

'She was still alive. You made me throw my own mother off the bridge for a thousand pounds?'

Doug was wielding the knife recklessly now; Hollie knew she had to intervene fast.

'Doug, wait!' she called. 'There's a chance for you to get justice here. You can avenge your mother's death. Don't make things worse by hurting McCready. If McCready rots in jail, your mother gets justice.'

She'd seen the look on Doug's face before. He was a man who was rapidly becoming detached from the situation surrounding him. He was getting swept up by his anger and frustration; it was beginning to consume him.

'This bastard told me the nun was responsible for bullying the girls. He told me she'd victimised my mother. He said she was a hateful woman and deserved everything she got—'

'You can make this right, Doug—'

'Let me help my mother!' Tony called.

Doug looked from face to face, confused, overwhelmed by the decisions facing him.

'We can make this right for you,' Hollie pleaded, 'but it helps nobody if you hurt McCready.'

For one moment, she really thought he was going to let McCready go. Tony had been edging towards Rose.

'Please let me climb over,' she begged. 'My hands are getting stiff, I can't hold on much longer.'

'Shut up! Shut up, all of you!' Doug screamed. 'Just give me time to fucking think—'

'Your mother despised you, Doug, she deserved everything you did to her.'

McCready was winding him up. If he thought that would make things better for him, he was seriously wrong.

'Let me help Rose, please,' Tony urged. He'd almost reached her. She was sobbing now.

'I can't hold on, please, please let me climb over.'

As Tony reached his mother, McCready made an attempt to get away. He almost made it; he'd caught Doug completely by surprise. Doug lunged at him with the knife.

'No!' Hollie shouted, rushing towards them. She reached

out for Doug's arm, but he pushed her away, crashing her against the barrier on the far side of the path. Doug dashed at McCready, ramming him hard against the rail of the barrier.

Hollie tried to recover herself. As she turned around on the ground, she caught Doug thrusting the knife deep into McCready's neck.

'Oh no, Doug, no.'

He'd hit an artery and the blood was pumping out of McCready's neck. McCready was in a blind panic, the life fast draining from his body, but with enough life still left in him to know he was dying. He choked as the blood filled his mouth and lungs. As he collapsed on the bridge, Doug caught him and pulled him up so that his body was hanging over the barrier, his head and blood-soaked neck aimed at the road below.

'Doug, you don't have to do this.'

Doug grabbed McCready's feet and flipped him over the edge of the bridge.

'Oh God—'

Hollie pulled herself back onto her feet.

'Get away from her!' Doug shouted at Tony, waving the bloody knife.

Tony was now holding onto Rose Warburton by her wrists, doing everything he could to prevent her from releasing her grip. She was clipped by McCready's foot as he went over. She faltered for a moment. Hollie thought the DCC was about to follow McCready, but Tony held tight, ignoring the danger from Doug Maybury and grasping his birth mother firmly.

'Doug, you don't have to be defined by your past. You're a better man than this. You can get justice for your mother now. That's what's most important—'

'That's all right for you. You weren't abandoned like I was,' Doug screamed. He was crying now, obviously frightened by what he'd just done and rapidly running through his options.

'We know what happened now. Patrick McCready and

Father Duffy were on the take; you were adopted out illegally. I understand how hurt you are—'

'How can you understand? Were you discarded on the scrap heap? Were you fucked by your so-called father more times than you can remember?'

He was unhinged now. Hollie had to put some distance between the knife and the DCC. She edged forwards to block the gap between them.

'I know what you're doing. Stand back!'

The knife swished dangerously close to Hollie's face. She thought of her children: Noah, Lily and Izzy, and she wanted more than anything to be with them at that moment.

Doug looked up at the police helicopter hovering in the distance. Hollie followed his gaze; he'd spotted one of the gunmen, their sights trained on him.

'Drop the knife now, Doug. You won't come to any harm if you give yourself up to me—'

'It's too late. It's gone too far. Why did I have to listen to that bastard McCready?'

Doug was pounding his head with the blunted handle of the knife now, tears of frustration and regret running down his face. He moved closer to Rose and Tony. Hollie rushed in front of him and held the arm holding the knife. They struggled, the blade dangerously close to his neck. Hollie tried to turn him, so the armed officers in the helicopter could get their clean shot if it came to that. He was too strong for her, and he shook his hand free, pushing her to the ground once again.

'Please, no, Doug—'

For one terrible, slow, torturous second, Hollie thought he was going to push Rose Warburton off the side of the bridge. Instead, he dropped the bloody knife and looked Hollie directly in her eyes. She saw a man broken, distraught at the horror he'd created around him.

'I can't live with this...' he began.

He placed his hands on the barrier and looked down at the road below.

'Doug, we can get help for you. It doesn't have to be over.'

Hollie pulled herself up off the ground once again, seeing what he was planning in the split second before it occurred.

Doug took one look back at Hollie then vaulted over the barrier. He was gone in a second, at the same place where his birth mother had met her tragic end at his hands only days before.

EPILOGUE

Hollie looked around the small area they'd taken over at the Three Crowns. Rose Warburton, Gilly, Theresa and Mandy were laughing at something or other. She could easily picture the group of women as the girls they had once been, and it was good to see Rose and Gilly reunited after so many years. There was so much water under the bridge, so many shared and appalling experiences, and it broke her heart that Violet was unable to share in these moments.

The investigation had been one hell of a baptism of fire for her, and she struggled to think of a case in which so many lives had been affected by one man's evil. Patrick McCready had stolen so much from these women. Doug Maybury's death was tragic; she could still picture his face the moment he realised what he'd done. It was the sight of a man whose misinformed decisions had snatched everything he ever wanted from his grasp, even when it was right in front of him.

At least some good had come out of it. Tony and Timothy were huddled together talking earnestly in the corner over a couple of pints. Even Clive, Mandy's son, had attended the event and was chatting to Duncan and DS Patel. Hollie had never seen a police officer jump on an invitation so fast when she put word around the office.

'Gilly Hodges is holding a get-together for the girls who were in the mother and baby unit...' she'd begun.

'Is that Gilly Hodges, birth mother of the handsome Duncan?' DS Patel had smiled.

'It is,' Hollie confirmed.

DS Patel had delivered a melodramatic sigh.

'It's another work-related event, but I guess it would be unprofessional for me not to attend.'

From what Hollie could see, they'd more than made up for lost time while the case was being resolved.

'Besides,' Patel had continued, 'I figure I've earned it after tracing that newspaper article about the house fire back to Sister Brennan. We've got a date match now. Sister Kay confirmed the date she and Father Duffy came across her in the church. It's likely she was involved in the deaths of the men found burned in the fire, and she may well have been the person who killed them, but we'll never know for sure. We can confirm why she was pregnant now and so distressed. The poor woman, what a life.'

DS Patel had pulled a blinder. Her painstaking research gave an insight into Sister Brennan's tragic life before she arrived at the church. At least it helped to explain to the women why she was so hostile towards them. And now it was confirmed; the Brand New Family adoption agency never existed – it was what McCready used to cover his tracks.

'So, what made you decide to bring everybody together like this?' Hollie asked as Gilly walked up to her. 'I'm not complaining, mind you, it's just that there are a lot of mixed emotions involved.'

'We've carried this sadness and anger for so long. What with Violet's death last week, it just feels like we're all too old now. We have to put all this behind us and move on. It's because people couldn't move on that it ended this way.'

She was right, too. Doug Maybury and Tony had both had the same wretched start in their lives, but Tony had made something of himself, while Maybury had chosen a different path. Of course, it had been painful and terrible. But as Gilly said, they'd got their children back. Violet's death showed how vulnerable they were. Gilly was right: they had to make the best of things.

Theresa, Mandy and Rose Warburton joined them, bringing over a tray of food. Hollie took a lamb samosa; it made a change to have the time to eat properly.

'Thank you for what you did, DI Turner,' Mandy said.

'Well, you all played your part in some way,' Hollie replied. 'I'm sorry that things got a bit tense at times, but I hope you'll understand that we have to be thorough.'

'I don't see Duncan complaining.' Gilly laughed.

'How is Clive now?' Hollie asked Mandy. 'Can he forgive us? I know he had a particularly hard time of things.'

She looked over towards Mandy's son, and he lifted his hand to acknowledge her. She'd make sure to speak to him later; she didn't want any hard feelings to remain.

'It's shaken him up, for the better, I think. Seeing Duncan and Tony, hearing about Theresa's boy, Colin, I think it's made him realise he might have ended up like Doug Maybury if he carried on playing a victim in all this. I've told him he can try living in my house again at the end of the month; let's see how it goes.'

Rose Warburton took Hollie's arm.

'May I have a quiet word?' she asked.

Hollie checked the bar area again, searching for DC Gordon. She'd heard on the grapevine that Jenni might be well enough to pay a flying visit. It was lovely catching up with everybody, but it was Jenni she most wanted to see.

'I want to thank you, DI Turner. Hollie. I thought I was dead.'

Rose Warburton's earnest tone made Hollie look up. She wiped her tears with her hand.

'Of course, it's what we do.'

'Do you know why I got you assigned to this case?' Warburton asked.

'No, but I did wonder. Why put a newbie like me on the biggest case the force has had in years?'

'I wanted a rookie on the job. Don't get me wrong, I know your record. I know you're formidable when you get the scent of a case. But I wanted someone with no local knowledge of the people involved. I hoped that way I might not get dragged into it. But when Gilly Hodges showed up, I panicked. Our paths never crossed professionally, though none of the girls would ever recognise me after all this time, and not with my married name. I was terrified the ghosts of the past were coming back, and I thought you were my best bet for keeping out of it. I should have known better. A good cop never misses a beat.'

'Well, it was a good call, because if it wasn't for Tony, I'm not sure I'd have been any the wiser. It was he who helped set us on the right course. Without that, we would never have got to you.'

'I'm not proud of myself. I've treated Tony horribly. And for a while, I thought it might be him who'd killed Sister Brennan. I hate myself for even thinking it now.'

'He clearly loves you deeply—'

'I don't know why. I don't deserve it. I knew exactly what was going on when I saw Sister Brennan's photograph on social media that morning. I didn't know who it was, or why, but it didn't take much figuring out. That woman won't be mourned in this city, I'm afraid, however sorry her past. She had a chance to change things and, instead, she chose to make our lives a misery. She could have been there for us and offered us the support we needed.'

'I guess people react differently to the crap in their life. I want to say to you, too, I'm so sorry for what happened to you as a child. Nobody deserves that. I don't know how you coped. The whole thing is wretched. Even after all these years, these terrible events still have a hold of us.'

'Thank you for being discreet about things. I've talked to my husband now, and my other children. I know it will all have to come out in Father Duffy's trial, but I just want to take it a day at a time.'

'How did they take it?'

'It's a difficult thing to have to hear, that your wife – your mother – was raped as a child and has a secret son she never revealed to you. Life just works like that. There was never a right time to tell them. And, you know, all the time I never spoke about it, I was able to keep it hidden deep down. When Tony reached out to me after so many years had gone by, I was delighted. But the lie had gone on too long by then. I had my career, my family. I couldn't risk it all tumbling down.'

'Is that why you joined the police?' Hollie asked. She was thinking about her own reasons for joining, all those years ago. Why she'd given up university and left Hull. She'd done it because she felt compelled to seek justice, and every bad guy she took off the streets felt like one small victory.

'Yes. I've locked up eighteen rapists in my career. With every single man convicted, there was a woman – or women – who never had to go through what I went through. Each one of these bastards I put in prison allows me to get a little piece of myself back.'

Hollie hugged her. It seemed the natural thing to do, despite their rank differences.

'I won't say anything more to the team. I'll let you handle it in your own way.'

'Thank you, DI Turner – Hollie. I knew you were a good appointment. It just took a little while to realise how good.'

'Oh, by the way, I take it Gilly is no longer out of bounds?'

Rose smiled.

'I just didn't want anybody to make the connection between us, that's all. It's been more healing than I ever could have hoped talking over what happened back then. I've a feeling this won't be the last time we meet up. I do feel that some good might come of this.'

DCC Warburton walked off, and Hollie finished her food. She'd been aware of someone hovering to their right. Now she could see it was DS Anderson. He looked like a different man in his black suit and long dark coat. She hadn't seen him arriving.

'What was that all about?'

'Nothing. It tends to bond you to a person when you were the officer who hauled them to safety from the side of a bloody great bridge.'

'Fair enough,' he acknowledged.

'Is Jenni going to make it today?' Hollie asked, trying her best not to sound too desperate.

'DC Gordon said he'll be along later. I'm hoping he'll bring her with him.'

DS Anderson paused and surveyed the room.

'Poor Jenni. She didn't deserve that. Thank God the surgery was successful. That was too close for comfort for my liking. You know we have her journey through the city tracked now on CCTV?'

'I didn't know that. The office has obviously respected my personal time and didn't bother me with it. I'd have liked to have known, though.'

'Yeah, there's enough CCTV to track it. She was chasing you all day to get that key back to you, and then when she went round to your flat after work—'

'I wish to God she'd called for backup.'

'Well, you can save your ticking off for when she's back in the office. It'll be gentle duties only for a while, I reckon. I'm guessing she thought she had it in hand. As a young kid, she wouldn't have wanted to call out the cavalry for no reason. She was just in the wrong place at the wrong time. It happens.'

'And Maybury was out there watching the house?'

'Yes. He followed you to the Old Town. It's all there, the entire sad journey.'

They stood in silence for a brief time, Hollie unable to stop thinking about Jenni.

'Have they charged Father Duffy?'

'Yup. The bank records came in at last. It wasn't enough to make the priest a rich man, but there are several large payments to his bank account, ranging from 1969 to 1978. McCready had corresponding payments, but much higher, because he wasn't making donations to church funds to assuage his guilt like the priest was. The boat cost him a pretty penny and he has an apartment in Amsterdam, too. It looks like he might have had other schemes on the go as well. It's a can of worms as far as he's concerned.'

'I can't believe Maybury killed his own mother. McCready was a monster; imagine deceiving him like that? Getting the poor guy to do your dirty work when it was the one reconciliation he'd been seeking all his life. There's a special place in hell for people like McCready. You've done well tying up the loose ends. Thanks for your help; we couldn't have done this without you.'

'I know I come over like a prick, but I'm not all bad, you know.'

She still hadn't got the measure of this man, but she had to give him that. He was good at the job.

'When are you back in the office?' he asked. 'I'm happy to keep your seat warm for as long as I'm needed.'

'I've got to see the mental health team first, then I'm back as soon as I get the okay.'

'Sheesh, good luck with that. They'll have you doing Pilates and lighting incense sticks before you know it—'

'Of course, you've been through this after MacKenzie's death.'

'Yes, just tell them what they want to hear, and you'll soon be back at your desk.'

He was about to turn away when he stopped.

'Look, I was a bit of a dick when you first arrived—'

'Just a bit?'

'Okay, okay, I'm sorry. I misjudged you. They were right to give you the job over me. I'm sorry.'

'No apology needed,' Hollie replied. 'You've more than proved yourself on this case. You're perfectly capable of doing the job and you're a worthy deputy.'

A ripple of excitement distracted them; it was Jenni. DC Gordon was pushing her in a hospital wheelchair. She was wearing a floral head scarf which covered her head, and she still had bruises and scabbed wounds on her face.

There was a cheer from DS Anderson, DC Hayes and DCC Warburton as Harry wheeled her over. Jenni waved, she seemed excited to be there.

Hollie rushed over to her, bent down and gave her a hug before saying a word. She stayed that way for several minutes, the tears streaming from her eyes.

'Don't ever do something like that again, do you hear me?' she sobbed. 'Or I'll consign you to desk duties for the rest of your career.'

Jenni laughed.

'Someone told me they needed some entertainment at this party.' She smiled. 'I thought we could reprise our double act.'

'I think we've had quite enough of the viral videos for now, don't you think?'

DCC Warburton had joined them.

'It's good to see you again, Jenni. I don't expect to see you back at work for some time.'

'I had to beg the hospital and my mum and dad to let me come today,' Jenni replied. 'I wouldn't have missed this. I'm allowed out for an hour, then I have to get back. Oh, and I'm on strict orders to stay in this thing.'

Jenni pointed to her wheelchair and screwed up her face in disapproval.

Somebody was tapping a spoon against the side of their glass to get everybody's attention. It was Gilly; of course it was Gilly. She was dressed the brightest in the room; Hollie wondered if she'd thought it was Eurovision they were celebrating.

'I just wanted to say a few words, while we're all together in the same place.'

The room fell silent. Timothy and Tony walked over with their drinks, and a semicircle of bodies formed around Gilly.

'Firstly,' Gilly continued, 'I want us to toast our good friend Violet—'

'To Violet!'

They raised their glasses.

'We experienced some terrible times in that mother and baby unit, but it was thanks to Violet and Theresa, and Mandy – oh, and not forgetting Rose – that we stuck together and survived that place. I'm only pleased that Violet got to spend some happy years with her daughter, Patricia; and Patricia sends her apologies that she was unable to make it today. She doesn't feel quite ready yet.'

There was a murmur of agreement and sympathy.

'Today is about putting the past behind us and moving on. Hundreds of girls just like us suffered terribly in that mother and baby unit and in other places like it. I have decided to use my influence as a councillor to bring together those families who were involved and try to help everybody make some sense of all this. I will also be joining the campaign to seek an apology from the government for what happened.'

There was a spontaneous round of applause. Hollie was so pleased Gilly wasn't involved in the murder. She liked her very much and the world needed people like Gilly Hodges to get things done.

'So, please raise your glasses to all of us here today. We're survivors – all of us. It's time to get on with our lives.'

Everybody made the toast, and they broke off into their small groups. The chatter was lively; Gilly had done a good thing bringing them all together. Hollie stood on her own for a while, watching Jenni laughing with DS Patel and feeling a rush of gratitude that she'd made it through her surgery. It had been a shaky start, but she reckoned she'd joined an excellent team, despite their difficult history.

'When are you back at work?'

Gilly had sought her out again. Hollie drew her gaze away from Jenni and turned to face her.

'I've got a few days left before anybody will start getting antsy.'

'What do you have planned? Will you be going away for a break? You certainly deserve it.'

Hollie looked up at her new friend and shook her head.

'Not quite a holiday,' she replied. 'I'm heading back to Lancaster for a couple of days. I've got a life and a marriage to sort out.'

A LETTER FROM THE AUTHOR

Phew! So now you know how it all played out on that fateful day when Sister Brennan died. Everything links together and, unfortunately, there are more victims in that little mess than there are victors. I think we'll all agree on who the real bad guy is, and hopefully, you'll be pleased that he gets what's coming to him.

Thank you so much for reading *The Fifth Girl*, I hope it's kept you on the edge of your seat. If you want to join other readers in hearing all about my latest releases, you can sign up for my newsletter here.

www.stormpublishing.co/paul-j-teague

Or sign up to my personal email newsletter on the link here:

www.paulteague.net/storm

I'd appreciate it very much if you would leave a review for this third title in the DI Hollie Turner trilogy, as this helps other readers to discover my stories.

It's been a great joy to write this series of books set in Hull. I lived and worked there for seven years, but having moved away from the city in 2000, it's been wonderful to revisit old haunts in my imagination and remember places that I'd forgotten.

I loved working in that area – including the other parts of BBC Radio Humberside's patch in places like Grimsby,

Cleethorpes, Barton, Goole, Brigg and all the villages in between. There's so much variety. It was wonderful to cover it as a journalist, but it also has so much potential when seen from the perspective of a writer.

Take North Ferriby's foreshore, for instance. When I relocated from my BBC job in Barrow-in-Furness to Hull, my wife and I rented for six months while we decided where we wanted to live. We were immediately drawn to North Ferriby, a well-served village that lies on the banks of the Humber.

North Ferriby had its own train station, so I was able to commute to work while I was presenting the evening news show, with splendid views along the Humber and the bridge all the way in. We could easily walk to the foreshore, where poor old DCC Warburton ran into a spot of bother while walking her dogs.

North Ferriby has a couple of shops, a school, a football club, a church, and a pub – I sound like an estate agent, but we loved living there and I had to use it as a location in my book.

Swanland is an equally nice village just along the road from North Ferriby. I always remember it having several big houses and some nice shops; they certainly know how to make lovely villages in that part of the world.

I stumbled across an excellent find while writing this trilogy and I ended up going down a bit of a rabbit hole with my research. As a journalist, I often covered news stories related to the fishing industry around Hull and Grimsby, but the one story I remember dominating my time there was that of the loss of *The Gaul*, a Hull-based fishing vessel which was lost at sea in February 1974, just a few months ahead of when the seventies scenes occur for Mandy, Theresa and Gilly.

However, when I was getting a feel of Hull in the 1960s for Sister Sophia Brennan's scenes, I came across the city's *Headscarf Heroes*, an amazing group of four women who campaigned for improved conditions for fishermen after the city's tragic triple-trawler disaster.

Although I only refer to the *Headscarf Revolutionaries* in passing, I wanted to acknowledge the impact the four women made in the city after three trawlers sank in just three weeks. Fifty-eight men died in those tragedies, and a group of ordinary women, led by Lillian Bilocca, set up a petition and galvanised an army of fishwives to get shipping laws changed in Parliament.

At the time of writing this book, there is a local campaign to mark the incredible achievements of those women by erecting a statue in their memory. You can find out more about their story in the book *The Headscarf Revolutionaries* by Brian W. Lavery, and I must acknowledge that text for the insights it gave me into life for the fishing families along and around Hull's Hedon Road.

I always like to point out that although I feature real-life locations in my stories, the characters and situations are completely fictional, although they might be inspired by real life. I also incorporate fictional settings, usually where there's a gruesome death or unpleasant incident that takes place in a public location. Sometimes, as a writer, you have to bend reality just a tiny bit, so please forgive any tweaks or liberties taken with actual locations. This is a work of fiction, and all characters are a figment of my imagination.

This trilogy began because of the female taxi driver who used to transport me to the BBC at an unearthly hour so that I could present BBC Radio Humberside's breakfast show. Our morning chats meant that we became more friendly, and I always used to hope the taxi company would send this lady to pick me up because I enjoyed our early morning conversations so much.

It was her story that inspired this book. I can remember us sitting outside the former BBC radio station in Chapel Street while she related to me how her son was in contact again after being taken from her as an unmarried teenage mother. I was late for work and needed to get on with my show preparation, but what she was telling me was so compelling.

At the time, I knew nothing about the girls and young women who had had their babies taken from them, and I was incredulous when she told me. It's the sort of thing you can't imagine happening in a country like the UK, but it did, to hundreds and hundreds of women.

Many of those women are still waiting for an apology for how they were treated. There will be many who were never reunited with their children, or who died before those reconciliations could take place.

This book is dedicated to my former taxi driver, and I hope I have treated her story with respect but have also managed to convey the mixture of anger, loss, and sadness that she inevitably felt. The storylines that feature Mandy, Gilly, Theresa, Violet and Rose are entirely fictional and no part of what happens is taken from the conversations that we had about the topic.

Her story was serialised on BBC Radio Humberside on our mid-morning show, which I was co-presenting at the time. I wish I still had a copy of it. It was recorded on a minidisc, if memory serves me correctly, and the broadcasting industry hasn't used those for a couple of decades.

I'd also like to acknowledge my time at BBC Radio Humberside and the good company and counsel of my colleagues there, many of whom are still working for the radio station. I had an amazing experience at that radio station and have some incredible memories of my time there.

So, what now for DI Hollie Turner? Will she head back to Lancaster with her tail between her legs or can she sort things out with Léon so that she gets to see her kids? Are there any more adventures awaiting her in the Humberside policing area, and if so, can she now count on her team of detectives to come to her aid?

We still don't know what happened to DI MacKenzie, the detective who she replaced, and there are hints of treachery, betrayal and corruption, which Hollie has only just skimmed the surface of. I hope that you enjoyed this trilogy of books. If you'd like to hear about future releases, please connect with me on social media.

Thank you very much for reading these books and I do hope that you'll go on to check out other stories in my library.

With best wishes, Paul Teague

 facebook.com/paulteagueauthor
x.com/PaulTeagueUK